ASKING

FOR

LOVE

ASKING

FOR

LOVE

and Other Stories

Roxana
Robinson

Random House   New York

Copyright © 1996 by Roxana Robinson

All rights reserved under International and Pan-American Copyright Conventions. Published in the United States by Random House, Inc., New York, and simultaneously in Canada by Random House of Canada Limited, Toronto.

The following stories appeared in slightly different form in these publications: "Sleepover" in *Glimmer Train*; "King of the Sky" in *Harper's*; and "Mr. Sumarsono," "Leaving Home," and "The Favor" in *The Atlantic Monthly*. "Mr. Sumarsono" was also published in *The Best American Short Stories—1994* (Houghton Mifflin, 1994).

Library of Congress Cataloging-in-Publication Data

Robinson, Roxana.
    Asking for love and other stories / Roxana Robinson. — 1st ed.
      p.   cm.
    ISBN 0-679-43902-1
    I. Title.
    PS3568.03152A9   1996
    813'.54—dc20   95-23719

Manufactured in the United States of America on acid-free paper

98765432

First Edition

Book design by Caroline Cunningham

This book

with much love

is for my father,

Stuyvesant Barry

Contents

Leaving Home   3

Sleepover   22

Slipping Away   34

The Nile in Flood   55

The Favor   70

Do Not Stand Here   95

Asking for Love   113

Mr. Sumarsono   137

Halloween 153

The Reign of Arlette 165

Breaking the Rules 187

Family Restaurant 210

The Nightmare 222

White Boys in Their Teens 237

King of the Sky 256

ASKING

FOR

LOVE

Leaving Home

E very summer when I was growing up we made the long drive from outside Philadelphia, where I was born, to the village of Devon, in western Massachusetts, where my father's family had lived for a hundred and fifty years.

The road to Devon turned off the river road, dropping suddenly down the riverbank, then leveling abruptly for the ancient covered bridge. Our car bumped sedately as it entered the bridge. This was dark inside, with huge crisscrossed beams. Going slowly and majestically through the nineteenth-century gloom, we could hear the hollow wooden echo of our passage.

This ceremonial crossing of the river was the moment I waited for. When we came out of the dark tunnel of the bridge I said contentedly, "Now we're in Devon."

"Now we're in Devon," my father always answered.

We drove up Devon's one steep street, over the railroad tracks, and past the small, neat shops that my grandmother had used: Bates the butcher, the dry goods shop, the grocery store.

"Wallace's is closed," my mother said. The grocery store was always closed by the time we got to Devon.

"We can stop at the farm for eggs and milk," said my father.

The farm belonged to Cousin Thomas, who was the only Thatcher still farming. Four generations ago the family had split: Thomas's great-grandfather had stayed in Devon, and my father's great-grandfather had moved to Boston. Thomas's line had stayed farmers, and the men in my father's line all went to Harvard. They were Episcopalian ministers, like my father, and judges and teachers and lawyers. Now the Thatchers lived all over the Northeast, but they had kept the land. The cousins, more distant with each generation, still came to Devon in the summers.

Cousin Thomas's farm was at the foot of Devon Hill. There were two big, gloomy hemlocks along the road, and a pond below the house for the flock of bossy German geese. The white clapboard house was symmetrical in front, with square pillars and a deep and generous front porch. In back, the house meandered, with lopsided additions. It was built around 1800, and now, in 1970, the shutters sagged, the clapboards showed cracks, and it needed paint.

We pulled into the driveway, next to the house. A flock of bantams with shaggy boots fussed in the weeds.

"Coming in with me?" My father turned sideways to talk to me; I was in the back seat. I could see his Thatcher nose, pointed and severe, his pale blue Thatcher eyes and limp blond

Thatcher hair. I have Thatcher looks, like his, and when I was little I liked this. I liked people saying, "Well, I can see *you're* a Thatcher." It made me feel a part of something larger than myself, part of a gentle tribe, a network that was invisibly spread across these Massachusetts hills. But the year I was thirteen, looking like a Thatcher made me uneasy. Looking in the mirror, I felt like a fraud, as though I were wearing a Thatcher mask I couldn't take off. I looked like a Thatcher but I knew in my heart I was not one.

The Thatcher family was famous for integrity: those judges, headmasters, ministers, were all high-minded and principled. They were models of rectitude. The Thatcher genes carried not just blue eyes but virtue, and when I was thirteen I had become aware that I was deeply deficient in virtue.

My mother turned and smiled at me over the back seat. My mother wore round flesh-colored glasses, which made her eyes pale and vulnerable. She had straight brown hair, very fine, held to one side with one bobby pin. She never wore makeup. Her clothes were unworldly: baggy woven skirts, sturdy comfortable sandals, limp tan cardigan sweaters. Appearances did not matter to my parents; the material world was unimportant. I knew that I ought to feel this way too, I wished that I felt this way, but I did not. When I was thirteen I was deeply, and shamefully, concerned with appearances.

"Go in with Daddy," my mother said, smiling. "You always do."

But that year I didn't want to go into the farmhouse with my father, though I didn't know why. Avoiding my mother's eye, I looked out the window at the dense green sea of corn rising up Devon Hill.

"Maybe Cousin Gloria will be there." My mother offered me the cousin closest to my age, but I didn't answer. My mother said kindly, "Go on. Don't be shy."

This sounded condescending, and I said crossly, "I'm not *shy*."

"Then what is it?" asked my mother.

There was another silence.

"Sounds like shy to me," my father said, brisk and certain. My father was certain about everything. "Better come in."

"I'm *not* shy," I said again, crosser. "I don't want to go in, that's all. I don't *care* if Gloria is there. I don't care about *Gloria*. I *hate* Gloria."

And now there was a terrible silence in the car. I had spoken a word that was never used in our household. The sound of it hung in the air—the short explosive syllable, with its fierce aspirate beginning, the powerful black vowel at its center, and the sharp closure, like a hissed threat. The shock of it quivered among us. It was as though I had thrown a rock through the windshield, and we now sat staring at the star-shaped fracture, the damage.

My mother gave a long sigh, her face sorrowful. "I hope that's not true, Alison," she said quietly. She sounded wounded, as though I had struck her in the face, and I knew that was how she felt. "I hope you don't really *hate* your cousin."

There was another thunderous silence. Brutally, I had betrayed my mother and disgusted my father. My father looked straight ahead now, the back of his neck rigid. My mother watched me, full of concern. They waited for me to answer.

I looked out the window. It was too late to take back the word, which I'd never meant to say in the first place. The word had come out before I thought, and now I would have to pay. I had no defense, no excuses. I never did. I could never argue with my parents: they lived in a separate moral universe from mine. They never swore, or spoke unkindly, or had uncharitable thoughts. My parents were guided by virtue.

I sat in the back seat and wished that God, for once, would take my side and erase the sound of the word from family memory. I told myself that it was just a word, but I was without conviction. I stared out at the jostling sea of green corn, waiting.

In the front seat, my mother sighed again. She said gravely, "What is it that you 'hate' your cousin *for?*"

I didn't hate Gloria. I hardly knew Gloria.

The farming Thatchers had five children: two boys, Tom and Charlie, and three daughters, Gloria, Karen, and Joanne. I hardly ever saw them. I spent the summers at the tiny club down at the lake, with its two soggy red-clay tennis courts and old shingle-sided boathouse. The farming Thatchers didn't go to the club. Their children were never seen fooling around out on the rafts, or playing tennis on the bumpy courts, or sitting on the tiny muddy beach with sandwiches and soft drinks. Tom and Charlie, in blue overalls, spent their days on slow, thundering tractors, cutting hay and plowing fields, lifting a laconic hand if someone waved from a passing car. I don't know where the girls were, but it wasn't down at the lake.

"I didn't mean I really *hated* Gloria," I said slowly.

My father turned sideways again. "Then maybe you should not have used that word, Alison." He did not, of course, say the word himself. "That word is very strong," he said. "You should think carefully before you use it. If you don't mean it—and I hope you didn't—then it's not a word you should use." He paused. "I hope you don't really feel that emotion toward your own cousin."

I didn't answer. I stared out the window again so I wouldn't have to look at my mother. My mother, her eyes shining through the colorless glasses, watched me steadily. She was ready to forgive me.

There was a long pause. I knew what would happen. If I didn't answer, if I didn't admit to my crime, we would sit here in silence for the rest of the evening, for the rest of my life. The black sound of the word I had used would hover over us forever. I closed my eyes. The weight of this bore relentlessly down on me.

"I'm sorry," I said.

My father nodded slowly, without looking at me. His face was bleak, and frozen by disapproval. His mouth was drawn in on itself, and his pale blue eyes were hooded and distant, as though I were someone he had never met. It would be hours before he approached friendship, even acquaintanceship. My mother leaned across the car and patted my shoulder. She gave me a brave smile, but her eyes showed damage: She had been wounded.

"I'm going in," my father said. His voice was remote. He got out and shut the door.

I looked sideways at my mother, who nodded urgently at me. She waved me toward the door. I waited a moment, for pride, then got out.

My father stood in the rutted driveway, taking a deep breath of Devon air. I moved tentatively next to him and he turned away, stepping up onto the side porch. A clothesline hung above its railing, wooden pins staggering along its length. Inside the house I could hear a radio—a trashy singer yearning to a sunset-colored melody.

My parents listened only to classical music. Once, in the car, I was rolling the dial along the radio band. I stopped it at a popular-music station, just for a second, as though I were just pausing to shift my grip on the dial. At once a hot red blare of sound filled the car, and at once my father reached over and clicked the radio off. He looked straight ahead, his mouth closed and tight. He didn't say anything. I didn't dare turn the radio back on, even for the news.

My father's footsteps thundered on the porch floor, and I heard chairs scraping inside. We went into the dark mudroom, where in one corner lay a mud-colored dog blanket, flattened and hairy. Faded jackets hung on the wall, tipped-over rubber boots on the floor below them. My father raised his hand to knock, and the kitchen door opened.

"Well, if it idn't Cousin James," said Cousin Florence, her sharp blue eyes seizing on my father. Cousin Florence stood outlined in the doorway. She was small and fierce, with pale red hair pulled straight back into a ponytail. She was thin, with a pointed nose, and small deft hands. She wore a housedress, and over it a faded flowered apron. She folded her lean arms and tilted her head cheerfully to one side.

"Hello, James," Cousin Thomas said, stepping forward and smiling. Cousin Thomas's nose was Thatcher, and his cheekbones, but he was half a foot shorter than my father, his body small and dense. His denim overalls were loose and waistless, like a clown's suit.

Thomas hugged his elbows, but my father put out his hand. Thomas unclasped himself and they shook hands slowly, smiling at each other. Cousin Thomas turned and grinned at me.

"Well, come on in," he said, amused and pleased, and waved us past. The mudroom smelled rank, but I took a deep breath before I stepped into the kitchen.

In the middle of the kitchen was a table covered with red-and-white-checked oilcloth. Battered wooden chairs stood unevenly around it: in two of them sat girls. I saw them out of the corner of my eye. I stood with my head cocked in concentration, my eyes fixed on my father's face as though I had to read his lips.

The farming Thatchers had dinner early, and we had arrived in the middle. Food filled the plates, and in the center of the table stood a pie-shaped piece of sweating yellow cheese. An overhead hanging lamp lit up the table; the rest of the room was shadowy.

"Come sit down, James," said Florence. She stood in front of the stove, her fisted hands set on her hips. She wore thin white socks, limp around her ankles, and her brown oxfords had a dull pale bloom of scuff at the toes.

My father smiled gently. "I'm afraid we can't, Florence. Diana's out in the car, and we're meeting Ted at the house. He doesn't have a key, so I'm afraid he's waiting there. And it looks as though we're interrupting your dinner, so we won't bother you any more than to ask for a few eggs and some milk. We'll bring the can back in the morning."

"A few eggs," said Cousin Florence. She moved to a table where a wide, cracked bowl stood. It was heaped with brown eggs, bits of feather stuck to them. "How many is a few?" Florence asked my father, twisting to eye him.

"Oh, two, I suppose," my father said, not sure.

"Six," I had to prompt him, in a whisper.

He looked down at me. "Six?"

I nodded and he repeated it to Florence.

Florence looked at us and shook her head, grinning.

"Sure now? Six? Or two?" she said.

My father smiled. "Six," he said, nodding. Florence turned again and began to count eggs into a wrinkled brown bag. "Gloria, get the milk," she said, her voice suddenly peremptory. The older girl slid off her chair, staring at me. Joanne, the youngest, in pajamas and a turquoise bathrobe, sat at the table, watching. Her curly hair was in a fine tangle and she held a comic book, forbidden in our house.

"Give them the can," ordered Florence.

Gloria went to the old-fashioned high-legged refrigerator. She took out a tall, silvery milk can and carried it carefully to my father, ignoring me. Gloria had Cousin Florence's small face and her restless blue eyes. Her elbows were pointed. She wore a white lace-edged blouse, unironed, and baggy jeans tightly cinched with a narrow plastic belt.

"That be enough milk?" Florence asked loudly. This was meant as a joke: the can was so full Gloria could hardly carry it.

"I think it will be just fine," my father said, polite.

Gloria came and stood directly in front of me, too close, invasive.

"Hi," she said. She lifted her chin suddenly and scratched under it.

"Hello," I said coolly.

Cousin Florence held out the bag of eggs to me.

"Don't forget the eggs," she said energetically. "All two of them. Or was it six?" She laughed again, staccato. She looked at me more closely and frowned.

"Happened to your hair? Caught in the mowing machine?" She looked at my father, then back at me. My father smiled.

I said, "I had it cut."

Cousin Florence laughed briefly. "I can see *that.*"

"Well, thank you very much, Cousin Florence," my father said. "Thomas." He bowed his head. "And you all are well? The boys? The farm?"

"Pretty good," Cousin Thomas said. Cousin Thomas had a nice smile, small and true. He put his hands comfortably inside the bib of his overalls, like a muff. "Things are pretty good. I can't complain. And you?"

"We're pretty good ourselves." My father nodded goofily, like a marionette. "Well, thank you again for all this," my father said, holding up the eggs like a prize. "I'll bring the can back tomorrow."

Cousin Florence flapped her hand at him. "Don't worry about it," she said. "Children can bring it back. Right, sister?" She stared at me again.

"Come at milking," Thomas said, smiling at me.

"Thank you," I said, smiling stiffly back. I knew he meant this as a treat, and when I was little it had been one. But now what I remembered was the row of dirty-haunched Holsteins with their slimy noses, the concrete gutter behind them clotted with green manure. The heavy-bodied flies everywhere.

When we were back in the car, my mother asked, "How are they all?"

"They were fine," my father said, backing the car out of the driveway. Our house was at the top of the next hill; we would be home in minutes. "Thomas was cheerful. He always is."

"He's good-hearted," said my mother. "So is Florence. I hope she didn't give you all their milk. She'll never tell you she needs any for herself."

"I wonder if she did do that," my father said, slowing the car down. "I wonder if she gave us all their milk. Maybe we should go back."

I sat in the back seat, the cold milk can against my chest. It was freezing, and I could feel the milk sloshing back and forth, nearly spilling each time. I closed my eyes, hoping that my father's conscience would not demand that he go back to the farm and reopen negotiations.

"Did she just give you the can from the fridge?" asked my mother. "Did they pour any off into a pitcher?"

"No," said my father. "They gave us the whole can." He turned the car in at a driveway to turn around. We set off back up the hill to the farm again. This time I didn't go in.

Our house in Devon was built by my grandfather. It was massive and rustic, with rough, dark-stained clapboards. There were huge stone chimneys guarding each end of the roof, and clusters of tiny-paned windows that huddled in groups under the eaves.

My brother, Ted, was waiting for us on the front porch, his knapsack beside him. He had hitchhiked here. Ted always hitchhiked, not in a dashing, carefree, gypsyish way but in an ascetic, puritanical way, as though he disapproved of the comfort and expense of other kinds of travel. My father shook Ted's hand and my mother hugged him. I stood off to one side, and when Ted was finished with my parents, he turned toward me and I lifted my hand in an awkward wave.

"Hi there," Ted said. He was eight years older than I was, serious and remote. He talked very little, and practically never to me. He was going to be a concert pianist, and he practiced six hours a day. While he played, his mouth went down at the corners, like my father's. I was afraid of Ted: I knew he disapproved of me. I knew that he could tell that I was vain and selfish, superficial, brutal, a false Thatcher.

While the others unloaded the car, I opened the house. This meant unlocking the back door from the outside and the front door from the inside. I always wanted to be the first person to enter the house in the summer. Carrying the key, I ran through the summer twilight. My bare feet knew the long springy grass of the unmown lawn, the narrow, rocky path down the side of the house, the splintery gray steps up to the back porch. The woods came right up to the back porch, and at night the raccoons made their secretive way up the steps to the scraps left out for them.

I set the key into the heavy lock, twisted it, and pushed open the door. The kitchen was cool and gloomy, deeply silent. The refrigerator door stood coldly open, declaring its metal racks empty. The big green back-porch rockers sat tipsily on top of one another in an uproarious still life. In the dark pantry, glass-fronted cupboards rose up to the ceiling, stacked with my grandmother's fluted white Wedgwood china. The rooms, as they always did, smelled of wood and wax. After the pantry's gloom the dining room was a burst of light, with its pale, shining birchwood floor, its long wall of French doors facing the lake. In the living room the huge blackened granite fireplace was flanked by oak bookcases. A giant iron cauldron stood to one side, for firewood. Facing the hearth were overstuffed chairs in their baggy slipcovers, and the faded chintz sofa. The house was unchanged since my grandmother had arranged it.

My bare feet made no sound on the polished floors, and moving through the silent rooms, I felt as though I were walking into the dense center of my family. I was breathing air that my family had breathed, my grandparents, my aunts and uncles, my cousins, my father. I was seeing the same images—these same chairs in their baggy slipcovers, these old china lamps, this Toby jug on the mantelpiece—that my family had seen each summer for generations.

Usually I liked this moment. Usually I felt as though I were somehow swimming into my own past, as though the whole liquid, transparent past of my family enveloped me, warm, comforting, nourishing. But this time it felt different. This year the house felt strange. The air seemed dense and heavy, and the rooms felt claustrophobic. I went straight to the front door without stopping, and when I unlocked the door and pulled open the heavy slab of oak, I stood still in the doorway, facing out of the house. The cool evening air, smelling of ferns and woods, swept into the house like a blessing.

The next morning I went, early, down to the lake. The air was fresh and minty, and the narrow downhill path through the birches was soft and padded with leaf mold. The wooden boathouse was empty, and the floor echoed hollowly beneath my heels. I walked out onto the deck and took a slow breath, looking around. The lake, ringed by low, wooded hills, was calm and light-filled. I could smell the weathered, sun-baked planks beneath my feet. The air was still, and there was no sound anywhere. In the middle of the lake, far out on the shimmering water, two fishermen sat motionless in a flat-bottomed rowboat. A filmy white mist traced the green shoreline. I walked to the edge of the deck and looked down: the water was yellow-green and translucent. A narrow fish hovered over the sandy bottom, its fins rippling like transparent flags. The early sun was warm on my bare legs, and I sat down between the stiff wooden arms of the ladder. I closed my eyes: I could feel the summer about to begin.

By the weekend I had met everyone my age who was there that year. Calvin Edgerley, fourteen, whom I already knew, was staying with his grandmother. This year Calvin's older cousin was there too, Trowbridge Small. And one afternoon we rode our bicycles over to Betsy Jordan's, whom the boys knew.

The Jordans' house was new. It was low and sleek, made of brick. Betsy's mother opened the wide white-painted door. She had short blond hair, curled, and she wore a flowered terry-cloth shift with ruffled edges.

"Hi, kids, come on in," she said cheerfully. "Betsy's here somewhere." She called behind her: "Betsy!" She turned back and smiled at us. Her lips were clear curves of raspberry. "She's doing her summer reading, so she'll be thrilled to see you."

Betsy Jordan was wearing blue-jean cutoffs and a tank top. She held a book negligently in her hand, a finger stuck between the pages. Betsy was short and rounded, with neat limbs and easy gestures. Her face was covered with dark freckles and her hair was sleek, like an otter's. She was completely relaxed, and I could see that she knew, just by instinct, how to be. I stared at her with admiration. At once I felt myself too lanky, long-boned, wrong.

"Hi," Betsy said. "Want something to drink?"

In the kitchen we got Cokes, which were forbidden in our house. We went back to sit in the living room, and I looked around. We sat on low built-in sofas covered in bright red jittery prints. There were low glass tables with metal frames, and the white wall-to-wall rug was thick, like the fur of an animal. On the shiny white shelves against the wall were a stereo system and a huge television set. The white brick fireplace was raised off the floor. All of this seemed perfect to me, exactly the way a house should be.

Trow, in tattered blue jeans, his hair falling across his eyes, sat next to Betsy. He leaned against her shoulder and pointed at her book.

"So, whatchou up to, Bets?" he asked.

"*Villette,*" Betsy said mournfully. "Brontë."

"Like it?" Trow asked, grinning.

Betsy snorted lackadaisically and shook her head slowly. "Hate it," she said. "*Hate* it." She used the word casually, as though it were no different from any other.

"Wait'll you get *Middlemarch,*" Trow said, raising his eyebrows, grinning. He shook his head. "Woo-woo!"

"*Middlemarch,*" Betsy said, wrinkling her nose. "Please. We read that last year. I hated it too."

I listened admiringly. At home I went to a church school, and no one talked like this. My parents did not allow complaints about schoolwork.

"What do you have?" Calvin asked me. Calvin had a long, comic's nose, pale skin, and fine dark hair.

"*Walden,*" I said.

"Henry David Thoreau-up," said Calvin, and laughed loudly.

"Where do you go?" Betsy asked me.

"Farmington," I said, proud. "I start this fall. Where do you?"

"Concord Academy," said Betsy, and I nodded knowledge-ably.

They were all older than me and already at boarding school. They told me elaborately how terrible it was. I listened, entranced. I could not imagine what it would be like. I was hoping for a new life, coarse and raucous: loud radios, friends who swore. I hoped we would all laugh behind the house-mother's back, uncharitably, without remorse.

Sitting on the jazzy red sofa, with a Coke bottle in my hand, listening to them criticize the grown-up world, I was proud. I thought we looked like a photograph of teenagers in a magazine. This was what teenagers did, I thought, and I myself was doing it. I was one of them, a member of this elect and glamorous group.

Of course I knew that there were things I had to conceal from them, things that would reveal me as an impostor. For one thing, there was the fact that I liked to read. I had already read the Brontës, on my own, and I liked the books on the summer reading list. For another thing, there was my hideous, unaccept-able old house and my virtuous, unacceptable family. But I thought I could keep my two worlds apart, and that I could keep these things hidden. And in the meantime, here I was, sit-ting in this golden group, holding a Coke. Two boys sat next to me, clowning. Betsy rolled her eyes languidly, and the boys laughed. I felt I had entered a charmed land. I thought that I had never been so happy. I thought my new life had already started.

Later in the month, I lay one afternoon in the big canvas hammock on the porch. I was reading *Walden,* and from time to time I put my hand underneath the hammock and gave myself a slow, peaceful push against the stone parapet. Below me, the wooded hillside was quiet, and the lake was calm. Far out in the middle was a single figure, paddling slowly in a silver canoe.

When I heard the knock on the front door I stopped reading, wondering. No car had come up the hill. My mother's footsteps crossed the polished floor.

"Why, hel*lo*!" my mother said to someone, effusive. "Come right in."

I heard a muffled, unidentifiable voice.

"She's right outside," my mother said. "Come with me. She'll be so glad to see you."

I sat up, appalled. I was wearing stained green shorts and an old, too-tight jersey. Worse, I was here in the house: the huge, blackened fireplace, the humped, flowered, monolithic chairs, the faded oriental rugs, the absent television. There was no Coke in the refrigerator and never had been. I was caught, trapped, in these clothes and in this house.

"Alison," my mother called, "you have a guest."

The screen door opened and Gloria stood there, a bundle in her arms.

"I come to play," she announced, and smiled, showing her flat front teeth.

I stared at her.

"I brought my bathing suit," Gloria added, holding up the bundle.

"Good," said my mother brightly, looking at me. "That's good. You can go down to the lake together for a swim. How about that, Alison?"

I was speechless.

The afternoon had, in a stroke, turned bleak and endless. Hours and hours lay before me, locked in Gloria's company. I would have to talk to Gloria. I would have to listen. And Gloria's presence, I knew, would ruin me. Everything I had built up, all the teenagerness, whatever borrowed glamour I had managed to acquire from the group, would all be destroyed by Gloria's presence. My true colors would be revealed, and I could never recover from this. Even if no one saw me, even if no one knew, a contamination would take place. I would be subtly expelled. The others would make plans, they would do things together, and they would not call me. They would expect me to spend the day with Gloria. It was the end of my new life.

Gloria looked diffidently at my mother. "Ma says I'm not to go to the boathouse, because it costs you. She says we can go down into the woods."

My mother looked awkward. "Oh," she said, blinking behind the colorless glasses. "Oh, that doesn't matter. Don't worry about that."

"No," Gloria said firmly, shaking her head. "Ma says I have to swim from the woods, I can't go to the boathouse."

There was a pause, and my mother nodded. "All right. There's a path that goes down to the lake on our property." She thought for a moment. "How old are you, Gloria?"

"Nearly twelve," Gloria said, proud.

I would be spending the afternoon with an eleven-year-old.

"And are you a good swimmer?" asked my mother.

"Not real good," Gloria said cheerfully.

"All right, then," said my mother. "Ted can go down with the two of you. Just to be on the safe side. He can take a book. The two of you can swim." She stood, smiling, surrounding us with warmth and approval.

Where would we swim? I wondered bitterly. Back and forth in the shallows, trying not to touch the muddy, squishy, loathsome, monster-filled bottom? By this time, that side of the lake was in shadow, and the water would be chill. And there was no clearing on the bank, nowhere to spread a towel, nowhere to sit but nettles. Ted would be no help; he would bring his book and say nothing.

We changed into bathing suits in my room. Gloria's suit was babyish, with smocking across the front and rows of ruffles across her rump. We went down the path, me in front. "The briers are bad this year," I called back in a grand way. I was trying to suggest some kind of superior knowledge, a connoisseurship of briers. I hoped Ted would answer, but Gloria did.

"Yee-ah," she said. She giggled loudly, then screamed as a thorn ripped a white line along her arm. "Ow," she explained. I turned off onto the faint trail down to our landing. The briers were worse here. Behind me Gloria shouted good-naturedly at each hostile touch.

At the water's edge, we put our towels down on bushes. Ted, who didn't care, sat down with his book among the brush.

"I'll go first," I said. I began to wade cautiously out into the cool water. Goose bumps appeared suddenly up and down my arms. The lake bottom was famously awful, and cold black ooze came up between my toes. I stepped on slime-covered rocks, slippery and unsteady. I kept my head down, trying to see into the sunless green depths.

Behind me Gloria screamed loudly with every step. "Oh my God," she said, over and over.

When the water reached my waist, I looked up. The silver canoe I had seen before was coming in from the middle of the lake. It was a new aluminum one, with a girl paddling. It was headed past us, toward the boathouse. The girl wore a sleek black tank suit, like Betsy's.

I started walking more steadily through the cobbly ooze, pushing urgently through the water, toward the canoe. The girl was watching me. She slowed her stroke and slightly changed her course. As she came closer I could see the flicked-up nose, the sleek wet head. It was Betsy.

I waved at her, lurching, trying to hurry through the heavy water. I could hear Gloria, now way behind me, shrieking in the shallow water.

"Betsy!" I called.

Betsy paused, her paddle lifted. Out where she was, the lake was still lit by the long late-afternoon light. The canoe was radiant on the glassy water, and long silver loops slid off the paddle.

"Betsy! It's me!" I called. "Alison!"

I threw myself forward into the water and began swimming. Betsy hesitated, then turned the canoe toward me with a long, strong stroke that sent the boat skidding across the water. I swam toward her, flailing my arms and splashing wildly. When I reached the canoe, I kicked myself up out of the water in a flurry, rising up and reaching for the gunwale. I grabbed it as though I were drowning, as though I were desperate and the canoe were a lifeboat.

"Go," I said urgently. "Just go. Quick."

Without asking, Betsy began paddling again. The canoe, clumsy with my awkward weight, swung back away from shore and headed for the boathouse. I clung to its cold, pale side and stared at the normal life going on at the boathouse: the bored lifeguard lounging in his canvas chair, his white hat pulled down over his eyes. Small children shouted in the shallows.

I didn't once look behind me, where Ted would be sitting among the bushes, his head now raised from his book, watching me, unsurprised. I didn't look back to see Gloria, who would be standing in the muddy shallows, quiet, no longer shrieking, staring at her cousin. Hanging on to the smooth, chill metal, my teeth chattering, I fixed my gaze ahead, as though I could put my family behind me forever, as though I would never have to look at them again.

Sleepover

"Lean over," her mother said, scrubbing at the child's milky skin. Bess bent her head over the sink, stretching her leg out straight behind. She craned her head around, trying to see the back of her own knee. Bess was seven.

"Would you be able to see it yet?" she asked her mother. "Could you see the red? I think it itches."

"You probably didn't even get it," her mother said. "This is just in case."

"But I was near it," said Bess. "I saw it. I might have touched it and not remembered. I might have touched it before I saw."

"There," said her mother, and stood up. The back of Bess's knee was covered with calamine lotion, a great, chalky, pink-white island. Bess straightened and then bent her leg, lifting her foot behind her in a slow, hypnotized gesture as she felt the tautness of the dried lotion on her skin. She looked up at her mother and smiled, her eyes focused inward, concentrating on the sensation. "It feels like a balloon when you touch it. Tight and squeaky."

Her mother screwed the top back on the calamine lotion. "I used to spend the summer covered with this stuff," she said. "I used to get poison ivy every day."

"Every day?" asked Bess, distracted from her back-of-the-knee experience. "Every single day?"

"Maybe not every day," said her mother, "but *nearly.*" She turned suddenly theatrical, and her voice dropped, urgent and mysterious. "Ve-ry nearly," she whispered to Bess, the words—absurd, nonsensical—transformed by her delivery into code, a message about unknown danger. Bess laughed, her mouth slightly open, her eyes unguarded. She watched her mother's face as she would a movie screen: rapt, expectant, ingenuous, waiting for splendor.

The bathroom, flooded with late-afternoon light, was suffused with a feeling of intimacy. Bess leaned easily against the porcelain sink with its deep blue stain. Everything in this room was familiar to her. Everything here was part of Bess's life within her family, everything proof of her mother's presence. Here was the soupy oval of soap in its dish, the soft, fraying towels, hanging neatly folded on their long wooden bars. Her father's huge terry-cloth bathrobe stretched its heavy folds on the hook behind the door; on top of it was her mother's pink cotton robe, with a white lace frill along its entire front. The pink tiles with their darkened lines of grout, the faint moldiness of the translucent shower curtain, the peeling paint on the window frame over the bathtub—everything suggested steam, warmth, privacy. Here was safety.

Bess, staring at her mother, waited for more. This was an unexpected image: her mother as a child in the long summer evenings, galloping through thickets of dense green, immersed in her own secret plans, heedless of risk. Bess hoped for more gypsy, more wildness, more of this strange vision of her mother as unreliable, irresponsible. Someone with a secret life.

Bess waited, watching the smooth oval of her mother's face, the neat rim of bangs that covered her forehead, the two thin beautiful lines that marked where her smile would be. She was hoping for more of this, but her mother was finished. She put the calamine bottle back on the shelf and with a soft multiple click closed the medicine cabinet door. She turned away, and Bess, seeing the signs, began to hop.

"It itches," Bess said warningly. "Already. I remember that Sammy pushed me. He might have pushed me right in it."

"If it itches in the night, tell Daddy to put some more pink lotion on." Her mother left the bathroom, switching off the light as though Bess were not still in there. She started downstairs. Bess followed sullenly, stepping stiff-legged onto each step and leaning resentfully into space until gravity forced her onto the next.

"He doesn't do it right," she called to her mother, who was now in the kitchen. Her mother didn't answer. Bess reached the bottom step and sat down on it. She fit herself into the corner, her shoulder beneath the railing, her feet side by side on the riser. She called again, louder, "Daddy doesn't do it right," and listened for her mother's answer. Bess could hear her mother's voice. She was talking on the telephone, the voice rising and falling, the tone private. Bess knew that particular voice. She hated it. Now, if Bess walked into the kitchen, her mother would turn her back. As though the person she was talking to were so important that her conversation could not be interrupted, even by the sight of her daughter. When her mother talked in this voice she laughed in her throat, playing with the twisted cord of the telephone. Sometimes she leaned against the wall, as though she were no longer going to hold herself upright, as though she had given in to something.

"DADDY DOESN'T DO IT RIGHT, I SAID," Bess shouted, as loud as she could, but the private voice in the kitchen went on. Bess leaned against the wall, hooking her wrists over the railing. Once, when she answered the telephone, "Hello who is it please?" she had heard a man's voice, friendly, familiar, as if he knew her. "This is a friend of your mother's," he said. "May I talk to her?" Hating the voice, Bess had given the phone to her mother, who had smiled and turned her back, playing with the cord.

That night, George, Bess's father, made dinner. He stood at the stove, his back to the children. He was tall and broad, and his body was slack, as though he were held loosely together by his clothes. He had taken off his jacket when he came home and was cooking in his gray flannels and white shirt, his sleeves rolled up.

"Come and get it," he said to the children behind him. He began spooning things onto a plate. "Here it is, the World's Most Honored Meat Loaf."

"Meat loaf again," said Bess in a neutral voice. Behind her father's back she made a wild face at her brother. Sammy was five. He rolled his eyes back energetically, putting his hands at his throat, strangling himself. Bess laughed.

"Come on," said George, a warning note in his voice. "Children, come *on*." He turned and held a plate out to Bess. She did not put her hand out to take it. "Bess, that's your plate." He towered, impatient. Bess waited as long as she dared, then raised her hand to take it. The meat loaf sizzled disgustingly in its hot fat. The frozen peas would be still cold in the middle, and the frozen french fries would be mushy.

"Where's the ketchup?" she asked accusingly, and George turned and looked at her.

"Where would you imagine the ketchup was, Bess?"

Sulkily Bess lowered her eyes. "In the fridge," she finally said.

"Right," said her father. "Here." He handed Sammy his plate and they sat down at the round pine table. The room was small, and the table stood next to the window. The sky outside was dark. When their father cooked, dinner was always late. Bess began to swing her feet under the table; her father and Sammy began to eat. Sammy ran a small metal car back and forth over the tablecloth in a short explosive pattern. Under his breath he made engine noises.

"Don't," said George, without interest. Sammy lowered his eyes and continued, more quietly, to roll the car up and down by the side of his plate. George looked at Bess. They had the same high forehead and straight-across eyebrows, though Bess was fairer than her father. Her hair was nearly blond, and her eyes were blue, like her mother's. Bess sat with her hands under her thighs, swinging her legs under the table.

"Bess?" said George in a warning voice.

Bess slumped heavily against the back of her chair, her spine rounded deeply as though it could never straighten again. She raised her chin and waited as long as she thought was safe. When she heard her father draw in his breath to speak again, she answered.

"What," she said.

"Is there some reason that you can't eat your dinner?"

Bess delayed again, then shook her head slowly, her fine hair swinging back and forth, making a neat triangle across each cheek in turn.

"Then would you do it?" said George. He had both hands braced against the edge of the table, as though he were ready to throw the table over. He leaned forward at Bess, unfriendly. Bess didn't answer. "Would you please do it, Bess?" he said, his voice thin and knify. "Would you eat your dinner?"

Bess dropped her head suddenly, her bangs brushing the meat loaf. She began to sniff, and her shoulders rose, then fell.

"Bess," said George, "*what is it?*" His voice was not kind. He put one hand out toward her across the table. Bess sniffed again, her head still down.

"My knee hurts," she said in a trembling voice. "I have poison ivy on it." She raised her face now, her mouth drooping and shattered, her eyes wounded. There was a long pause. "Mommy put pink lotion on it," she said, her voice wavering. "But it still hurts."

George leaned back in his chair. "I'm sorry your knee hurts, Bess," he said. "You will still have to eat some dinner, however." He stared at her through his large horn-rimmed glasses. "When did she do that?" Now his voice was different, and Bess retreated.

"Who?" she asked.

"Your mother."

"Don't say it like that," said Bess.

"When did she do it?"

"Before she left," said Bess. "This afternoon."

Sammy ran the car up and down beside his plate. He kept his eyes down and made whispering sounds for the car. "Room," he whispered, "rooom."

"Before she left," said George. He folded his arms and leaned back in the Windsor chair, its narrow spindles creaking against his weight. Behind him, on the white stove, pots stood disorderly on the burners. The oven door was still open.

Bess hunched her shoulders and pushed them against the edge of the table. "She said if it itched in the night, you would put the pink lotion on."

George laughed unhappily. "She did," he said. Bess stared at him, and he sobered. "She's right. I will."

"What if it still hurts, though?" asked Bess.

"Then I'll put even more lotion on it," said George severely. "Your mother will be back tomorrow. You can show it to her then."

Bess swung her legs under the table. "Tomorrow, tomorrow, tomorrow," she said in an infuriating singsong.

Sammy broke in before George could start. "Bess," he said in a patronizing voice, "don't hunch."

She looked at him, furious. "*Sammy,*" she said vindictively, "don't munch. Don't punch. Don't sunch. Don't lunch." She laughed in a high, annoying manner. George pushed his chair back and stood up. He did not look at the children. He picked up his plate and took it to the sink. He stood with his back to them and scraped off the leftovers into the disposal.

"Not the meat!" Bess said. He did not answer. "Not the meat, Daddy! Mommy gives that to Charleston." Charleston, the springer spaniel, had come in with the smell of dinner and was standing, polite but interested, in the doorway, his ears alert.

"Daddy," said Bess, but more cautiously.

George turned around, the rinsed plate in his hand. "What I do and what your mother does are two different things. When your mother is here, she does things her way. When she isn't, I do them my way." He stared at Bess. "Do you understand?"

"Okay," said Bess. "Okay, Daddy. *Okay.*"

George left the room, and the two children sat on alone. The table now looked abandoned. The thick blue tablecloth still had crumbs on it from breakfast, and there were some dark spots on it. The children's messy plates lay in front of them, and their half-empty milk glasses. No one had told them to put their napkins in their laps. Sammy, his mouth full of meat loaf, put his head down on his arm, stretched out flat on the table. Chewing steadily, he closed one eye and rolled the car up and down. "Rooom," he said quietly, "rooom."

George went into the living room. It was long and narrow, with french doors opening out onto a terrace. A big deep sofa stood in front of the fireplace, flanked by overstuffed armchairs. The colors were handsome and comforting: deep reds and browns. When they had first moved here, his wife had created this small world: She had had curtains made; she had covered the furniture and bought rugs. Big swatches of material had hung confusingly in layers over the arms of chairs and sofas, for months, it had seemed, before the final choices were made. His wife had seemed to have an inner vision of what she wanted, something precise, lucid, beautiful. This had seemed a wonder to George, her certainty, her care. He had felt deeply grateful, fortunate to have a wife with such power, such conviction about this place, the core of their life. He had pretended to complain to their friends about the length of time it took, the cost of it all. Really he was using this as an excuse to draw everyone's attention to her skill, her grace, her love for him. He was respectful and proud.

Eight years later, the fabric on the arms of the chairs was thin and faded; in some places it had worn through entirely. There were subtle stains on the carpet, and Charleston's white hairs were everywhere, in all the folds and creases. The cleaning lady came twice a week, rolling the vacuum slackly across the carpet, but George felt, looking around the room at the wrinkled rug, the crooked lampshades, the mysterious topographical stains, as though he were on a doomed island, a tiny decaying principality that was slowly sinking, lowering itself into destruction.

He put on the padded earmuffs of his headset and chose a compact disc from his collection. This was large and entirely instrumental, mostly Baroque, but with some early Renaissance. He liked music that was pure, abstract, intricate. George was a lawyer, and he liked sitting down in his chair in the evenings, leaning back, and losing himself. When George put on his headphones, once the music started, he was gone: silent, invisible, passive. He could hear nothing in the old world; he was in another place. He felt that he was part of a mysterious current, this fluid, beautiful sound that swept him along and immersed him.

For the children it was like having an effigy of their powerful father, something they could treat in ways they would never risk in his actual presence. They played games around the deaf, immobile figure, daringly shouting bad words, tiptoeing up behind him and pretending to touch him, to tickle him, to bop him on the head, then falling back, chortling. Sometimes they forgot he could see, and sometimes he startled them. Sometimes he broke unexpectedly into their games, reaching out and grabbing one of them. When this happened to Bess, she screamed with fear and joy: fear at this threat of sudden danger from her father, who was the true source of her safety; joy at being so selected, kidnapped, loved.

Left in the kitchen, the two children now stared at each other. Bess's plate was untouched, and the World's Most Honored Meat Loaf had become cold. The liquid had turned into flat orange blobs, opaque, dotting the grainy gray surface.

"Now," said Sammy, "he's mad. Because of you." His head was still down, pillowed on his arm in its striped jersey. His bangs fell sideways on his high forehead. He eyed her, then the small car.

"I don't care," said Bess. She picked up her milk glass fastidiously. She swallowed lengthily, each gulp audible. When she stopped drinking she gasped for breath, a white shadow left along the upper rim of her mouth.

"Why does she go away?" Sammy said. One eye was closed; he was focusing on the car at close range.

"She has to. It's business," Bess said, officious.

"Business," said Sammy. The room off the kitchen, with a computer in it and a telephone, was their mother's office. The children knew the word: "consultant."

"Daddy goes to business, and he doesn't go away," said Sammy.

"She only goes for one night," said Bess.

"She shouldn't," said Sammy.

"She has to," said Bess firmly.

"Anyway, she went on business before, and it wasn't like this," said Sammy with conviction.

Bess said nothing, silenced: this was true. When her mother had first told her about these trips, one night a week, it had been different from the other times. This time her mother had not knelt down in front of Bess to tell her, she had not put her arms around Bess and played with her hair as she talked to her. This time she had told Bess while she was rinsing off dishes in the kitchen, not looking at her, her voice raised over the sound of the running water, loud and remote. And there were other things that were different now: the voice her mother used for those telephone calls. Their father's temper. And there were shouts, sometimes, and doors slamming, late at night.

Still, their mother left them for only one night at a time. It had happened twice. She left in the afternoon while Mrs. Garcia was still there. Mrs. Garcia stayed until George arrived. The next day, when the children came home from school, their mother was back again. The day of her return she was affectionate, full of energy, her voice high. Dinner that night was fancy. The day she came back, she was triumphant, and George was silent. He did not look at her, even when he spoke to her.

Bess pushed back her chair from the table. She left her plate and the half-empty milk glass. It would still be there, this abandoned meal, when their father made breakfast, but later her mother would be back. When Bess came home from school the kitchen would be clean.

Bess went into the living room. Her father, in his deep faded chair, did not see her. His eyes were unfocused, staring into the air at the wall above the carved Italian chest. He was settled into his chair, the earphones covering his ears. His big hands lay on the torn chair arms. One of his fingers was moving, marking a rhythm that Bess could not hear. She twitched her shoulders in a rude way. George did not see her, and she put her hands on her hips and walked forward until she was directly in his line of vision. He raised his eyes and stared at her, his eyes level with hers, and hostile. Bess arched her back insolently and stared back at him.

Looking at her father, Bess saw how ugly he was, how his hair was thinning along the top of his forehead, how stupid that looked. How mean his mouth was, how his face was full of nastiness. She thought how she hated him.

Her father was no longer looking at her. He was staring straight through her, as though Bess had become invisible. To test him, Bess slowly raised her arms, straight out, as though she were about to fly. Her father looked straight ahead, one forefinger tapping out his rhythm on the arm of the chair. Bess leaned to one side, her arms still out, but her father's eyes did not shift. He looked in a straight line. Bess opened her mouth, wider and wider. Slowly she stuck out her tongue at her father, leering, twisting her face into a gargoyle of distaste. She focused on him hard, sending him everything she felt, rage and hatred and disgust, for the gray-brown meat loaf, the chilled peas, the abandoned house. Her eyes closed with her efforts, and she leaned forward, delivering her message to her father in ferocious mime. Her whole body was engaged, and she forgot that her father was there. When he spoke, she jumped.

"Do you think I like it?" her father said, shocking the silent room. His voice, raised above sounds only he could hear, was loud and frightening. He was nearly shouting. "Do you think it's my idea? Don't you think, if there were anything else I could do, I'd do it?" He had stopped tapping his fingers, and his hands had closed into fists. His mouth was tight at the corners, pinched, as though he were holding himself away from something, as though he were just barely holding himself away from something terrible.

Bess took a step back from him, her heart pounding. Seeing her father like this was frightening, and she did not know what to do now, where to turn. Her knee hurt, and her mother was not there.

Slipping Away

J ames had begun listening in on my phone calls. I could tell when he did it, of course—you always can. It's not that you hear a sound but that the silence on the line has altered. It has deepened and expanded. Suddenly, in the middle of your conversation, out beyond your friend's voice, you hear space. Suddenly you have the whole black universe on the line, and that's not who you were calling.

The first time it happened, I thought James had just picked up the phone and didn't know I was already on it. I said, "James?" to let him know. There was no answer.

Then I thought it must be our housekeeper, and I said, "Lita?" But there was still no answer. For a long moment there was that listening distance, and then, soundlessly, the audible space closed in. The line became close and intimate, and it was only my friend and I again. After that, I knew who it had been. And I knew there was no point in asking James to his face. We've been married for seven years, and I know that James answers questions only when it suits him. If I asked about this, he would just smile in a private way and shake his head.

But it was getting more and more frequent. It began to seem as though every one of my phone conversations contained one of those black spaces, the sound of the Great Beyond suddenly intruding on the talk. Every time it happened I said, "James?" I was trying to shame him into stopping, but it had no effect.

On Tuesday James and I had breakfast, as always, in the dining room. The big round table in the middle is too big for the two of us, so we sit at a small drop-leaf table, under the window that overlooks the park. We get two copies of the *Times* delivered, because James doesn't like to wait if I haven't finished with the section he wants. We read while we eat, trading comments on the paper.

At eight-thirty Lita brings in a tray. I have coffee and whole-wheat English muffins, and James has coffee and orange juice and scrambled eggs and buttered toast and bacon. I've told him all this is bad for him, but James just smiles at things like that. He doesn't believe them. James believes that he is somehow protected from bad things: cholesterol, heart disease, airplane crashes, hard work. He's forty-two, and, so far, experience has proved him right. He is still alive, and so are both his parents, so the biggest trust funds are still to come.

In the meantime, James invests the income from the smaller trust funds. James does that, and I do everything else. I run the household. I make the arrangements when we go away, and when we don't. I buy James's mother's birthday present; I write the thank-you notes. I found our apartment, I arranged for the mortgage, and I got the letters for the board. I pay the bills, and I talk to the accountant about our taxes. I don't mind this. James needs someone to look after him; I'm here, I'm fond of him, and I'm good at it. I like making things run smoothly. Besides, this isn't all I do: I'm a book designer and illustrator; there are other things in my life.

James sees no reason to worry about cholesterol, or anything else. Why should he worry? There he sits every morning, at his table overlooking the park. Lita brings in his breakfast at eight-thirty, the eggs cooked just the way he likes them.

"*Buenos días, señores,*" Lita said, sliding the tray onto the table. Lita is from El Salvador. She is short and broad, with silvery-olive skin and jet-black hair. She is twenty-one years old and has a tempestuous private life.

"*Buenos días, Lita,*" I said. "*Gracias.*"

My family is from Boston, but when I was growing up we lived in Mexico City, where my father worked for an American bank. Spanish has always been with me, and speaking it is like entering another country. Every morning, when I talk with Lita in the kitchen, I slip back into it. We are only talking about the mechanics of the day, about groceries and the electrician, but everything in Spanish is different. The talk is rapid, the words click and rattle, the gestures are vehement. This is a world of high energy and powerful emotion. Even if it is only groceries and electricians, emotion gets into it. Every transaction in Spanish involves feelings.

When we have done discussing the day, Lita turns back to her work and I go on to mine. But sometimes Lita's face, as we talk, is stormy, and finally I ask her what is wrong. I know already: it's always her boyfriend, Paco. Lita tells me her story, and then we are well and truly in Spanish, where things happen that would never happen in English. We are in a landscape of drama and passion, one that rings with accusations and denials, amorous declarations, cries of betrayal and rage.

Lita stands before me, her eyes glittering, her hands on her hips. "*Mentiras! Mentiras!*" she cries, thrillingly. *Lies! Lies!* She holds her head high, like a heroine. Music rises in the background, and the crimson glow of a last sunset stains the backdrop. It is like having the third act of an opera in your kitchen, every morning. It is always like this in Spanish. I love it.

"*Poco más de mantequilla, por favor,*" I said now to Lita, looking at the small pat of butter on the plate.

"*Sí, señora,*" Lita said, her voice muted, her eyes lowered. She turned at once, silent in her crepe-soled shoes, and vanished through the swinging door into the kitchen. In public, Spanish is very formal.

James speaks only English, and he is not interested in Lita's thrilling life. He knows nothing of the passion and drama that take place in Spanish. James mostly ignores Lita, and seldom speaks to her. Sometimes he will say an English word to her in a loud voice, naming something that he wants, and smiling radiantly. James sees Lita as a kind of miraculous apparition: deaf, mute, and willing, there only to serve him. James wishes all women were like this.

That morning at breakfast James was in a pale blue and white pin-striped dressing gown, Egyptian cotton, very elegant, and blue pajamas and his Brooks Brothers leather scuffs. James is handsome, in a charming, boyish way. He has tousled reddish-brown hair, with a kind of electric sunny gleam to it. He has blue eyes and wears reddish-brown tortoise-shell glasses. He has a wide brow, a wide jaw, and a wide, beguiling smile.

James was reading the paper and turning irritable. I don't know why it is that the *Times* puts all the upsetting news on the front page. It takes the whole rest of the paper—the heart-warming reunion of a separated family, or the story of a home-less man finding a job—to put you back in a mood in which you can face the day.

"Just look at this," James said, shaking his head. "Now we're going to have the death penalty again."

"I didn't vote for him," I said. "He's your governor."

I was not in the mood for politics that morning. I had skipped the whole first section and was reading the metropoli-tan news. "Listen," I said. "This says that a dead body left out in the air will become a skeleton in a matter of weeks." I looked up. "Isn't that amazing?"

James looked at me over the top of his paper. "What's amazing about it?" James has uneven eyebrows, and always looks slightly quizzical.

"Well, it seems amazing to me," I said. "I thought you had to be buried. I thought it had to happen underground, like com-post. What happens to all the flesh? I thought worms ate it, or lit-tle tiny organisms, bacteria or something. If the body was just sitting on a chair in the cellar, where would all the flesh go?"

"What are you talking about?" James asked, now frowning. It irritates him when I talk about something he considers unimportant.

"This article," I said. "Here's an elderly Chinese woman in the Bronx, who speaks no English. Her husband is missing. The meter man comes around, and she keeps refusing to let him in to read the electricity meter. Finally the meter man calls the police. They all arrive, push past the old woman, and go down to the basement. The cellar is dark and full of cobwebs, and in it is the skeleton of the woman's husband, sitting bolt upright on a wooden chair."

James looked back at his paper. "How did she kill him?"

"They don't think she did," I said. "It says she's not a suspect. And then it says, just by the way, that a body will become a skeleton in a few weeks."

I like mysteries, and I particularly liked this one. I was pleased that I'd skipped the first section of the paper.

"Well, what was her husband doing down there, then, if he wasn't murdered?" James asked. He was barricaded now behind his paper. James doesn't like mysteries unless they're his.

Lita appeared with a plate of butter pats.

"*Gracias,*" I said.

"*De nada,*" Lita murmured. She turned, erect in her neat gray uniform, and left us.

"Nothing," I said to James. "He was just down there."

James lowered his paper. "What?" He sounded deeply skeptical.

"He was missing," I reminded him. "He's been missing for some time."

"But so what? Obviously she killed him," James said. "Why don't they suspect her?"

"They just don't," I said. "It says there was no suggestion of violence."

"Absurd," said James, impatient. He mistrusts all women. "Of course the wife did it."

"Maybe not," I said. "Maybe they had a fight and he went down to the cellar to hide from her and then had a heart attack. Maybe his wife thought he was still wandering around Central Park in a two-month huff."

Central Park is where James goes when he's mad at me. He did not reply.

I looked over at James's plate. In principle, I don't eat bacon, but James's plate always looks so appealing, with its sunny rumpled bed of eggs, the little twinkling triangles of buttered toast, the dark glistening strips of bacon. Sometimes the whole thing is irresistible. James had his paper up in front of him and I knew he couldn't see if I took a slice of bacon, so I did.

"I saw that," James said at once, not moving from behind his paper.

"I'll get us some more," I said, conciliatory. I wondered how he had seen me.

Looking toward the kitchen, I saw that the swinging door was open, just a crack. Lita was behind it, invisible in the dark slit, watching us, waiting to see when we were finished. I called to her for more bacon, and the door swung silently shut.

"Of course the wife killed him, it's obvious. But why did she do it?" James asked. He closed his paper with a huge rattle and clatter and reopened it importantly to the next page.

"You mean, what had her husband done? It could have been anything," I said. "He could have been listening in on her phone calls, for example. Or calling *The New York Times* for answers to the crossword puzzle and pretending he figured them out himself. There are lots of things."

James looked at me over his paper and over the tops of his glasses. "Most people," he said, "would not think those things were capital offenses."

"Those would be people who have never experienced them," I said. "The pain and anguish."

James shook his head and went back behind his paper. I broke my stolen bacon very quietly up into three pieces and laid them on an English muffin. I bit into this gingerly, muffling the sound by making a sort of hollow cave of my mouth.

"I can hear you," James said, "eating my bacon."

I didn't answer.

When I had finished my second cup of coffee I stood up and folded my paper. James had eaten the eggs, the toast, and the extra bacon and drunk two cups of coffee, but he wasn't ready to move. I saw Lita hovering in the open kitchen door, the tray held down, flat against her leg.

"She wants to clear," I said.

"She can," he said, not looking up.

"*Puede despejar,*" I said to Lita. Then, as I was leaving the room, I said to James, "Are you going to the office?"

James put down the paper at once. "Why?"

"No reason," I said. "I just wondered if I was going to have the pleasure of your company all day."

James shares an office downtown with two other partners. The three of them look at deals. They have secretaries, and telephones and desks and file cabinets: it's a real office, but since James is one of the partners, there's no one who calls up sternly if he doesn't appear. And if he decides not to go in on Monday, his money will still be there on Tuesday. Most days he goes in, some days not.

"I haven't decided yet," he said, and went back to his paper. Just as James resents questions, he resists decisions.

I left the dining room and went into my study. I was working at home that day, on a book jacket that was due on Friday. I had started it the day before, but I hadn't gotten a lot done. I'd had trouble concentrating. James was restless. He was in and out of the apartment all day long, leaving without explanation, returning just when I thought finally he was gone for the day, leaving again just as I sat down to a sandwich, back again suddenly in the middle of the afternoon. It set my nerves on edge, those wordless arrivals and departures. I kept hearing the big front door open suddenly and then shut with a big crash. I'd think, There, that's that, now he's gone, I can settle down and work. Then he'd be back, fifteen minutes later, with another crash. Sometimes I'd call out, just to make sure it was him. "James?" He never answered, but sometimes Lita would hear

me, and she would come to the door of my study and an-
nounce, "*Ya se fué, señora.*" He's just gone out. Or, "*Acaba de lle-
gar.*" He's just come in. James himself never came in to tell me
what he was doing, it was just those crashes.

The book I was working on was a mystery, the old-
fashioned nonthreatening, domestic kind. The cover was
meant to be a lighthearted combination of charm and sus-
pense. This is difficult to do without being cartoony, and I was
having a hard time. James's erratic openings and closings of the
door made the atmosphere more and more unsettled.

Finally, hearing a crash, at one point I shouted, more from
frustration than curiosity, "James?"

There was no answer, and this time I went out into the big
dark front hall. James was standing in front of the closet, struggling with the sleeve of his coat and holding a small paper bag.

We faced each other. James was now dressed in his work
clothes, a sober suit and tie. I was wearing my work clothes:
hot-pink sweatpants and a navy sweatshirt, thick wool socks,
and slippers. To judge from appearances, James was the grown-
up and I the adolescent.

"Is that you?" I asked pointlessly.

James raised his eyebrows haughtily. "Certainly not," he
said, removing his arm from his sleeve. He hung his coat in the
closet, still holding the paper bag.

"What did you get?" I asked.

"A pear," he said. He opened the bag and held the fruit out
like a magician with a rabbit. "I had a sudden urge."

The pear was a soft, lustrous yellowy-green. I thought of
biting into it.

"It looks delicious," I said, feeling the same urge he had.
"Did you get me one?"

"Certainly not," James said again, and vanished with the
pear into his study.

Later I heard the door slam two more times. James going out and returning, I thought. Now he's in. But I must have lost track, somehow, because when I finally came out of my study at the end of the afternoon, thinking James was in, he was out. This meant that there had been a crash I hadn't heard, which bothered me. If James normally slammed the door hard, without thinking about it, why had he shut it softly once, on purpose? Or was he deliberately slamming it loudly every time but once? There was no point in asking him.

The next day, on Wednesday, as I left the breakfast table, I said, without looking at James, "Are you going to the office today?"

James's head snapped up. "Why?" he asked, as before. It was as though he'd just been called to attention.

I turned around and looked at him. "I just *wondered*," I said, holding my hand elaborately against my heart, as though he had given me palpitations. "I just *wondered* if I would have the pleasure of your company, *again*. That's all."

James leaned back in his chair, his paper in his hands, his face turned watchfully to me. Lita had come in to clear, and behind him I could see her steep Mayan profile, her lowered eyelids, as she bent over the plates.

"Well, you might," James said. "You might have the pleasure of my company all day. Or I might go down to the office."

"O-kay," I said, raising my eyebrows and smiling. "Right-o. Just wanted to know." I left to get dressed. I was not happy.

The thing was, I was seeing someone else. Guy was totally different from James: he was a grown-up. I had been seeing him for some time, and for a while we had been very careful, supremely discreet. We were still being careful, but things were starting to change somehow, and move faster. I wasn't sure anymore that I could be careful, or that I could keep things under control. I wasn't even sure if I wanted to; I didn't know what I wanted. I wasn't sure if there was some subversive part of me that didn't want things under control. Something was slipping. I didn't know if it was me, or everything around me.

That day I was meeting Guy for lunch. By itself, that would have been all right, since I often go out for lunch, whether or not James is at home. But this time Guy had planned to pick me up at the apartment. If James was going to be popping in and out of the apartment all day, then I should tell Guy not to come, but if James was listening in on all my phone calls, how was I going to tell him not to?

We have two phone lines, and when one is being used, a little yellow light on the telephone goes on, to show which line it is. Every time that light went on, I knew, James would stealthily lift up the receiver. He would do it utterly noiselessly, holding the twin plungers down until the receiver was completely still, the mouthpiece held away from his mouth, the earpiece pressed deep against his ear, his whole listening brain ready to plunge into the middle of my conversation.

I went into the bedroom, working on this problem, and also the problem of what to wear. I wanted Guy to look at me and think: brainy and sexy. I chose a black short tight skirt, black tights, black cashmere sweater. I stood in front of the mirror, examining myself. The risk was that he would look at me and think: brainy undertaker. I tried on a gold chain and a gold bracelet: rich brainy undertaker? I took off the gold.

It occurred to me that maybe right now would be the best time to call Guy, while James was reading the paper. The dining room was the only room in the apartment that didn't have a telephone, with its two little yellow lights. But was James still in there? It would be just like him to sneak after me as soon as I left, and go into his study to watch for the yellow light.

I went into the front hall, where I could see into the dining room. James was still sitting at the table with the paper. He was leaning over the puzzle, a pencil in his hand. He looked placid and settled.

The kitchen phone was the closest. Lita was standing at the sink with her back to me. I dialed Guy's number. I stood facing the room, my head high, my chin lifted. I wasn't going to turn my back, or whisper and act secretive; I was going to act perfectly normal, as though everything I was doing was respectable. Still, my heart was pounding a bit.

When Guy answered I said, "Hi." My voice sounded perfectly normal (I hoped) and cheerful, as if he were any old friend, and as if everything were fine. "It's me. About lunch."

"Still on?" Guy asked.

"Ye-e-es," I said, dragging the word out to suggest complications. "But we can't meet where we planned."

"You mean at your place," he said.

"Exactly," I said.

"Okay. What's going on?" Guy asked.

"It's hard to say, exactly," I said cheerfully.

"You can't talk," said Guy. "Can you call me later?"

"I certainly hope so," I said, laughing and emphatic, as though I would be shocked and offended otherwise. "Okay, then. Talk to you soon. Bye." I hung up.

I hoped that I had made it sound, to anyone listening from the dining room, as though the conversation was quite different from what it was. But the whole thing had been more alarming than I had expected. My heart was still pounding, in fact it had gotten worse: this was more excitement than I had hoped for. Lita turned around and looked at me without speaking. I smiled at her in a perfectly natural way; she doesn't speak much English anyway. She couldn't have picked up anything from my conversation. Everything was still perfectly all right: Guy had been warned off, and James was still out there working on raising his cholesterol content.

Still smiling perfectly naturally, I walked past Lita to the swinging door. I cracked it open and peered out into the dining room the way Lita did. James was gone. My anxiety level shot up. Where had he gone, and when? If he'd left when I arrived, and had been in the bedroom or in his study, he'd have seen the yellow light go on, and I was dead. If he'd been in the bathroom, shaving, or if he'd only just now left the dining room, then I was safe. My heart was pounding even more, but the main thing, I thought, was not to panic. I would act natural, and do everything as usual.

I went back to where Lita stood at the sink.

"Lita," I said.

"*Sí, señora,*" she answered at once, turning to face me.

"This afternoon, when you go to the dry cleaner's," I said, "can you ask them if they have my red skirt? I need it for tonight."

"*Sí, señora,*" she said. There were other things that needed to be done, a water stain I wanted removed from a coffee table. I added pears to the grocery list. Lita's face was stony, her expression grim. I could see that there was turbulence beneath it. I knew there was something she wanted to tell me, but I couldn't afford to listen to her life right then. I couldn't hear another story about Paco, I couldn't bear to see her face turn thunderous, hear the music rise. I was having enough trouble with the turbulence in my own life.

I went into my study. Out of nerves I left the door slightly open, which I never do. I knew I couldn't concentrate on real work, so I did sketches and layouts, peripheral things, as I waited for the next thing to happen. The worst of it was that I didn't know what I was waiting for. Even if James had listened in to the phone conversation, he wouldn't confront me. I tried to imagine what he would do: something bizarre and convoluted. Would I be found, in a few weeks' time, sitting upright in my chair, my bones immaculately clean?

It was ten past eleven, and Guy and I planned to meet at one. I would have to call him soon. I hadn't heard a sound from James in half an hour or so, so I walked very quietly across the rug to the door of my study and peered out. Why was I walking so quietly? If I wasn't feeling guilty I'd make noise, I thought. But I couldn't help myself. I had to tiptoe. My pulse was still racing. I peered soundlessly out into the front hall. There was no one there. I listened: no noise.

I stepped out into the hall, onto the big Oriental carpet. I took three more silent steps until I could see the dining room: empty. James was either in the bedroom, in his study, or in the bathroom, or he'd gone out. I would go in and see if he was in the bedroom. I could do this quite naturally, as though I were in there getting something. I walked quietly back down the hall—I seemed incapable of making noise—and opened the door to our bedroom. It was terrifying. I felt as though I were opening the door to an enemy camp. I stepped inside.

Someone was leaning over the bed, and to my panicky eyes it seemed to be James in his pale cotton dressing-gown—doing what? What was he doing to the bed? Poisoning my pillow? Guilt and nerves assailed me.

It was Lita, in her pale gray uniform, pulling the bedspread smooth. She turned around and looked at me.

"Oh!" I said, confused. Then, since I had started the conversation, I added, "*Buenos días.*" Ridiculous. You don't say "Good morning" every time you see someone, all morning long.

Lita nodded without smiling. "*Buenos días,*" she answered politely, and turned back to the bed. She tugged firmly at the bedspread.

I hesitated, wondering whether or not to go through the bathroom, into James's study. If he was in there getting dressed, I would have to produce some reason to be there. I would have to have something ready to say, something better than "*Buenos días.*"

"*Señora,*" Lita said. She plumped one of the pillows hard, thumping it on the bed. "*Se fué.*" He's gone out.

"*¿El señor?*" I asked. How did she know what I wanted?

"*Sí,*" she said. She gave me a long, sober look.

"Oh," I said, "*gracias.*"

I was safe for a few minutes. Back in my study I called Guy. This time I couldn't help myself, I spoke in a near whisper. I was listening for the front door.

"It's me," I said.

"Hi," he said, "what's up?" It was unspeakably wonderful, hearing his voice. Guy is totally, totally focused, and whatever he says he will do, he will do. I find this incredibly sexy.

"Things have gotten very weird," I whispered.

"Listen, if this is a bad day, we don't have to meet today, you know," Guy said reasonably. "We can change it."

But that was not possible. I couldn't bear the thought. I had been waiting for this day to arrive for decades, it seemed. And the day itself had started slowly, and quietly, in small dry trickles, like an avalanche, moving from the trickles into steep meaningful slides, gaining speed and mass and thunder. It was now hurtling downward in a huge sliding roar, carrying me with it, carrying all of us, headed straight toward this lunch, and my meeting Guy. My heart was thundering too. The thought of it all not happening was impossible. Putting it off meant meeting him sometime in another era. It was not possible. It had to happen today.

"No," I whispered, "it will be fine. Only we'll have to meet on the street. The corner of Madison and Ninety-first, the northeast corner. Same time," I said, not naming it, in a desperate attempt to leave something unsaid.

"See you then," Guy said, and we hung up.

I straightened. In my urgent secretiveness I had hunched myself over the phone as though I were trying to keep it warm. I stood up, not looking around. I was consumed by the horrible certainty that I was being watched. The skin on my neck felt cold, and my heart was galloping along, loud and wild, like a runaway horse. I made myself walk to the window, very naturally, and look out onto the park. I stared out for a few moments, seeing nothing, and then allowed myself to turn. James was standing in the door.

"Hello," I said, breathless. "I thought you'd gone out." Damn Lita, I thought, wild. I'll kill her.

"No," he said. He smiled. "I hadn't." There was a pause. I walked back to my desk and sat, very naturally, down.

"Are you going out for lunch?" he asked.

"No," I said instantly, and my heart sank at once. A fatal error. How could I have said something so stupid? It was a denial reflex. I was really answering the question: Are you guilty? Right then I would have said "no" if James had asked if I'd ever seen him before.

If I hadn't been such a fool, I could easily have told James I was going out for lunch with someone, anyone. Now I had trapped myself into staying here.

"What are you doing? For lunch?" I asked. Maybe he was going out, I thought hopefully.

"I'm not sure yet," James said. "I may be going out."

I nodded casually, as though it meant nothing to me. James stood there a bit longer, as though he was waiting for something else, and then he turned, looked back at me, then left.

I turned back to my sketch pad. Had he heard me? How would I know? I had an hour and a half before meeting Guy. I started making useless sketches. If worst came to worst I could call a friend, and tell James afterward that she had asked me to lunch. An hour and a half. I looked at my watch. My heart was not going to last the day if it kept up like this. "Shh," I whispered, but it kept on.

Then the door began its sporadic crashing again. This time, every single time it crashed I had a wild urge to go out and look. Had James gone out? Come in? And why had Lita told me he was gone when he was not?

At twelve-fifteen I decided to make a move. When I heard the next crash, I went out into the hall. It was empty. "James?" I said, loudly. I looked in our bedroom, and in his study. They were empty. He was definitely out. When he came in, when I heard the next crash, I would tell him someone had called, and I was having lunch out after all. I went into the kitchen and fixed myself another cup of coffee—as though what I needed was caffeine—and started back to my study. Crossing the hall, my mug in my hand, I met Lita.

"*Señora,*" she said, meeting my eyes with some urgency. "*Lo siento. Creí que se fué.*" I'm sorry, she said, I thought he had gone out.

"*No importa,*" I said, waving my hand. I didn't want Lita to think I was spying on my husband.

"*Está en el armario,*" she said. He is in the closet.

I stared at her for a moment. In her life, this sort of thing was always happening. Paco was constantly lying in wait for her, banging on doors, leaping out from alleys, accusing her of infidelity, trying to seduce one of her friends, or doing some other wild and alarming thing. But these things never happened in English. It's true that I was seeing another man, but quietly, decorously.

I wondered if I had misunderstood Lita, if she was continuing with some story about Paco she'd started earlier.

"¿*Quién está en el armario?*" I asked.

"*Su esposo,*" she answered. Your husband. She stood very straight, her face solemn, as though she were a scout reporting on enemy activity.

"¿*En cual cuarto?*" I asked. In which room?

"*Su escritorio,*" Lita said.

James was in the closet of my study. He was standing there, dressed for the office, in his suit, in the dark. He was probably standing on my shoes, crushing the insteps. Was he hunched over, his ear against the heavy door, listening? Was his hand on the doorknob, holding it still? What if I tried to open the door? Would he hold on to it and keep me out? Would we wrestle, through the door? What if I managed to open it and we stood there, confronting each other? What would he say?

I didn't want to find out.

"*Gracias,*" I said to Lita. My stomach felt terrible.

"*De nada,*" Lita said, soberly, and we passed by each other, she on her way to the kitchen, I on my way into my husband-infested study. I sat at the desk, doodling on my sketch pad. I thought of leaving the room again so that James could slip out, but of course it was possible that he didn't want to slip out. It was very possible that he wanted to wait there until something incriminating happened.

The phone rang and I jumped. "Hello?" I said nervously.

It was only a friend, but I knew James was listening to every word. This made me feel very strange, and I must have sounded odd, because Susan asked if I had a call on the other line. I told her I was working on deadline, which was true, and we hung up. The hands on my watch moved so slowly that I kept looking at the clock, to see if my watch had stopped. Every time I did, I thought of James, breathing quietly, still standing on my shoes in the closet, for whom the time was passing even more slowly.

Finally, at twenty-five past twelve, I stood up. James would be ready by now to get out of the closet, I thought. I went into the kitchen, to give him a chance to slip past. I stood well back inside, across the room, where I could see out into the hall if James went by.

Lita was in there and turned, her eyebrows slightly lifted, as I came in. I smiled at her and put the kettle on again.

"*¿Está todavía adentro?*" she asked. Is he still in there?

I nodded, smiling slightly, shrugging my shoulders lightly, not looking at her. I wanted to act casual, as though we were not really talking about this, my husband standing in a dark closet for over an hour, listening to me make doodles on my sketch pad. Lita gave a decisive and disapproving shake of her head, then turned back to the silver she was cleaning.

It was now twenty of one, and I had one last hope. If James was going out to lunch, it would be soon. He refuses to eat lunch any later than one o'clock, because of his theory about digestion. He might be leaving any minute. I was so unnerved by having him in the closet that I didn't think I could now manage to tell him someone had called earlier, while he was out, and asked me to lunch. I couldn't even be sure, now, that he had been out. For all I knew, he'd been crouching in the hall coat closet all morning, tiptoeing out periodically to slam the door, and rushing back in after each crash.

I closed the door from the kitchen to the front hall and turned to Lita.

"Listen," I said. "I want you to go out and stand on the corner of Madison and Ninety-first." I told her what Guy looked like. I told her to tell him to wait, that I'd be there within ten minutes. "Okay?" I asked. "*¿Me entiende?*"

Lita washed her hands as I talked, listening carefully, with a frown of concentration. When I was finished she wiped her hands firmly downward on her apron, like a salute.

"*Sí,*" she said. "*Entiendo.*" She went to get her coat. I stayed in the kitchen. Lita came back, her coat on, her face sober. Walking past me she turned. "*¿Por qué no sale a la oficina, como los otros?*" she asked contemptuously. Why can't he go to the office like other men? She set off on her mission.

I stood in the kitchen, hoping to see James leave my study. I turned off the kitchen light so I wouldn't be seen. I had forgotten to ask her this, but I hoped she would slam the door loudly, loud enough to be heard by someone standing inside the closet in my study. I waited, holding my breath. There was a huge crash.

In a second James strode rapidly down the hall toward his study, past our bedroom. I waited, wondering what to do. I looked at my watch: four minutes to one. If James had a lunch date nearby he could still make it. Even if he didn't have a date, he'd leave if he thought I'd gone out. Wouldn't he? There would be nothing else for him to overhear, but maybe he'd stay in, out of sheer perversity: I had no idea what he would do. I could take the bull by the horns and walk out boldly myself. That would throw him into confusion, but was that what I wanted?

I couldn't think what I wanted. All my talent for organization had vanished. I couldn't think of what would be the best thing to do. I had no idea. As I stood there, hesitating, I heard the front door slam again. I looked out into the hall at once: it was empty. James was gone. The heavy botanical green wallpaper, the big oak chest, were alone, the room silent, unpeopled.

Everything in me had now started up like a factory. My heart was hammering, my blood was pulsing, my nerves vibrating. My ears were ringing. I was sweating, and I couldn't remember how it was I normally breathed. I went to the hall closet and took out my coat, but I had a hard time putting it on. I couldn't remember which one I normally wore, or if there was a reason for wearing a different one today. I was going to see Guy in moments, moments. He was already waiting outside, on the street corner. Lita would be standing surreptitiously nearby, on guard, having delivered her message but unable to tear herself away. The message was brief, one she could say in English—only a few words, the name, the phrase "ten minutes." Her sober Mayan features would be her credentials.

Guy's car would be parked along the sidewalk, right on our corner. James, long and lanky in his tweed overcoat, might stride right past him, his hands stuffed deep into the pockets of his untidy overcoat, his face enigmatic. James might stop when he saw Lita, and then she might, in her excitement, glance at Guy. Then James might follow her glance, and look at the man in the car parked alongside her. Then their eyes might meet, James's and Guy's. Oh, God, I thought, anything could happen, now, anything at all. The music was rising, the sunset colors coming up.

I was buttoning up my coat as I was thinking all this. I felt hot and cold at once. I couldn't remember what season it was outside. In the elevator, the door slid shut behind me and I turned to the mirror. I had fastened my own coat all wrong. The brass buttons were out of alignment and the hem was awry, like a crazy person's. Looking at myself in the mirror, I felt the floor suddenly plunge out from under me, dropping away, leaving me aloft with nothing beneath my feet, leaving me breathless.

I felt unprepared and helpless: I could do nothing about any of this. It was alarming, but it was also thrilling. I could feel my whole known, orderly life slipping away. I could feel it slipping into Spanish, right before my eyes.

The Nile in Flood

When Nora woke, the cabin was dark except for a rumpled strip of light under the curtains at the window. This was not dawn. Outside on the docks, where their ship was moored, the big sodium lamps stayed on all night. Their sizzling glare struck directly at the cabin window.

This was not how Nora had imagined things. She had thought that only the moon would shine into the cabin at night. She had thought that the window would be small and round, a porthole, opening easily so she could lean out into the jeweled night. Instead, the window was big and square, like a motel's. It did not open at all, and anyway was almost entirely blocked by a huge television, set between the bunks. Nora thought of the cool breezes outside, sweeping down the wide brown Nile.

The cabin's air was thick and fumy, as though the ventilation system were circulating exhaust from the engines. These throbbed steadily, though the ship was moored. By morning the cabin would smell like a garage. This was the second night that Nora had awakened, alarmed, her head pounding, the throat-closing stench overpowering sleep in the tiny room.

She looked through the gloom at Gordon's bunk, at his motionless silhouette. Perhaps he's dead, she thought. They had been married five months. She watched his dim shape: slowly the angle of his shoulder rose, then dropped. He was only asleep.

The Egyptian trip was their belated honeymoon. Nora had not expected something so majestic, so exotic, so old-fashioned. She had thought vaguely of a week spent driving through England in a rented car. Or a week anywhere, or even a weekend: she was forty-nine, and her expectations had diminished.

Nora had never been to Egypt before. She had read about it, but the reality surprised her. There was the heat, for one thing, which was violent and relentless. Standing in the desert, outside the tombs at Giza, Nora felt dazed, assaulted by the sun, which threatened madness and death. Still, once inside the silent, shadowed passages, the heat was forgotten: Nora had also been unprepared for the paintings. In the books, the text was in charge of the paintings, decoding and diminishing them. In reality, the paintings were in charge. They needed no text: they had a life of their own. They drew her into their own world, rich, powerful, intimate. Nora was entranced by the vivid, graceful, warm-limbed bodies, by their magical energy. At the temple of Dendera, deep in an underground passageway, she had put her palm on one of the glowing figures, as though she could absorb its power. The guide frowned sternly, and Nora withdrew her hand. Of course touching would be forbidden.

Lying in the dark, Nora squinted at the clock Gordon had given her: three-seventeen. The cabin was small and coffin-shaped, narrow at each end. Even in the dark it was oppressive. Nora was wide awake, and hours lay between her and the daylight world, movement and speech. She pulled the sheet over her head, covering her face. She breathed slowly, through the sheet, trying to filter the worst of the fumes. Last night she had gone back to sleep like this, the sheet tented over her face. In the morning she had been covered with sweat and had a pounding headache, but at least she had slept.

She breathed shallowly, trying not to draw carbon monoxide inside her. She imagined tiny capillaries in her lungs, clogged and sluggish from the poison. She noticed her heartbeat, and a pulse in her temple. Panic and claustrophobia began to flicker in her mind.

The sheet was heavy, and sweat broke out on her forehead. *Don't think about suffocating,* Nora warned herself. At once she threw off the sheet and sat up, her heart noisy, her face damp. The walls of the cabin pressed in. The black television loomed over her pillow, and the air was unbreathable.

Nora climbed out of bed quietly and opened the closet door. She felt inside for a caftan and slid it over her head. She took her pillow, her quilt, and the room key, tightly wrapping her fingers around its clattering rings. Gordon shifted, and Nora paused. When he was quiet, she opened the cabin door.

The corridor was bright and airless, and under her bare feet the carpet bristled, dry and synthetic. Holding her runaway's bundle, Nora padded past door after door to the lower lobby. At the top of its angular staircase she pushed open the last door, onto the deck. Outside she stood still, taking a slow breath.

Around her was the Egyptian night, vast, deep, spangled, the air a rich translucent black. The night came down to the deck, surrounding and embracing her. Overhead was space, high, luminous, star-filled. Learning the dimness, she saw low black shapes, like sarcophagi, lining the deck: deck chairs. She pulled a mattress off the stack, dragging it to the stern. The wooden deck was cool beneath her feet, and around the ship the river moved and murmured.

On the eastern shore, cold spotlights glared over the docks, a cluster of gas tanks, and a chain-link fence. On the western shore—close, the Nile was narrow here—a low and ancient village hugged the river's edge. Whitewashed buildings fitted neatly into one another and a small mosque raised a bulbous dome and elegant spire above the flat roofs. A night wind moved through the palm trees, and their long splintery leaves swayed, shifting black patterns across the whitewashed walls. The street was empty and silent, and it stopped abruptly: a few palms, then blackness. Fields would lie along the river, Nora knew, and behind them would be useless sand: the land was fertile only as far as the Nile had flooded. The Aswan Dam had ended the annual rampages; the river now lay meek and obedient between its banks forever. But in the past, the river's wild spates had been the source of life as well as death. The invading floodwaters bore a cargo of bountiful black soil, dense and fertile. On the way to a temple they had seen the high-water line: it lay precise and absolute, like a boundary on a map. There was no gradation, no shading: the dark luxuriant soil stopped dead. Beyond it the earth was dry and empty, barren.

Nora lay down on her mattress and tucked the quilt around her. The deck was dry, the air cool and sweet, and the sky radiant with stars. The engine throbbed far below, barely audible. Calm, like the night, settled on her. Peacefully Nora watched the village, full of secrets. The palm leaves shifted in the wind, and shadows moved against the white walls. Nora was safe and warm: encircled by water, enwrapped by her quilt, invisible in the dark. She was alone and happy in the strange Egyptian night. She pulled the quilt closer; she slept.

The breeze was steady, the night silent, and Nora half woke often, half dreaming, tranquil. She blinked, confused, then pleased, to find herself by the mysterious village, in the deep parts of the night. Toward morning, though it was still black, the muezzin appeared in the mosque, and Nora woke to his thin, urgent cry. White-robed men appeared, gliding like dancers with long, hurrying strides, the heavy folds of their caftans swaying. The men made no sound, slipping in and out of the shadows like spies. Lit theatrically from below, the minaret was radiant, glowing and irresistible in the surrounding dark.

Nora watched the hurrying men and wondered how it felt to be striding through the freshening air toward that ancient cry. She closed her eyes, opened them, and closed them again. She would never know. The only Egyptian Nora knew was Mr. Fouad.

The first night, after dinner, the passengers were invited to the murky, lurid bar, with its gold-mirrored tables and smoked windows. Nora and Gordon sat on low banquettes, a strange sweet drink before them, in tiny, fussy glasses, ruby-red, with gold rims. On the dance floor a spotlight suddenly irradiated the ship's manager, holding a microphone. He was dark and slim, with soulful brown eyes and a thick black mustache. His neat suit was somber, his collar and cuffs dazzlingly white. He spoke a precise and heavily accented English.

"My name is Mr. Fouad," he said, and bowed slightly. "I welcome you to Egypt, one of the Great Wonders of the World." His voice was rich with pride, and he bowed again, ceremonially. He explained that the syrupy drink was a symbol of welcome; everyone took cautious, dutiful swallows. "I wish also to welcome you to the ship *Hathor*, another of the Great Wonders of the World." He smiled happily at this modest joke, but it was clear that his pride was real: Mr. Fouad thought the grim geometry of the soulless boat was, simply, perfect. What Nora saw as bleak, disheartening, and artificial, Mr. Fouad saw as the triumph of technology over the old, antiquated ways.

Mr. Fouad smiled, waiting hopefully for a response, and the passengers applauded politely. Mr. Fouad bowed again, and then, meticulously, he introduced each member of the staff. They stood lined up next to him, all smiling. "This is Miss Nadia, the housekeeper," he said respectfully, and the passengers clapped. Miss Nadia, her smile gleaming in the dim light, stepped forward.

Afterward, in the cabin, Nora sat cross-legged on her bunk. There was no room for both of them to stand at the same time, and Gordon, who was tall and portly, towered majestically before her, unbuttoning his shirt. The top of his head was perfectly smooth and burnished, like an objet d'art or a piece of polished alabaster.

Nora asked, "Didn't you think all that was wonderful?"

" '*Wonderful*'?" repeated Gordon. He raised his eyebrows. "I'm not sure that 'wonderful' would be the word I'd choose." He sounded tolerant, amused. "Why did you think it was 'wonderful'?" He put quotation marks around her word.

At his tone, Nora turned cautious. "Oh, I don't know," she said. "I just thought Mr. Fouad was sweet, with his big thick mustache and his white shirt. I liked the way he was so proud of *every*one, the waiters, the stewards, the housekeeper. And they were all so proud. And they had such beautiful, brilliant smiles." Mr. Fouad's dark, glowing face, his elegant gestures, the ceremony and strangeness, had reminded her of those figures in the paintings, lithe and vital and mysterious.

Gordon laughed briefly. "My dear girl, you sound as though we'd seen some ancient tribal ritual. This is like showtime in Las Vegas. These people do this at the start of every cruise, every week, fifty-two weeks a year. It's not exactly a spontaneous outburst."

"But that's *why* it was so nice," Nora protested. "Even *though* they do it all the time they were still so proud of themselves, proud of the boat, proud of Egypt." Nora could see Mr. Fouad, turning courteously from side to side, the spotlight shining down on his narrow shoulders, illuminating his precise and radiant smile.

Gordon shook his head, still smiling. "Well, you're rather easy to please."

Nora, pulling her dress over head, did not answer.

After a pause Gordon turned to her again. He had a majestic voice, deep and resonant. "I must say, I'm a bit mystified. I'd have thought you'd like the tombs, the temples, the paintings. I didn't think I'd brought you all the way to Egypt to admire the headwaiter." He smiled again, as though this were a joke they could share, her sophomoric response to Egypt.

Nora looked steadily back at him. She smiled, but said nothing.

Before she married Gordon, Nora had made a vow: she would not fight with him. She did not have the heart for another divorce; she could not afford a second failure. She would never permit a fight to begin. Any anger he felt, any hostility, any criticism, she would absorb. None of it would be reflected back at him. Nora believed she could do this; she believed she had to. All her life she had relied on passion, and it had always betrayed her. This time things would be different. This marriage would be based on sympathy, loyalty, affection. She would take responsibility for its success. She would be vigilant; she would not allow anger to make its chaotic inroads into her heart.

Nora's dress lay in a green pool in the cradle of her lap. She reached behind her back and unhooked her bra. Naked to the waist, she waited for Gordon to finish so she could stand. His back turned, he held on to a shelf with one hand as he stepped ponderously out of his trousers. On either side of his pale solid back a crease of thick skin slanted diagonally down. The flesh itself was somehow womanly, heavy and slack, loosened forever by age. The skin was soft and pale, but not smooth: moles, pockmarks, bumps, stood out on its pallid landscape.

Gordon turned to face her. Along the ridges of his shoulders were meandering hairs, long and white. His chest was androgynous. On either side of the sternum, flesh that would once have been hard and flat now drooped, pendulous, like breasts.

It distressed Nora to see the damage done to Gordon's body by age; it distressed her to feel her own response. She did not love his flesh, which shamed her. I should have known his body when it was young. I should have grown old with him, seen him change beside me, she thought. But she had known him for only eight months, and had seen none of his changes.

"Don't you think?" Gordon asked.

Nora had not been listening, and felt doubly guilty. She had been disloyal and inattentive. "Yes," she said, at random. Stiffly Gordon leaned over her, putting his hands on her bare shoulders for balance. The touch on her skin was unexpected. As he leaned his body toward her, pale and massive, Nora felt suddenly at risk, her breasts naked and vulnerable. She wanted to cover herself, to protect herself from him, as though he were some stranger, not her husband.

"Good night," Gordon said loudly. He kissed Nora on the mouth. The kiss was firm and dry, a seal on the day.

"Good night," Nora said.

Gordon turned his back again and began the cumbersome process of lowering himself down into the narrow bunk. As he maneuvered, Nora kept sympathy on her face, in case he wanted it, but he did not look at her again. When he was settled on his back, he lapped his hands, one over the other, on the crest of his high firm stomach and closed his eyes for the night.

Now, up on deck in the cool air, Nora thought of him, below. She hoped that he was sleeping peacefully, and that he had not waked up to find her mysteriously absent. She wondered what he would think if he did. She had no idea. She did not know him well enough. She had married a man she did not know.

All her life Nora had believed that things were improving. She had seen impecuniousness, haphazard living arrangements, arguments with her first husband, disappointments at work, as temporary. She had always trusted that the landscape would open at last into a broad and sunny plateau. When she left her husband, she felt she was doing something brave and commendable: her ideals would not permit her to lead a second-rate life. She felt that she was rejecting something shoddy, unacceptable, and that she would move on to something finer: a real marriage. And at the small publishing house where she worked, she had thought she would keep moving up, to better things.

One evening last winter Nora had opened her front door and stepped into her dark foyer. As she did so she thought suddenly, This is the best apartment I will ever have. I will never live in a better place. The thought was startling and painful, a blow. She closed the door, and the sound of the locks clicking into place behind her was sickening.

She stood still, in the dark. She did not turn on the light; she did not want to see the cramped and awkward living room beyond the tiny hall, or the hall itself, with its rickety table piled with mail and books and out-of-place objects, or the grimy, cracked plaster walls. She would be here in this dreary, inconvenient place forever. Even worse, she thought that she would never need more space: her daughter was nearly through college. Diana would not come back to live in the tiny second bedroom, with its thin curtains hanging slackly at the barred window. Nora's life was drawing in. Standing inside the door she felt hollow, as though something had dropped away beneath her. She closed her eyes.

She would not go on to better things at work either, she thought. Her publishing house was being taken over by a conglomerate, and though Nora had been assured nothing would change, it came her to now that this was, of course, not true. It would all become more commercial; the new staff would be uninterested in the books Nora wanted to publish. She would be lucky to keep her job. And she would not marry again, she could see. New York was full of divorced women, and men her age married women twenty years younger, smooth-faced women who lied about not wanting children. She would be alone.

Nora put down her plastic bag of groceries and sat down on the battered chair, jammed too close to the table. Her shoulder touched the stack of mail, and a stream of papers, magazines, and catalogues spilled smoothly off, like a pack of new cards, into a glossy, layered pool of chaos on the floor.

It was soon after that awful evening that she met Gordon. He was seventeen years older, which was surprisingly comforting. Men her own age were prickly with competitiveness, challenge, anger. These brutal edges seemed to have been worn smooth on Gordon, who was courtly and protective. His wife had died, and he had retired from the law. He spent his time on boards, of companies, museums, the opera house. The opera was his great love, and this seemed appropriate to Nora, that he should be so drawn to something so elegant, so dignified and civilized. He seemed wise and lofty, and it was a relief for her simply to be in his presence. He lived in a handsome duplex in the Eighties: there was room even for Diana. When he asked Nora to marry him, it seemed a miracle.

Her head still deep in her pillow, Nora opened her eyes. Something was intruding on the steady vibration of the engines: a rhythmic overlay of slow footsteps. A watchman, she thought, pacing the deck. She hoped it was a watchman and not someone less bound by duty: it was very dark, and very late. Nora was lying down, in her nightgown, and did not want an encounter. She drew her legs up to her chest and pulled the quilt over her head. She hoped he would think she was asleep and leave her alone.

The footsteps approached slowly. Maybe he wouldn't see her. Nora huddled into the hollow of the mattress, crossing her arms on her chest and closing her eyes, as though this made her invisible. What if he shouted at her, officiously citing some rule and ordering her back to the cabin? What if she had to stand up ignominiously before him, clutching her bedding, stumbling back along the deck in the gloom? Nora thought of the airless cabin and its fumes. She hugged her knees to her chest.

The footsteps were louder. They had quickened and changed direction: he had seen her. The footsteps stopped at Nora's head, and she heard a faint positioning shuffle. She held her breath and did not move. Perhaps he would think this was a pile of bedding and try to pick up her quilt. She would hold on to it, and they would struggle absurdly. She could feel his presence next to her, she could hear him breathing. His feet were directly at her head. She wondered how long she could hold her breath. If he thought she was asleep, surely he wouldn't wake her up.

"Excuse me," the man said. His voice was low and very serious. Nora's heart was pounding, and she began to sweat. The voice was right next to her head: he had crouched beside her. Nora wondered if he was going to touch her. If she feigned sleep, he might touch her to wake her up, but if she admitted she was awake, she would have to speak to him. She waited, hoping that he would leave. She ran out of breath, and let out the air from her lungs slowly, in a long silent stream. He did not move. She thought of the Rousseau painting *The Sleeping Gypsy:* the figure stretched out in an open field beneath the brilliant moon. In her mind, he seemed so calm, the Gypsy, in his bright clothes, so confident of his safety. The animal—a lion? a leopard?—stood over him, lashing his tail, regal and murderous.

"Excuse me, madam," the voice said again, very close. Nora raised her head from the pillow. Trying to sound aloof and testy at being disturbed, she said, "Yes?" She hoped that she did not sound weak or helpless. She hoped that she did not sound as though she was in her nightgown.

It was Mr. Fouad. He was squatting at the head of her mattress, gazing straight down into her face. She saw the dark *V* of his legs on either side of her, the solid line of his joined hands above her. He was still in his dark suit, his collar and cuffs gleaming.

"Mr. Fouad," Nora said. He smiled at her, not moving. He was very close to her. His upside-down face hung over hers, and she could feel the warmth coming from his body, from his legs.

"Ah, Mrs. Newhall," he said gently.

There was a long pause, and Nora could hear him breathing. She wondered what he was thinking. She felt her armpits dampen, her heartbeat quicken. Holding her head up was uncomfortable, and it brought her face very close to Mr. Fouad's legs, close to the center of his body. She could smell his strange, cinnamony smell, warm and strong. His hands, his brown, long-fingered hands, were very close to her face. One finger gently stroked another. Mr. Fouad was watching her intently, and she could not help thinking of his fingers touching her. Nora dropped her head back down into her pillow, to withdraw, but she wondered if it suggested yielding, giving way.

"Are you all right?" Mr. Fouad asked her. His voice was soft, as though he knew her very well, as though he knew secret things about her. His dark eyes were calm. He waited for a moment and then repeated the last words. "All right?" he asked again, even more softly. It was really a whisper, and he spoke the words as though they meant something else, something private that she would understand.

Mr. Fouad, crouching so close to Nora, his legs spread over her, and his hands hovering over her face, seemed like one of her dreams, on this strange night, another of the flickering scenes she had seen as she opened and closed her eyes, drifting in and out of sleep: the black Egyptian sky, the dark, moving shadows, the men in white robes striding urgently through the streets. She felt mesmerized, as though it no longer mattered what she did, as though she herself were hardly in her own life. She felt as though her life had been taken over, and things now would be unpredictable and exotic.

"I'm fine," Nora said. She heard her voice: it was as low as Mr. Fouad's. Her breath had turned erratic, as though she had been climbing stairs.

Mr. Fouad smiled at her, upside down. He leaned closer. "Are you sure there isn't something . . . that you want?" he asked. His hand dropped to her face and for a tiny instant she felt his long narrow finger briefly cup the curve of her chin. The touch was very light, and so gentle that Nora could not bear it.

At once she sat all the way up, drawing herself very straight. Under her caftan, she could feel her breasts against the soft cotton of her nightgown.

"I am perfectly fine, Mr. Fouad. I would like to sleep out here on deck. I am perfectly fine," she said. She tried to sound dignified and self-assured, like a married woman. She looked directly at Mr. Fouad. He looked silently back at her. His eyes were startling, so close—they were so very deep, so quiet. And he seemed to know her, his hand had seemed to know her skin.

"All right," he said gently, as though she had asked him for something that he could give her, and he smiled again. He did not move, and there was another pause. He leaned closer, tilting his head, so she could see how it would be if they kissed. "You are sure?" he asked. His question, his voice, was gentle, deeply courteous. He was offering her a chance to confess her secret, to admit the truth.

"I am sure," Nora said.

Mr. Fouad stood beautifully. He gave a small bow, still watching her. Nora nodded in return. Mr. Fouad turned and began walking away, his footsteps measured. Nora stayed upright long after she had lost sight of him in the gloom, sitting up until his footsteps lessened, until they were finally lost in the hum of the engines.

Nora lay back down again, shaky, her pulse still hurtling. She pulled the quilt up around her shoulders and closed her eyes, though sleep was now beyond reach. She had done exactly what she should have done. She had behaved properly, like a married woman. There was nothing to feel ashamed of. Yet lying there, Nora felt frightened, bewildered. She was frightened not of Mr. Fouad but of her own confusion: nothing seemed now to make sense. She thought again of Mr. Fouad's gleaming smile beneath his luxuriant mustache. His white teeth. The low, tender voice in which he had asked her, "Are you all right?," and the butterfly touch on her chin. Nora wanted to weep, thinking of Mr. Fouad.

She felt that she understood nothing. Her life seemed mysterious and unreadable. Nothing was the way she had imagined it. She had never imagined herself on this strange, old-fashioned voyage. She had not dreamed that she would marry a tall and courtly stranger. And she had not known that this courtly man, her husband, would never touch her body. She had not known that his only kiss, ever, would be a firm, neat one on her mouth. She had not known that his tumult would be over, that he would never invade her soil. She had not known that the line at the end of passion would be so clearly marked, that the life that lay before her would be so pale, so dry.

The Favor

Driving back to his mother's house from the tennis courts, Roger rounded a slow curve just past the golf course and saw a woman at the side of the road. She was standing at the end of the sandy lane that led to the little club beach. Against the Caribbean sun she wore a turban and a terry-cloth robe. Her legs were white and stalky, and on her feet were plastic bathing sandals. As the car approached, her hand fluttered up, undecided: not exactly a flag, but different from a wave. Roger stopped the car and she came over, taking tiny steps across the hot sand.

"Well, I suppose you're in a *terrible* hurry," she began.

Roger shook his head. "Not at all," he said politely.
"What's the problem?" Roger was forty-eight. He had hazel
eyes and a narrow face. His cheeks were lined and his forehead
was high; his hair was beginning to recede.

"Well, my *cah* has broken down, you see," said the woman.
She talked very quickly, with an old-fashioned accent, stylized,
rather grand. There was an outraged lilt to her sentences, as
though it were a scandal that she had to say any of this at all. "I
came ovah for a *swim,* and now it won't start, don't you see, and
I have to get back home somehow."

Roger leaned across the empty passenger seat and opened the
door for her. "Here, climb in," he said. "Where do you live?"

The woman pointed back the way Roger had come. "Parrakeet Peak," she said, getting in.

It was just past noon, blazing hot. Beyond the scrubby trees,
the sun was reflected by the ocean and sent back up into the
shimmering air. Settling herself into her seat, the woman now
took a good look at Roger.

"Aren't you a Pickering?" she asked, accusingly, as though
he were trying to sneak his family past her.

"Roger Conrad, hello," he said, giving her a grave nod as
he backed the car and turned it around.

"Oh, you're Roger *Conrad,*" said the woman. "I used to
know your fohthah."

"Did you," said Roger, pulling back out onto the road.
"Now, where is it again that you'd like to go?"

"Parrakeet Peak!" said the woman, surprised that Roger
had already forgotten.

"And just where is that, exactly?" Roger asked.

"Oh, it's way back in, near the Janeways'," said the woman,
waving her hand in a long-distance gesture.

Roger started back toward the clubhouse. The road here
ran along the wide white beach, which was edged with a line

of palm trees. The trees leaned haphazardly toward each other, scattering shaggy leaves on the fine sand. Across the road, the golf course rolled its smooth gray-green mat across the rising slopes. Beyond the golf course there were low inland hills, covered with dense jungly growth. A few isolated houses were scattered along the crests and ridges. The island was very dry, and next to each house was a whitish open patch—a concrete catchment for rainwater.

The club owned a thousand acres in the southeast corner of the island. Except for the shorefront and the golf course, the club land was uncleared, covered with dense wild scrub. Most of the rest of the big island was open. Brown cattle grazed across broad, peaceful fields of pale grass, where sugarcane had once grown.

Roger's parents had chosen this place, years ago, for its clean white beaches, the low pretty houses, the golf, and their kind friends there. When Roger was little, the family had come every winter after Christmas. He remembered those times as green, warm, easy. The life of the island was brilliant and foreign to him: the hot spiky growth and the brilliant flowers, the dry swift lizards. The black, black people, with their loose bright clothes and syncopated speech. Roger and his younger brother, Steven, had spent their days outside—on their bikes, or snorkeling in the easy washes around the small coral islands. Paddling slowly through the lucid surges, magically powered by his limber flippered feet, he heard his breathing loud and hollow in his ears. Roger felt privileged to be in this exotic place, following the silvery underwater life, the schools of wary fish, shifting and glittering before him; he felt like a fortunate traveler from another planet.

In those days the weather was steady, the sun benign, the rains brief. In the evenings, his parents went out to parties on wide stone terraces. His mother wore flowered dresses, a white sweater over her smooth brown shoulders.

Roger had not been back in nearly twenty years, but it seemed now that little had changed. The original premise of the club had been simplicity—the houses were modest, and there were no telephones. Now there were some new houses, bigger than the old ones, but still no telephones. The club seemed just the same: a cluster of low stucco buildings, clean, cream-colored, freshly painted, set into the low bluff above the long, perfect crescent of the beach. Vigorous foursomes in bright clothes moved across the golf course in the dazzling sunlight. In the evenings, in the club dining room, with its high thatched ceilings and polished stone floors, Roger's mother waved and smiled at her friends. These were women who looked like her, in flowered dresses, with white earrings and necklaces. The women were with pink-faced men in colored trousers, men who looked like Roger's father. It seemed, all of it, just as Roger remembered it: gentle, pleasant, protected.

Roger drove along slowly. The club roads were narrow, made of uneven concrete slabs. On the inland side the brush was hacked short for a scant yard, then gave way to heavy tropical growth, spiky-leaved and hostile. As Roger's car came around a corner, a honey-colored mongoose, soft and bright-eyed, raised his head at them, then rumbled into invisibility among the gray-green leaves.

"I have to get back, you know, because I have to meet the architect. *And* the decorator." The woman shook her head. "It's so *difficult* to get things done down here. Of course I haven't been here for five years. I've been in Palm Beach. It's up along here on the right."

Roger turned the car inland and started up the long spine of the hill. This road was one he did not remember, though he and Steven had biked around most of these narrow lanes. In those days his family had stayed at the clubhouse. It was before they built their house.

"I'm at the top of the hill," said the woman. "The highest point on the island. You can see the sun rise and see it set from our house. I joined this club forty-five years ago but I didn't buy a house until years later. I wanted this one, and I waited until it came on the market. Wiggy Newcombe called me up and said, 'Cynthia, your house is for sale.' I couldn't believe it." She looked at Roger expectantly, then asked, "Didn't your fohthah join about the same time we did?"

"And my mother," said Roger, nodding. "That sounds right."

"I used to know him well."

"Ah," said Roger. This seemed unlikely.

"I knew your mothah, too, but not as well. She wasn't a golfah. Your fohthah was a golfah."

"He was," said Roger.

"But your mothah wasn't a golfah, was she."

"She plays golf," Roger said.

"I don't remember it," the woman said flatly. "Are they down here, your parents? Is that where you're staying?"

"My mother is here," said Roger. "My father died last summer."

"Oh, I'm *sorry* to hear that," said the woman, turning in her seat to look at him. "Oh, I'm *terribly* sorry to hear that. Your fohthah was *such* an attractive man. A *terribly* attractive man."

"He was," said Roger.

"Give your mothah my sympathy, would you? I don't know that she'll remember me. Cynthia Harrison. I used to see her at parties. Tell her I'm terribly sorry about your fohthah. I'd love to see her," she went on unconvincingly. "Will she be here long?"

"We're leaving tomorrow, actually," Roger said.

"Tomorrow, oh, that's too bad. Oh, I'd love to have seen your mothah," said Mrs. Harrison, now more confident. She patted her white turban. Her hands were large, and the joints of her fingers thick. She wore deep red nail polish, and her skin was milky. A faint dusting of freckles, like nutmeg, went up the backs of her arms. There were traces of dark lipstick on her mouth. She had an aura of faded and dreadful glamour.

"I used to see your fohthah at Saratoga, too," said Mrs. Harrison. "He loved it there."

"Yes," said Roger.

"Do you go to Saratoga too?"

"No," said Roger.

"It's a beautiful spot," said Mrs. Harrison. "Right along here. Turn left again. It's really rather spectacular. We can see the sun rise *and* set from here. You'll have to come in and see the view. I'll just be a minute. I'll have to find my man and send him back down to the cah. Can you take him down? It's right on your way. Because it won't start."

Mrs. Harrison's house was like all the old ones: low white stucco, with a palm-thatched roof. A tree with violent purple blossoms stood by the front door. On the garage roof squatted three black men wearing shorts and sunglasses. Mrs. Harrison rounded her hands into a megaphone and called up to them.

"Hoo-oo!" she called. "Where's Mar-tin?"

The men looked at her and shook their heads. Mrs. Harrison turned back to Roger.

"Wouldn't you know the roof had termites. I wasn't here for five years—that's why it's all such a mess. I'll get Martin. Rose will know where he is. Because he has to fix the cah. It won't start."

She made her way across the scrubby lawn in her transparent plastic sandals. On the other side stood a small whitewashed cottage; a radio inside blared ragged music. Mrs. Harrison stood outside the nearest end. Elbows pressed tight to her chest, she put her hands to her mouth.

"Ro-ose!" she called through the music. Rose did not appear, and she tried again. "Ro-ose!" Her voice was high and impatient. Roger looked up at the men on the roof. One of them, in yellow shorts and reflector sunglasses, was looking at Mrs. Harrison's narrow back, her bathrobe and turban. He was laughing.

Rose came out of the other end of the cottage. She was black, with an injured expression and a large middle. She wore a loose paisley dress and a white apron.

Mrs. Harrison, not seeing her, leaned into the window full of music. "*Rose!*" she called despairingly.

"Hello!" shouted Rose, right behind her.

"Oh, there you are, Rose," said Mrs. Harrison, turning around. "Where's Martin?"

Rose shook her head with finality. "Don't know."

"But I have to find him," Mrs. Harrison pointed out. "I need him to fix the cah, you see."

"Don't know," said Rose again. She looked at the ground and jumped her hands up and down under her apron.

Mrs. Harrison did not answer. She turned her back on Rose and walked toward Roger. "It's no good telling them anything," she said loudly. "They don't listen to a word you say." She gave Roger a fretful smile. "Now come inside and let me show you the house." Roger started to speak, but she held up her hand. "You have to see it. It's the best view on the island. Come in for one minute. I know you need to get back."

Roger did not need to get back. No one was waiting for him, and it might be useful to see inside of Mrs. Harrison's house. Roger was here to help his mother put her house up for sale, and seeing other houses would give him a better idea of the market. He stepped inside.

A large open room led through a wide doorway to a terrace beyond. The ceiling was high and airy, the struts and beams exposed. The sight of this—the orderly right-angled pattern, the architectural skeleton—reminded Roger suddenly of the structure of his parents' house here, and of the night he had first seen the plans of it.

This had happened in the big gabled brick house in Greenwich where Roger had grown up, and where his mother still lived. It was Roger's senior year at Middlesex, and he and Steven were both home from school for Thanksgiving. Before dinner that evening their father called everyone into the library, which was his room. It stood off the big, square front hall, and was a narrow room with two tall windows. The walls were paneled in dark wood, and there were high built-in bookshelves. A fire was burning, and the room was warm and lit up. The whole house smelled of the roasting turkey. Roger's grandparents were coming, and the air was full of anticipation.

Roger, Steven, and their father were all wearing ties, blue blazers, and gray flannels. Roger's mother, Charlotte, was in a dark green dress. She sat on the leather Chesterfield sofa, and the black Lab, Troy, had crept surreptitiously up next to her. The dog smiled widely at the boys, his eyes narrowed in happiness, his rose-colored tongue hanging out. Their mother, too, was smiling, and their father, who seldom smiled, was jingling his keys in his pocket. He did this when he was either pleased or annoyed, and tonight he was pleased.

"Ready?" he asked the boys. He was a tall man, broad-shouldered and thick-waisted. He had a high beaked nose, fierce eyebrows, and a florid complexion. At his temples were bushy gray tufts of hair. He was mostly bald, in a gleaming, powerful way.

Roger and his brother nodded alertly, though they did not know what it was they were ready for. An easel stood in front of the fireplace, a white linen napkin draped over the top of it.

Their father looked at the easel, then back at the boys.

"Get that dog off the sofa," he said irritably. Troy was strictly forbidden to sit on the furniture, but only Roger's father enforced this rule.

"Troy," Charlotte said. At her tone, Troy's face turned mournful and his body became immobile. "Troy," Charlotte said again, loudly. She pushed at him, carefully. Everyone watched while Troy climbed reluctantly down and curled up dolefully on the rug.

"All ready?" Their father asked again, brusque. "Stand up straight, you two!" Roger and his brother moved their shoulders dutifully.

Their father lifted up the linen napkin. "Look at that!" he said proudly. On the easel was a drawing of a house, the boys had no idea why.

"Wow," said Roger politely.

"Wow is right," said their father severely. "Wow is right. The best-looking house in the whole damn club." His face was stern but he jingled his keys, radiating satisfaction.

It was an architect's rendering, drawn in straight and perfect lines. It was an ideal, a paradigm of a house, orderly, calm, supported by logic. Roger stared at it intently. He tried to imagine the drawing as an actual house, built, made real, with the sound of real waves beyond it, real palm fronds crashing around it, in real sea wind. Roger tried, but the transformation from theoretical to real was beyond him. He felt he was encountering his own limitations, and the vast reaches of his father's strength. He knew the plan would be made real, and it seemed as though the house would be created out of his father's sheer willpower.

This made Roger feel both proud and baffled, as though his father knew some empowering secret and Roger himself were stretching toward this knowledge, trying to live into what his father possessed so easily—his stern certitude, his absolute grasp of the laws governing the real world. Roger pulled his shoulders back farther, drawing himself up. At his feet, Troy thumped his heavy tail hopefully; Roger, usually his ally, frowned down at him severely.

Now Roger looked around Mrs. Harrison's living room. It was large and light, but it looked as though it had not been touched in decades—since the nineteen-fifties. The turquoise plaster walls were covered with long, complicated cracks. Black kidney-shaped coffee tables stood on looping wrought-iron legs, and the big curved sofas were made of contoured foam-rubber cushions. At each end were square pillows with abstract shell designs on them. Whatever was not faded turquoise was faded yellow. On a table stood a huge conch shell, glossy, gum-pink inside, with a hard white undulating edge, like congealed icing. A faint, sharp odor of mildew hung in the air.

"Look at that," said Mrs. Harrison, pointing with satisfaction out beyond the terrace. Below them was the long, sloping hillside of tropical thicket. Roger gazed dutifully at the ocean spread out in the distance, flat and gray-blue, glittering restlessly.

"That's where the sun sets, right there." Mrs. Harrison pointed, authoritative. "You can see it in the evening."

"Very nice," Roger said.

"Now let me show you the rest of the house," said Mrs. Harrison. "It's quite a remarkable place. Martin will be back in a minute, and you can take him down to the cah."

"Mrs. Harrison—" Roger began, but she interrupted at once.

"Let me just see where Martin is. I hate for him to keep you waiting like this. I've told him a hundred times *not to go off without telling someone where you're going.* You can't get them to listen to a word you say."

"Mrs. Harrison, I'm afraid I have to get back for lunch," Roger said. He was beginning to think of his retreat.

"I know that, I know that," Mrs. Harrison said. "That's why I'm so cross at Martin. Let me just go and find him." She vanished outside.

Roger did not follow her. He was reluctant to leave her stranded here, with no car and no telephone, but Roger had seen enough of Mrs. Harrison's house, and of Mrs. Harrison as well. He did not look up again at the rafters. There was a second part to his memory of the house plans; it came back to him unasked, unwelcome.

The next morning, Roger had been called back into the library alone. When he came in, silent on the thick carpet, his father closed the door behind him without speaking and walked to the fireplace. The sky outside was overcast, the light inside was dull. The room was now cold. Thanksgiving dinner was over, the house silent. Roger's father stood again by the fireplace, which was now black and empty. The easel still displayed the calm and perfect house plans, but this now seemed pallid and irrelevant. Roger's father did not look at it. He looked at Roger. His face was dark, his eyebrows drawn fiercely together at the top of his high curved nose. He jingled his keys.

"Know why you're here?" he asked Roger. It was an accusation.

Roger thought he did.

The trouble at school had started with minor offenses— skipping study hall, lights on after lights-out. There had been a forgotten appointment with his adviser. He had missed chapel and been caught. He and some friends had gone off campus without permission one Saturday night and were found walking along the road by a master driving by. There had been warnings about Roger's attitude. Then, just before Thanksgiving, Middlesex had played its annual football game with its great rival, St. George's. The game was at St. George's, and Middlesex won, for the first time in years. It was a great and important victory, and the way to celebrate it had come to Roger in a moment of happy inspiration.

Roger still remembered the silence of the empty stone chapel, the smell of damp walls, the ecclesiastical perfume of hymnbooks and pews, the lightning thrill of illicitness. He remembered running easily up the stairs to the belfry, finding the long coil of heavy rope unguarded. The moment of setting himself onto the rope, fixing his grip on the rough, twisting surface, throwing his whole weight into the effort. He hung in the air, clamped onto the rope, his feet pulled up under him, his whole body willing the great change to begin. For a long moment there was nothing. Then, triumphantly, he felt the rope begin to give ponderous way beneath him, to begin its slow descent. Above him he heard the great sonorous clamor begin, the clanging jubilation sent out into the clear air. It had been his doing. It had been wonderful. He had nearly been expelled.

"You know why you're here or not?" his father asked again. He walked back and forth in front of the fireplace, his hands in his pockets, his strides menacing. Against the somber sky, the heavy dark green curtains looked black.

"I guess so," said Roger. He stood up straight, his shoulders pulled back.

His father stopped. "Why do you think you're here?" His tone was belligerent.

"Ringing the bell, I guess," said Roger bravely.

His father snorted. "You guess?"

"Ringing the bell at St. George's," Roger said.

His father glared at him. "You're goddamned right. You're here because of the goddamned bell." He stopped and stared at Roger for a second, then turned again away. "I don't know who you think you are," he said.

Roger said nothing.

"I drove up to your school on Tuesday to talk to the headmaster."

Roger had known nothing of this. The thought of his father at his school, talking to the headmaster, unbeknownst to him, gave him a chill feeling. He could see his father in his gray suit, frowning, walking rapidly across the gravel of the parking lot toward the brick administration building. It had happened three days ago. Roger felt a darkening of the room.

"Drinkwater said he'd never had a boy like you. He said no one had ever done a thing like that before at the school." His father turned and faced Roger. His thick eyebrows were pulled angrily together. "I told him I thought he should expel you."

There was a silence in the room.

"I said, 'Kick the boy out. Teach him a lesson.' " His father looked at him. His mouth was a wide, bleak line, set by a rigid jaw.

Roger said nothing. He did not know what it would be possible to say. He felt cold, as though the November wind were sweeping right through him, as though the house itself were no protection. The room seemed colder than anywhere he had ever been.

Roger's father fixed him for a moment, narrowing his eyes, and then began again, walking back and forth before the blackened fireplace.

"He wouldn't do it," his father said, his voice contemptuous. "Drinkwater said he wanted to give you another chance." Roger's father shook his head.

Now, in the tropical air, Roger could feel again the cold of that morning, hear his father's voice as he said the word "expel." He saw the easel, the drawing of the tropical house still there. He had felt ashamed that the house plans had been witness to this.

Roger moved out onto Mrs. Harrison's terrace. By now his mother would be back from golf, and changing for lunch. Charlotte was tall and thin, with long limbs and dry, mottled skin that wrinkled diagonally along her arms. A spray of fine lines radiated from around her mouth, and her pale blue eyes had milky rims. Her short, dust-colored hair was in neat waves, held back by two combs at her temples. She wore no makeup.

Charlotte had told Roger her plans at breakfast. "I'm having lunch with the Simpsons," she announced. She squeezed a slice of lime over the narrow prow of a pale green melon wedge. "I doubt they'd interest you. They're a hundred years old and he's had a stroke. I've known them all my life. Betty's a saint. I don't think you'd have much fun with them. Better have a sandwich at the club. Come if you want." She did not look at him; she was concentrating on spooning a perfect half-moon out of the melon. "You'll do better at the club. Betty's cook is famous. Worst on the whole island."

Roger had not minded his exclusion from lunch at the Simpsons'. In fact, he was relieved at the prospect of solitude: he and Charlotte had spent three whole days almost entirely in each other's company. Roger had never before spent three days alone with his mother, and before coming down he had wondered if the trip would be uncomfortable, if it might produce some kind of awkward intimacy. What he dreaded, vaguely, was some disclosure from his mother, some unwanted revelation of grief, loneliness, regret—something ghastly, unavoidable. Of course this had not happened. Charlotte had been as she always was: cool, pleasant, composed. Roger was proud of her for this, proud of her emotional reticence and her sense of propriety. And he was proud of himself, too: he gave himself modest credit for maintaining an atmosphere—decorous, civilized—in which an emotional storm would not occur.

Cynthia Harrison now came out behind him. "Rose thinks he'll be back soon," she said. "Let me get you a pick-me-up."

This surprised him: "pick-me-up" was his father's phrase. Roger did not answer. Mrs. Harrison bustled smoothly back inside to the ice bucket, and Roger followed her. She scooped ice into two fat plastic glasses. "I will say, Rose makes the best rum punch in the whole club. Everyone says so."

But Roger had not gotten a sandwich at the club, and he did not want his empty stomach invaded by rum punch. He answered in a no-thank-you tone.

"I'm afraid—" he began. But his voice was not quite firm enough, and Mrs. Harrison could hear through it that he had no plans. She waved her hand and interrupted.

"He'll be back in a moment, Rose says. Because he has to fix the cah." Mrs. Harrison handed him a glass, took the other for herself, and guided him to a chair. She sat on a sofa, where she leaned back theatrically against the cushions. Her long white legs were crossed at the thigh. The veins in them were bold and blue. Roger wondered how old she was: seventy? A bit more.

"Go on," she said, "try it. Everyone says she makes the best."

Roger took a sip: sweet and strong. He would drink half of it and leave, he decided. Then, if Martin was still not back, Roger would drive up to the club and ask the manager to take care of Mrs. Harrison and her car.

"Now, tell me," said Mrs. Harrison. "Tell me about your fohthah. I'm so sorry to hear that he died. What happened?"

"There's not much to tell," said Roger. "He had a heart attack last summer, in Greenwich. He was playing golf. The eighth hole," he added politely, in case she knew the course.

"Oh, your poor mothah," said Mrs. Harrison expansively, shaking her head. "I know just what she's going through. I remember when Eric died. I was devastated." Her tone had become relaxed and intimate. "It changes everything, death. I mean apart from the grief, from your feelings. Everything is different. You don't know what time you should get up in the morning. Should you have lunch? Should you go on having the paper delivered? You don't know what to do, you haven't the first idea." She gestured widely. "And then people stop asking you out. They do at first, out of pity, but pretty soon instead of being a widow you turn into a single woman, and then they stop. No one wants a single woman at the dinner table. Your best friend will only ask you to lunch. She thinks you're after her husband. As though I'd look at John Addington: a drunken sheep!" Cynthia Harrison laughed and shook her head. "But we can't be picky, of course. None of us can. We aren't such bargains anymore ourselves." She suddenly smiled disarmingly, tilting her head self-deprecatingly. Her white hands with their gnarled knuckles fanned out on either side of her face, as though displaying some disappointing merchandise.

Roger looked down at his drink, uncomfortable. He did not want Mrs. Harrison's sympathy. She was wrong, too, about his mother: Charlotte had been entirely self-possessed when his father died. She had been sad, of course, but calm and rational, not lonely and dithering. Roger could not imagine his mother wondering scattily whether or not to have lunch, any more than he could imagine her wearing blood-colored nail polish and a turban, flagging down cars on the road, asking strangers for favors.

"How long has your—how long have you been alone?" Roger asked. He looked at his watch. He would stay for five more minutes and then leave, Martin or no Martin.

"I was divorced in nineteen fifty-six," said Mrs. Harrison promptly. "I remarried in nineteen fifty-seven, and then my second husband, Eric, died in nineteen seventy-nine. But I had already known your fohthah long before all that. He was *such* an attractive man."

"Did you know him well?" Roger asked, sure she had not.

"At one time I knew him well," said Mrs. Harrison thoughtfully. "I used to see him in Saratoga. I never saw your mothah there."

"She didn't go," said Roger authoritatively, as though he knew. In fact, the trips to Saratoga had been in the summer, when he and Steven were at camp. He didn't know whether his mother had gone or not. Still, he refused to let Mrs. Harrison be an authority on his parents.

Mrs. Harrison took another long swallow of Rose's famous rum punch. So did Roger: it had actually begun to seem like a good idea. The rum was sweet and comforting, and it felt somehow energizing.

"No. I never saw your mothah there. Your fohthah said she didn't like it." Mrs. Harrison looked at Roger and paused. "Saratoga, I mean." There was another pause. Mrs. Harrison seemed to be about to say something more, or waiting for Roger to ask her something, something more about his father.

Whatever it was she wanted, Roger refused her. "I don't know what my mother likes," he said abruptly. "Bridge. Golf. She has the garden club. I don't know what she does. What do you do all day?" he asked, surprising himself by the question. It was the rum, he decided. But he wondered if his mother did get invited to dinner by her friends. He had never thought of this before.

"Oh, I have so much I can hardly get it all in," said Mrs. Harrison, raising her hand to stem the tide. "You've seen what's going on down here. It's just as bad at home. Things seem to fall apart as soon as you notice them. Oh, you know what I mean. As soon as you've got the pool filter fixed, the maid quits. I've quite a lot to do. And I've got my boards. I'm very active on my boards. Have been for years."

"I suppose my mother is on some boards," Roger said, frowning. He wondered if she was.

"Of course your mothah's on boards," said Mrs. Harrison, waving her glass generously. "What else would she do?" She paused and looked at Roger. "What do you do? Are you married?"

"I'm a lawyer," Roger said shortly.

"Ah!" said Mrs. Harrison inattentively, and stood up. She brought the pitcher of punch back over to the coffee table. She replenished both glasses and sat back down.

"Are you married?" she asked again. Her tone was gentle, and she cocked her head kindly.

"Not anymore," Roger said, stiff.

Mrs. Harrison shook her head sympathetically. "Oh, it's so *painful,* getting divorced. I went through *agonies,* myself, even though it was my own idea."

Roger took another swallow of Rose's punch and did not answer. He would not discuss his divorce with this woman, his failure.

"Well, it's one thing my parents didn't do," he said, reminding her instead of his family's success. "They always stayed together."

"You mean they always stayed married," said Mrs. Harrison lightly.

"They stayed together," said Roger stubbornly.

"They stayed married. They didn't always stay together. I knew your fohthah very well," said Mrs. Harrison.

"And just how was it that you knew him so well?" Roger asked, nettled.

"Saratoga," said Mrs. Harrison.

"I suppose he stayed with you there?" Roger asked, belligerent. He was now trying to goad her into indiscretion, falsehood, something he could challenge, deny.

"Oh, of course he stayed with us," said Mrs. Harrison, surprising him with the pronoun. "Lots of times. We had a lovely big house at Saratoga, and he always came to us. Sometimes we'd all motor up together from New York. He loved Saratoga. We had a wonderful pair of linden trees by the terrace. Your fohthah was crazy about those trees. He used to stand underneath them and look up into the branches and close his eyes. He said he liked the sound the wind made in them. He said the sound was different from the wind in other trees."

Roger made a small noise through his nose. He had never seen his father look up into a tree.

Mrs. Harrison shook her head. "Oh, we always loved having him up to stay. And of course he was wonderful company. He was so funny."

"Funny?" Roger said, offended. "Roger Conrad?" His father had not been remotely funny.

"Oh, yes," said Mrs. Harrison, smiling reminiscently. She took another swallow of rum punch. She looked past him out the doorway. Without any warning she called out suddenly, "Martin!," in a loud high voice. She listened, frozen, her head raised, frowning. She had put on more lipstick, Roger noticed, and the dark mouth glistened horribly in her faded face. There was no answer from outside. Mrs. Harrison looked back at Roger.

"They laugh at me, you know," she said in a conversational tone. "The help. It's all changed here. When we first came down, years ago, they loved us here, because we gave them work. And we loved them, because they gave us this beautiful place. We used to be friends. Now, they hate us because we have money. They hate the scholarship funds we set up for their children, they hate the library we built them, they hate everything we do. Now they laugh at us behind our backs, and now we lock every room when we leave it." Mrs. Harrison shook her head. "I miss it all," she said. "I miss being friends with them. My old cook, Rachel, I miss her. Oh, how she used to make me laugh. We used to tell each other the most dreadful things, about our families, and laugh together. Now Rachel's dead, and I have Rose, her niece. You saw her. Rose barely speaks to me. She won't look at me unless she has to, and she won't smile at me at all. Not a glimmer." Mrs. Harrison shook her head again. "I miss my friends." She paused, and looked at him candidly. "Of course it's our fault, too, you know. It's not just them."

Roger said nothing. He wanted to deny flatly everything Mrs. Harrison said, but he found he could not. It was true, now that he thought of it, that attitudes had changed here. He saw few smiles now from the island people, and he remembered many when he was young. But Mrs. Harrison was wrong to blame this change on club members. Roger remembered only courtesy toward the island people—meticulous courtesy—from his parents, from their friends, from everyone he knew. This animosity, the change, was not their fault. He was on the point of saying so when he remembered something that had happened that morning.

In the club store he had seen a couple in their early seventies. They were white-haired and pink-faced, the man in bright green pants, the wife in a yellow golf skirt. Both wore round white canvas hats with wrinkly brims, pulled low. They were newcomers—someone's guests—and they moved through the crowded aisles with an air of gentle confusion. The woman bumped slightly into Roger and turned, giving him an abashed smile.

"I *beg* your pardon," she said charmingly.

At the counter, the man paid the black cashier in American money. He was given his change in something else—small darkish bills, rumpled, faintly greasy.

"What's this?" he asked, moving the strange bills between his fingers. He looked up at the cashier, the bafflement in his blue eyes magnified by his horn-rimmed glasses.

"That's island money," said the cashier, impassive. He was a man in his forties, with ashy-black skin, a broad nose. A white short-sleeved shirt.

"But what am I suppose to *do* with it?" asked the pink-faced man, still holding out the grimy bills, faintly outraged.

"That's their *money,* dear," said his wife. "That's their *money.* They use it to buy things." She gave the cashier a nice smile and plucked at her husband's sleeve, urging him along, kind, confident.

Roger had paid no attention then to the exchange, but now it came back, vivid and troubling. Now he remembered the cashier's cold stare when Roger had set his newspaper on the counter and smiled. It made him wonder about those other memories: perhaps what he'd seen as courtesy had been something else, something covering a blithe and insufferable assumption. Roger felt unhappy, less and less certain. Everything seemed so complicated, so opaque.

Mrs. Harrison returned to Roger's father. She shook her head, smiling. "No, he was wonderful to have around. He was such fun."

But here Roger was on firm ground. "My father," he said reprovingly, "was a very serious person."

"Oh, of course he was," Mrs. Harrison said, shaking her head. "I don't mean anything *against* your fohthah. He was a *marvelous* man. So funny!"

Roger straightened, magisterial. "Mrs. Harrison, I think I know my own father," he said. "He was *not* a funny man."

Mrs. Harrison raised her eyebrows kindly. "Well, maybe we saw different sides of him. But he used to tell those wonderful stories on himself. You must have heard them. Of course he was a terribly bad boy when he was younger. You've heard about all that. He must have told you."

"No," said Roger.

"Well, you've heard how he was fired from his first job?"

"Fired?" repeated Roger, smiling now. He shook his head. "My father was never fired, from anywhere."

"He was fired from his very first job, at a bank. For throwing paper bags of water out the window. He hit one of the tellers on her lunch hour." Mrs. Harrison leaned back, rubbing her papery white throat, and laughed expansively. "You wouldn't think they'd *fire* him just for *that,* would you?"

"It sounds quite reasonable, actually," Roger said stiffly. He could not imagine his father leaning out into the air, supple, hilarious, looking for targets.

"Not to me," said Cynthia Harrison. "But it turned out that he'd already done something worse. It was the two things together, you see. You haven't heard this story?"

Roger shook his head, skeptical.

Mrs. Harrison leaned farther back against the sofa. "Oh, it was years ago. I think he and your mothah were just married. One night they'd gone out somewhere, out to dinner with some friends. It got late: he wanted to go on; she wanted to go home. So she went home and he went on. When he finally

went home to the apartment your mothah was pretty cross."
Cynthia Harrison looked sympathetically at Roger. "It was
quite late by then. Well, your mothah refused to let him into the
apartment. He stood out in the hall, trying to persuade her, but
she refused. I think he must have gotten a little loud, you know.
The neighbors got involved. Everyone came out into the hall
and had a point of view. It got quite lively. But your mothah
was determined, and she stood firm. Finally your fohthah realized she wasn't going to let him in. By then it was around six
o'clock in the morning, maybe later. He'd had, really, quite a
lot to drink. And so it seemed to him that the best thing to do
was to go straight to the office. He didn't have any other place
to go, and he had to be there in an hour or so anyway. It
seemed to solve all his problems at once: not being able to get
in, finding a place to sleep, and being at work on time." Mrs.
Harrison's face lit up, as though she herself had just solved all
her problems.

Listening to her, Roger could feel his heart pounding more
and more urgently. There was a turbulence inside him he did
not understand. He felt angrier and angrier at Mrs. Harrison.

"So he took a taxicab downtown. He let himself into the
office, which was empty. He sat at his own desk and put his
head down and tried to take a little catnap, but you see it felt
cramped. So he got up and set off to find a bigger space, somewhere he could be more comfortable. When he found one he
settled down and went straight to sleep. And that was where
the president of the bank found him at nine o'clock, when he
went into the boardroom for a meeting with a client. Your
fohthah was fast asleep on that big mahogany table, stretched
out full length, flat out. He was still in black tie. Hadn't even
taken off his pumps." Mrs. Harrison laughed again, closing her
eyes with delight. She opened them finally and looked at
Roger. "Oh, you *must* have heard that story."

Roger had nearly finished his second rum. "I have never heard that story," he said severely. "And frankly, Mrs. Harrison, I have a hard time believing it." He stood up to leave. He was dismissing her, her ridiculous story, her ridiculous getup.

"Oh, it's true, all right," said Mrs. Harrison, smiling. She leaned back, pulling her legs up sideways underneath her and stretching her arms out along the cushions like a very old starlet. The flesh along her arms was loose and quivery. She took a long sip of the rum and looked up suddenly at the ceiling. "Ticky Cobb was there too, at the bank. Everyone knew about it." She drank again. "Well, but he was *famous,* your fohthah."

Doubtful, Roger said nothing. Ticky Cobb was a very old friend of his father's. And there had been some business connection, he knew. For some reason this enraged him, it enraged him not to be able to deny this monstrous story flatly, totally.

Mrs. Harrison leaned forward. "Let me freshen your drink. It would be *rude* not to, since I'm keeping you here."

"Thank you," said Roger, "but no. I'm afraid it's really time for me to leave." He set down his glass. "I'll run over to the club and ask them to see about your car. Thank you so much for the drink." His voice was cold, loaded with contempt: he loathed this woman. He loathed this terrible cacophony she had loosed into the air, the turbulence in his chest, the clamor in his mind. His father had not been like that: this woman was a liar.

Mrs. Harrison stood up too. "You look like him, you know," she said, and smiled.

But now he had her, Roger thought, triumphant. This was false. Roger did not in the least look like his father. He smiled.

"I'm afraid you're wrong," he said with satisfaction. "I don't at all. Everyone knows that."

But Mrs. Harrison only smiled back. She was not flattened by his denial, she was not even dismayed. She shrugged her shoulders. "Maybe no one else does, but when I look at you I see him," she said gently.

Mrs. Harrison seemed to have done it again. She had said something that Roger knew was false, but that he couldn't deny. He couldn't disprove this, any more than he could disprove the terrible, unwelcome story about his father. For there it was, the thing he had so dreaded hearing down here: the unwelcome revelation, the ghastly disclosure. Only the anguish was his, not his mother's.

Roger stood looking at her, without speaking. It was rude, but he hardly knew what to say, he felt such confusion inside him. There was something rising up in him, a great surge of rage at Mrs. Harrison, contempt for her, but there was something jubilant that had been loosed as well. Roger felt as though he were again racing up those narrow chapel stairs, alone, running upward toward the wild, dangerous song that only he could make. He felt in a state of chaos, rage and jubilation shifting and glittering together in his head. What held him, what he could not bear, was the thought of his father. His father, stretched out on that mahogany table, in his dinner jacket, his black grosgrain tie limp against his stiff white shirt, his patent leather pumps still on. The terrible, contented smile on his father's face.

All Roger knew now for certain, the only thing, was the fact that he hated Mrs. Harrison. How could he not? How could he ever forgive her? How could he thank her enough?

D o N o t S t a n d H e r e

"You did talk to William last," Emily said to Richard. She was looking not at her husband but out the side window of the car. They were driving west somewhere, away from London. The motorway here ran along the edge of a vast green plain that stretched to the horizon. They had been driving into the countryside for over an hour; by now the landscape should have been quiet and pastoral, but the green plain was disturbed by three red-brick cooling towers. Their size, their shape—their curved and tapered waists—suggested to Emily sinister depths, poisoned blue water, glowing and deadly.

"That's not the point," said Richard. "Who talked to him last." He did not turn when he spoke, but stared straight ahead at the broad gray motorway hurtling toward them. The rented car was small, and the roar of their own speed filled its interior. Emily did not answer.

"The point is, you made the arrangements, not me," Richard went on. "You're the one he invited. And in any case, he's your friend, not mine."

"He's not my *friend*," said Emily. "He's my *publisher.*"

"Oh, I see. And you don't like him." Richard laughed unpleasantly. "I thought you *loved* William."

"Don't be ridiculous," said Emily. "Of course I like William. *You* like William. But you're *always* the one who gets directions when we go on trips. Anyway, you're the one who knows England."

Richard had lived in England, years ago, with his first wife. When they quarreled, Emily held this against him.

"I don't even know what county we're in," Emily went on, scanning the countryside. "Where are we? I doubt very much that William lives in a nuclear park," she added crossly.

Richard had turned off the motorway, and the road now led toward the three brick towers. Wisps of white smoke drifted from their huge open tops.

Richard did not answer.

They had been quarreling since they arrived in England, four days earlier. That morning, leaving the hotel in London, they had entered the tiny mahogany elevator in stubborn silence. When the door shut they stood stiffly in the cramped space, close together, not touching, their chins high with aggrievement.

"The trouble with you," Richard had said, facing the closed door, "is that you cannot say you're sorry. You're incapable of it."

"I have no trouble at all saying I'm sorry," Emily said coldly. "None whatever. If I have something to be sorry for. I fail to see what I have to be sorry for at the moment."

"Being consistently unpleasant to me all last night and this morning," said Richard severely. "That suggests nothing to you? No fault on your part?"

"I wasn't *unpleasant*, Richard. I was angry. I don't pretend to be pleasant when I'm angry. You're unpleasant when you're angry, everyone is."

"So you won't apologize," said Richard, with satisfaction.

"No," said Emily. "For what?" Rage blossomed in her and she turned fiercely. "What about the things you said to me last night at dinner? Are you going to apologize for those?"

The elevator, lowering itself ponderously within its narrow shaft, arrived just then at the main floor. As Emily spoke, the door slowly scissored open to reveal the Victorian lobby: paneled walls, polished brass, a densely patterned carpet. An American couple, middle-aged, well-dressed, ill-at-ease, stood among their brand-new suitcases. Clerks bustled quietly behind the high reception desk. Richard, without answering her, stepped out of the open door, his face dark. Emily followed, her chin still high, her face matching his.

They had carried the fight along with them in the car. During the drive they had hardly spoken, and Richard's face was closed and tight. Emily had sat looking out the window, watching England move past her and brooding over the things Richard had said over these last four days. They had seen almost no one else in London; they had been trapped with each other at every meal, at the hotel, at the theater and museums. Emily now sat silent, picking through the things Richard had said as though they were jewels, spoils of a battle. She held each one up to the light, marveling angrily at its hard, glittering edges.

The road now dropped down into a small hollow among the broad green hills. It curved narrowly in between tiny shops and pubs, past an undistinguished eighteenth-century stone church with a modest spire, a row of half-timbered houses with deep, dense thatched roofs. Two elderly women in long black sweaters made their way along the sidewalk. Richard slowed the car and rolled down his window as they approached.

"Excuse me," he said, leaning out. "Could you tell me where Welnore Court is?"

The woman nearest to them had pink cheeks and short gray hair. Her eyes, through her colorless glasses, looked astounded, as though Richard had asked the way to Saturn.

"Welnore Court?" She shook her head slowly, with some satisfaction. "Not here."

Good, thought Emily.

"Do you know where it is, by any chance?" Richard asked politely.

"This is *Chipping* Letcombe. You want Letcombe *Regis,*" said the woman. Her words were loud and careful, as though Richard did not speak English. Emily stared straight ahead.

By the time they found the house it was growing dark. The trees had become dim and powerful silhouettes. As they drove up the long driveway, somber arboreal shapes loomed up at each turn, as though to block their way. When they reached the gravel court in front of the house they parked diffidently to one side, still not sure they were at the right place.

What they hoped was Welnore Court was a small manor house with a hill rising behind it. In the fading light the setting seemed cramped and claustrophobic; the trees on the hillside behind pressed heavily down on the building. The house was eighteenth-century, neoclassical, handsome but not grand. It was only two stories high, made of greenish-yellow stone. The windows were leaded; the murky walls were deeply stained with damp.

Emily walked first across the pale gravel. Over the front door was a hand-lettered sign: DO NOT STAND HERE. DANGER. FALLING STONE.

Uncertain, Emily moved away from the house and looked up. Above her, threatening black eaves hung out over the driveway. "Does this mean us?" she asked, with some alarm. "Then where *are* we supposed to stand?" She was calling a temporary truce; they could fight again later.

Richard ignored her. He set down the suitcases and read the sign. He pushed the bell, saying nothing.

"We still don't even know if it's William's house," Emily said doubtfully.

Richard still did not answer. They stood in the doorway, not looking at each other. They heard footsteps, and the heavy door swung open.

"Hello," said the woman inside. She was in her thirties, fair and thin, with long, light, messy hair. She wore a faded rust-colored turtleneck and a long denim skirt with a droopy flounce at the hem.

"Hello," said Emily, still uncertain. "We're the Brandons." They had never met William's wife.

"Yes, come in," said the woman, giving them an awkward smile. The hall was large, paneled in dark oak, dull and unpolished. Above the paneling the plaster walls and ceilings were dim and grayish.

"I'll just get my husband," said the woman, and left them.

"What's her name?" whispered Richard, driven to speak at last.

"Rachel," Emily whispered back. "If that's her. If we're at the right house. But then why didn't she introduce herself? Do you think she's the housekeeper? Or one of those upper-class girls who cooks?"

The big double doors at the end of the hall opened on charming William. He was tall, fair, narrow, always rumpled.

"Oh, good. Here you are at last!" he said, smiling, full of welcome. He came forward at once, his hands held out. His gestures were loose and boneless, like a marionette's. He kissed Emily on both cheeks. "How *lovely* to see you here," he said. "And Richard. How *very* kind of you to come." They shook hands. "And you've met Rachel." Rachel now stood behind him. They all nodded at each other, smiling.

"I'll take you upstairs," said Rachel. Her manner was brisk but anxious, and she scuttered quickly up the stairs ahead of them. She led them into a low-ceilinged room looking out onto the hill behind the house.

"How pretty this is," Emily said, meaning it. Everything in the room was fresh. The plaster ceiling here was brightly white, the woven rush carpet pale and clean, the flowers on the chintz clear and delicate.

"I've just done it up," Rachel said, looking vaguely around the room as though she had just noticed it. "It's come out rather well."

"It's lovely," Emily said, but Rachel did not answer a second time.

Left alone in the cold bedroom, Emily and Richard abandoned the truce at once. Without speaking they moved back and forth, unpacking, avoiding each other's touch or gaze.

They did not speak until they were ready to go down again. Richard, with his hand on the doorknob, turned to Emily and asked in a patronizing voice, "Now, before we go down, do you have anything to say to me?"

"Such as what?"

"Such as that you're sorry?"

Emily gave him a look of contempt and pushed past him, opening the door herself and going out into the dark hallway.

Before dinner they all sat in the drawing room. The children, two girls and a boy, Giles, the youngest, came down with the nanny to be introduced. Emily watched William's face as Giles, his favorite, was led forward. The child was fair-haired, like William, with huge bright patches of pink on his broad cheeks. Bold, triumphant, he stood with his arms crossed on his chest. He grinned precociously when he was introduced, and did not hold out his hand.

"Now, Giles," said his nanny. She was a nice young Welsh woman, plump, with pale skin and very black short hair. Watching Giles she was full of anticipation.

"Giles," William said, warningly, but with delight in his voice. Audacious, Giles waited, his legs apart, his eyes cast down, a private smile on his face. The moment lengthened. Just as the nanny and William simultaneously drew stern and audible breaths, Giles, without looking up, suddenly pulled out his hand, like a conjuror with a rabbit. Pleased with himself, he then shook hands, meticulously.

"Hello," he said, looking first up into Emily's face, then Richard's. His older sisters watched him, full of suppressed hilarity. A performance was obviously expected.

Finding Giles to be the center of attention did not surprise Emily. She had heard about William's family for years, over their lunches in New York. At a certain point in the meal Emily would ask, "And how is everyone at home?"

William would smile. "Everyone is very well."

He was always reticent at first, but Emily had discovered the key. Next she would ask, "And how is Giles?"

At this, William's face would light up.

"Giles is *frightfully* well," he would answer, delighted. Then he would begin to talk.

It was one of the things Emily liked best about William, the great and evident joy he took in his family. It was how she knew him, and why she trusted him. It was one of the things she and Richard had fought about, here.

The day before, at breakfast, Richard had said, "Now, tell me about this household where we're going."

Richard had a meeting later that morning, and he was already dressed for business: gray suit, striped tie. He was sitting at a linen-covered table that the waiter had wheeled in. He was addressing a huge English breakfast: kippers, poached eggs, cold, crustless toast.

Emily was still in her bathrobe and still in bed. On her knees was a tray holding her breakfast: jugs of tea and hot water, croissants, a little pot of honey. The papers were spread haphazardly around her on the bed.

"William has a wife and three children," said Emily. Her voice, like Richard's, was carefully neutral: in between fights they were excruciatingly polite. "But they live out in the country. He only sees them on weekends."

"Why is that?"

"Because the house is too far from London for him to commute," said Emily. "He has to stay in the city during the week."

Richard sliced his eggs with a neat crosshatch stroke.

"He hates it," Emily went on. "It's like living in exile."

"Then why does he do it?" Richard asked. He took a bite.

"I just told you," Emily said. "The house is too far to commute to." She tore a tiny piece off the end of a croissant.

Richard looked skeptical. "If he really wanted to see his family every night, he would."

"He *can't,*" Emily said, nettled. "He can't afford a big place in town. And it's a family house. He can't just sell it and move in closer."

"He could do something different," said Richard loftily. "Trust me."

Emily looked up at him. "Why should I trust you? Why are you suddenly an expert on William's life?" she asked. "You don't know what their situation is."

"A man who lives apart from his wife does it for a reason," said Richard. "I do know that." He took a long swallow of coffee without looking at her.

"Richard, it's just possible that you're wrong," said Emily. "You hardly know William. It's just possible that he does this because he wants his children to grow up in the country, not because he loathes his wife."

"Well, it doesn't sound like much of a marriage to me," said Richard.

"Maybe it doesn't," said Emily, "but it's not your marriage. As far as I know, William is happy."

"Happy," said Richard. He shook his head slightly, not looking at her.

But Emily would not answer him. She buttered the curly horn of a croissant and began to eat it; she picked up a section of the newspaper in a terminating way. She refused to say anything more on the subject; she refused to explain William to Richard. She knew William; Richard did not.

At their lunches, Emily had learned what William was like: warm and accessible, funny and responsive. From their conversations she could see how he was, glowing and benign. She saw him in place among his family like a sun. She could see him at home, radiant, generous, giving off heat and light to them all, without end or effort. Simply sitting across the table from him, Emily could feel William's benevolent warmth. Richard was wrong. He knew nothing of William's kindness, and nothing at all of his marriage.

The dining room at Welnore Court was long and bare, furnished haphazardly. There was no rug; skimpy pale-green curtains drooped at the tall windows. The satinwood table was very formal, highly polished, and much too big for the four of them. William and Rachel sat miles apart, at each end, and Richard and Emily confronted each other, at the center of the long sides. As soon as they all sat down Rachel sprang up from her seat.

"I'll get the soup," she said. She was sitting at the foot of the table, the farthest from the door to the kitchen. She walked rapidly the length of the table, past them all, her heels clicking loudly on the bare floor.

"Can I help?" asked Emily, but Rachel did not answer. She vanished through the swinging door.

William leaned forward. "Now," he said attentively, "tell me what you've been doing in London." He sat with his hands folded neatly in front of him on the table. He looked earnestly at Emily, his head tilted forward, one eyebrow lifted, as though he cared about every word of hers, every thought. Rachel reappeared, holding a shallow bowl of soup on a plate. She walked slowly, with cautiously hobbled steps, staring commandingly at the soup, as though her gaze would prevent it from slopping.

"We've had a lovely time," Emily began. Rachel set the soup down in front of her. "Oh, thank you," she said, looking up at Rachel, but Rachel had gone again.

"Have you been to the theater at all?" William asked, turning to Richard.

"Yes, we saw the new Pinter play," said Richard. Rachel pushed through the swinging door again with another plate of soup.

"And?" asked William. "How did you find it? Do you *like* Pinter?"

"Well, what's brilliant about Pinter is what he doesn't say, what's left out of the dialogue, don't you think?" said Richard.

Emily looked up. She was still angry at Richard, but her rage had begun to lose its heat. There was something here that she had not expected and could not decode. These cold half-empty rooms seemed increasingly strange; so did the atmosphere. She had begun to wish for an ally, a friend. She was no longer trapped alone with Richard, and now, hearing him talk to someone else, hearing him relaxed and thought-ful, Emily saw him in a different light. He no longer seemed an enemy.

"Those wonderful, ambiguous, ominous silences," Richard went on. "They mean whatever you want them to mean. Pin-ter gets the audience to furnish the subtext with their own thoughts. Which means that intelligent people, or the people with the most interesting thoughts, think the play is intelligent, and that the silences are complex and full of subtle layers of meanings. Stupid people, whose own silences are *not* full of subtle meaning, think the play is stupid. But they aren't the ones who write the reviews, or the essays on theater. So the work has a self-selecting audience of intelligent supporters. It's quite neat, really, the way it all works."

Emily was now reminded that Richard was someone she liked—his company, his thoughts.

Rachel set down Richard's soup. "Thank you, Rachel," he said, but she was heading back to the swinging door.

"Do start, both of you," said William, "before it gets cold." Emily and Richard murmured; they did not start.

"Would you call Pinter a charlatan, then? Does the emperor have no clothes?" William asked Richard. He listened with meticulous attention, as though Richard were a famous British theater critic and not an American lawyer.

"Not a charlatan," said Richard, "not at all. I find some of his plays brilliant. I like ambiguity."

"Oh, Richard. How can you say that? You don't, really," said Emily, but her tone was friendly.

"In plays, at least," amended Richard. He smiled at her. "I suppose not so much in real life."

"Which is where ambiguity is, of course, rampant," said William.

"And where everyone furnishes their own subtexts," said Emily. "Where we interpret things however we want to."

"And where we change our interpretations continually," said Richard, looking at Emily, "and drastically. The way you saw something earlier, even an hour ago, may now seem absurd. Don't you think?" He held her eyes steadily, friendly.

Emily could see what he wanted: a real truce. But though she was thawing, she was not yet warm. She still remembered the things he had said the night before, they were still piled up, her spoils, her private hoard. Her gaze was mild but unresponsive, and she let it drift through Richard's face as though he were clear glass.

Rachel set the soup down in front of William, who picked up his spoon. At that, Emily and Richard picked up theirs. When Rachel brought her own soup in and finally sat down, the rest of them had begun eating.

"I do hope you don't mind, Rachel," William said, giving her the same extravagant and courteous attention he had given Richard, his eyebrows raised solicitously. "We've started."

Rachel looked up at him without speaking. They all were looking at her. She glanced at Emily, as though it had been Emily who had spoken.

"It's quite all right," she said, and picked up her spoon.

It seemed to Emily that the conversation went very well while Rachel was clearing and bringing in. It was when she was sitting with them that talk flagged. She refused to let Emily help, and with each course they all sat while Rachel walked determinedly back and forth to the kitchen, carrying one plate at a time: she would not stack. The lamb was pink and tender, but stone cold by the time they began to eat it.

"I was admiring your garden as we drove up," Emily said to Rachel when she finally sat down with her own plate. "I hope you'll show it to me tomorrow."

Rachel looked up. "Have you a garden?"

"A small one," Emily said.

"Oh, Emily has a perfectly lovely garden," said William, who had seen it. "A perfectly lovely garden."

"Yes, of course," Rachel said, frowning slightly. "Of course it's the wrong season, but if you'd like a look round tomorrow, I could take you. I could show you the shrubbery."

"That would be lovely," Emily said.

Rapid steps were heard outside in the hall, and the nanny burst into the room.

"Mr. Langdale, it's Giles," she said, excited. Her cheeks were pink, and she had a screwdriver in her hand.

"What is it, Julia?" asked William, putting down his napkin.

"He's locked himself in your bedroom," said Julia. "We can't get him out."

"Good Lord," said William. "What in the world was he doing in there?"

"He was a bit *overwrought,* you see," said Julia. Her eyes were shining. "I told him he could start off in his mother's room, just to get to sleep. He does that sometimes. And then, since you were here, he changed his mind just as he was getting into bed, and ran down the hall and into your room. I was running after him and he got quite excited, I think. Just as a joke, you see, he banged the door against me. 'Giles, you open that door,' I said, and I'm afraid he locked it, just as a joke. Only now he can't get it open again. I've had the gardener up there. He can't get it open either. We've all tried. Shall I call the fire department, or will you have a go?"

William got up, shaking his head. "Excuse me," he said, without looking at anyone. He left the room, focused as a hound.

As he left, Rachel called after them. "Julia!" Julia turned back. "Is Giles all right?"

"Oh, he's fine, Mrs. Langdale," Julia answered. Her voice was high and animated, as though she were at a carnival. She trotted eagerly off after William.

Rachel watched them go, but stayed where she was. There was a pause, and Emily tried to revive the conversation.

"Do you do all the gardening yourself?" she asked.

Rachel glanced at her doubtfully. "No," she said, "I have help."

"Have I made a gaffe?" said Emily cheerfully. "Am I at Hidcote? Are your gardens world-famous?"

"Oh, no," said Rachel, forbiddingly, and did not continue. Snubbed, Emily subsided.

Richard took a turn, asking politely about schools.

"And will you send Giles away when he's seven?"

"Oh, I should think so," Rachel said. All their questions seemed to surprise and alarm her.

"You won't miss him?" Emily said. She thought this custom cruel and barbaric, sending infants away from their parents. If it was the lower classes who did it, she thought, the state would intervene to prevent it.

"Everyone does it," Rachel explained, as though this justified the orphaning. "All his friends will go."

William reappeared in the doorway with a suppressed smile at his son's triumphant naughtiness.

"Did you get him out?" Rachel asked.

"I got him out," William said, sitting down. "Please excuse this appalling circus," he said to Emily. "Giles is a perfectly dreadful child. His behavior is quite intolerable." He sounded pleased.

When they finished eating, Emily, without asking, stood when Rachel did. She took her plate and Richard's, carrying them firmly through the swinging door behind Rachel. The kitchen beyond was terrible—prisonlike, low-ceilinged, and cement-colored. The floor was dirty linoleum, the old refrigerator turquoise. The white tiles behind the stove were yellowed with grease, and old dirt seemed to fill the cracks on all the surfaces. Two windows looked out over a kitchen garden, and the light from the house illuminated the frost-blackened carcasses of vegetable plants.

"What a nice view," Emily said.

"It's nice in summer," Rachel said. In silence they scraped the plates, and Emily loaded them into the dishwasher. Emily kept hoping that a cheery gray-haired woman with stout forearms would appear and tell them energetically to leave the rest for her, but she did not. Emily thought of Julia, upstairs with the three children, playing uproarious games, giving them baths, reading aloud, while Rachel toiled down here alone in this ghastly kitchen. Why would you pay someone to have fun with your children, Emily wondered, and assign yourself to drudgery? But how could you send your child off among strangers at the age of seven?

Emily thought longingly of her own small, faraway daughter, the glowing wistful face. Now, in this dark place, the thought of the distant child was agonizing: a bright star in deep space. Emily could not imagine, now, how she could have left her daughter for these two weeks. She remembered Richard, saying good-bye to her. He knelt down on the hall floor, pressing the small body to his chest, wrapping himself tightly around her, closing his eyes. Remembering that, remembering his closed eyes, his fervent face, the last of Emily's anger at him loosened and dissolved.

After dinner they had coffee in the sitting room. Rachel set a tray on an upholstered bench in front of the sofa. The sitting room, too, seemed half empty: the one sofa and the few chairs were scattered awkwardly about, too far away from each other for conversation. The chairs matched neither each other nor anything else. All the rooms except the guest room seemed bare and unfinished.

"This is a lovely house," Emily said, stirring her coffee in its tiny cup. She looked around the bleak room. "Have you been here long?"

There was a pause. William was sitting on the sofa, his legs crossed at the ankle. He was leaning back among the silk pillows, supple, at ease. In one hand he held his emerald-green demitasse, in the other, a cigar. Rachel was walking behind the sofa, and at Emily's question she stopped. She stepped close to the sofa, stood behind her husband and put her hand on his shoulder. It was not a clasp, her fingers did not seem bold enough to take possession. Her hand lay lightly against his dark wool jacket, pale, uncertain, brave.

"We've been here four years," Rachel said. She showed for the first time a trace of cautious animation. "A sort of cousin of William's had it before us, and it was in rather a bad state. We've done quite a lot, though you can't see it. We're doing things slowly, as we can afford to." There was timid pride in her voice.

"We've decided to do the most important things first," William said, his tone dry and sardonic. He drew on his cigar, tilting his chin up at them. "We thought we'd do the garden, for example, before the roof. We thought we'd put in a really good shrubbery before we decorated the drawing room."

His wife's hand lay without moving on his shoulder; William took no notice of it at all. Emily, watching, found herself suddenly afraid to watch, afraid that he would reach up and brush the hand away as though it were a fly, his gesture heedless, dismissive.

William stirred his coffee with the tiny spoon, then set the spoon down neatly in the emerald-green saucer. He leaned back with his cigar into the cushions. He did not brush his wife's hand off, he ignored it altogether, as though it did not exist.

There was a long moment of silence. Emily, frozen, could say nothing. She felt as though the air in the room had turned to ice.

"Well, that sounds like a sensible plan," said Richard, nodding agreeably. He turned to Rachel. "Now, a shrubbery sounds very important. But we don't have so many of them in America. Would you be very kind and explain to me exactly what a shrubbery is?"

Emily, watching her own good-hearted Richard try to shield Rachel from her husband, felt a wave of gratitude. She was reminded now of Richard's compassion, the real tenderness of his heart. The last of her anger was gone, and she was sorry.

Now she longed for the evening to be over, for the moment when she and Richard would go upstairs. When they reached the end of the long, grim hallway, as they entered their cold, flowery room, she would turn to Richard as he closed the door. She would not let him take even a step inside the room before she reached him, before she wrapped her whole self around his body, reminding him that he liked her, liked her company, her presence, her skin.

Unpleasant, she thought, repentant, ashamed. She had been, and she was sorry. She was sorry she had been unpleasant, she was sorry she had been argumentative. She was sorry to have hoarded, so malevolently, the things Richard had said. She had been wrong about William, and arrogant about it, and she was sorry for that. But mostly she was sorry she had brought them here. She was sorry they had witnessed what they had—the undisciplined child, the separate bedrooms, the deadly chill.

Here was the risk, and she was sorry to have seen it, terrified.

Asking

for

Love

"Goodnight, Melissa," I called up. I waited, but heard nothing back from my daughter. I tried again: "Melissa, I'm leaving now." I was standing in the front hall of my parents' summer house in Maine. I was at the bottom of the wide staircase, listening, and Melissa was up on the second floor and did not answer.

Melissa had arrived that morning from a friend's in Boston. I had come up ten days earlier from Philadelphia, where we live. We were alone in the big shingle house that week, since my parents had gone cruising in their sailboat. Melissa's room is at the back of the house, over the kitchen, in what was once the servants' wing. I knew she had the door shut and her Walkman earphones on: she was sealed off from the outside world, and in one of her own. Tacked up on the old soft pinewood walls were her posters of rock groups: images of chaos, explosive, acid-colored. Melissa would be in her faded jeans, torn at both knees, and sitting cross-legged on the sagging iron bed. I could see her, face curtained by the long fall of her soft hair, her eyes rapt and unfocused as she nodded to herself, marking time. She was deep inside a web of syncopated rhythms, staccato sentences, and mocking phrases.

Last year I could have gone upstairs, opened her door, and walked right in. I could have stood beside her and smoothed her hair, and she would have raised her calm blue-eyed gaze to me and smiled. But now things are different, and when I heard no answer, I turned away from the silent stairwell.

John was standing behind me in the hall. Behind him hung an old gilt-framed mirror, its silvery surface flecked with dark spots. With the mirror I could see both his front and his back, both his long, earnest face and the place at the back of his head where his scalp is meekly becoming evident. He is forty-eight years old, tall and slightly stoop-shouldered. He is what he will be, and I like knowing this.

John was wearing a dark green sweater, tweed jacket, khaki pants, and blue boat sneakers. These are clothes worn by all the men I know, including my father, and though I haven't known John my whole life, he looks as though I have. I know things about him just from the way he looks: I know who he is, and I know I can trust him. This is a comfort, and right now I am eager for comfort. I have just become single, after twenty years of being married. This was my doing, and it was necessary, but it has been terrible in ways I never imagined, and much larger, as though I'd stamped my foot and started an avalanche. So I am grateful for John's calm presence.

John was listening too for Melissa's response. He raised his eyebrows politely. "Well?"

I shrugged my shoulders. "Let's just go."

"Are you sure?" John asked. "You don't want to just run up and tell her we're leaving? We're in no hurry."

John was thinking of his own daughter, Julia, who is nine, and lives with him. There is a live-in baby-sitter, Hannah, but even so, John would never leave for the evening without saying good night. John compares my behavior with his own, and he believes that I am irresponsible, a lax and heedless mother. I can't tell him I am not; you can't tell someone who you are. John will discover for himself what sort of mother I am.

"Melissa's all the way up in her room," I said, "with the door shut and the music on. She's seventeen years old, and she knows we're going out. Let's go."

Still John didn't move. "But then when will I meet her?" he asked plaintively. "I've primped."

"Primped?" I said, smiling. Only John would use this word.

John nodded solemnly. He smoothed a lock of hair back severely, in a parody of fussiness. At once it fell back over his forehead.

"You primped for Melissa? I thought that was for me. Thanks a lot." I pushed open the screen door. "Come on, we're out of here."

John and I have been seeing each other for eight months, which is long enough for him to have met my daughter. Melissa's been away at boarding school, but there were times they could have met. At first I put it off because I wasn't sure John and I would go on seeing each other; later I put it off because I was sure we would. I pictured it going badly: Melissa sullen, John stiff, the air dense with hostility. Later, I was afraid, alone with me, each of them would be self-righteous and critical, each claiming my alliance against the other.

I think John thinks adolescents are like wild animals, leopards or water buffaloes, unpredictable, vividly dangerous. And Melissa doesn't want to see her mother with anyone except her father. She doesn't want to see me perfumed and earringed, ready to go out. She doesn't want a strange man in her living room, smiling at her winningly. She doesn't want to hear his footsteps, later, on the stairs. She doesn't want me to be single; she wants me to be a mother.

But now Melissa is here for the summer, and John is here for July. He has rented a house for himself, Julia, and Hannah. He and Melissa will have to meet soon now, but I was relieved to put it off, even for one more day.

Leaving the heavy silence of the house, John and I went down the long staircase that slants across the stone foundation. The house is on a hill, and on the downhill side the rusticated masonry rises as high as a whole story. The rough stone wall is entirely different from the wood-shingled house above it, as though the big, airy, summery rooms were supported by a dungeon.

As we descended, the darkening house loomed over us—the deep porches, the gabled windows, the broad, shingled roofs. Below us was the pallid circle of the driveway, and beyond it the pine-crowded bluffs that dropped steeply to the shore. Chill air rose up off the channel in tingling, invisible clouds. It was nearly eight o'clock, and the evening was deepening rapidly around us like a dark snowfall, the darkness settling in corners like drifts.

John's car was a shadow, its silhouette revealed only by reflections, faint gleams along its rounded edges. As we opened the doors, the car filled with light, and we climbed into a radiant private space. Closing the doors with solid thumps we shut out the night, its chill, its dark, its distances. John and I were now shoulder to shoulder, thigh to thigh within a glowing cave. Outside sounds were gone, and inside ones—breathing, the rustle of clothes—were suddenly loud. I heard the gentle rasp of tweed as John stretched out his arm to the key. The glow fell over us like a tent, like a blessing. I put my hand on his shoulder.

"Hello, John," I said. I was nearly whispering, but my voice sounded huge.

John turned at my touch and I heard him draw in his breath. He is always surprised by affection, and humbly grateful for it. This saddens me: I think humility should play no part in love. I think love should be inexhaustible, like air, that we should give and take it freely, without thought, without having to ask. I think John deserves love in vast quantities, but he has spent his life among cold and parsimonious women. He doesn't know what he deserves, and he doesn't believe me when I tell him.

As he turned to me now, his face lit up.

"Hello, Sarah," he said. My name in his voice sounded wonderful, those ordinary syllables honored.

"It's nice to see you," I said, and I stroked his rough brown shoulder.

"It's *always* nice to see you, Sarah," John said.

John can't use the word "love." He is like someone standing on the edge of a high diving board and looking down. He is wavering, riven, churning with terror and longing, unable to risk that vertiginous step into the singing air. He'll do it, I know, he'll choose passion and jump. He'll give himself up to that swift, ecstatic freefall, to the wild explosion of foam, the jubilant embrace of deep water. I know this, so I don't care how long he takes. He'll find the moment, and he'll take the leap.

John's long face looked fervent and noble, and his eyes shone behind his polished glasses. John actually is noble, honorable. It is one of the things about John that I love; another is the way he kisses.

I closed my eyes, breathing in his cool, dark, salty smell as he put his mouth on mine, and it happened again. This is something that never fails to surprise me—this sudden melting, turning-to-gold sensation. Before I married Michael I thought all sex was good sex, I thought good sex was a given. Now I've learned that it's not a given but a gift. Now I know that a man you believe you love can turn your body to lead. He can slow your blood and chill your flesh and make you ache for solitude. So when John kisses me, I let everything go, and give myself up to this remarkable thing. I close my eyes, and sometimes there are tears in them, I am so grateful. Now I know that what I feel is rare, rare, and I am so glad that John and I have found each other.

The overhead light went suddenly off. John and I were left again in the larger darkness of the night, and we pulled decorously apart: we were saving the rest for later. We smiled at each other, and John smoothed the hair off my face. He reached out again to the ignition, and this time we set off.

The driveway hugs the side of the house, and we drove along the kitchen wing, where Melissa's room was, through a grove of vast old pines. Here it was suddenly pitch-dark, as though we had passed into another time zone: among those shadows it was deepest night. The artificial glare of the headlights caught the undersides of everything, and the grove looked suddenly unkempt, threatening: the rough bark, the trashy litter of dead boughs and pine cones lying on the rust-brown floor of needles. It looked like a grim Germanic forest, the lair of some malevolent operatic creature. I was glad of John's comforting profile, the gleam of his glasses in the dashboard's dim glow.

The one street in the village was empty, except for a few cars in front of the new restaurant. There are now boutiques in this lobstermen's village, and the old apothecary shop sells cashmere sweaters and tortoise-shell picture frames. But nothing has been built here in seventy years. The street is still lined with two-story houses, clapboard and shingle, and its silhouette is still a low, nineteenth-century stitchwork of gables, pitched roofs, and brick chimneys.

Inside, the new restaurant was fresh and cheerful, with red-and-white-checked tablecloths, cream-colored walls, and cream-colored wooden chairs. Local views by local artists hung on the walls: sunset on Great Cranberry Island, fog in the pines on Cadillac Mountain. Everything seemed innocent and unpretentious, and in that sturdy comfortable chair, surrounded by images of places I had known all my life, I felt happy and safe. I was proud that I could offer all this to John, and glad that he was here. He had chosen to enter my world, in a serious and public way. We speak through signs as much as words, and though John can not use the word "love," I knew that by coming here for the summer he had stepped openly to my side.

Our waitress turned out to be an old summer friend of Melissa's. This year Lainie was suddenly tall, her features subtly altered. She was now a young woman, and beautiful, with a long, fragile face and starry dark eyes.

"Lainie!" I said. "How nice to see you."

"Hello, Mrs. Talbot," Lainie said, smiling back. She filled our water glasses from the heavy pitcher, and I watched her narrow tanned wrists flex, the tendons suddenly visible, then vanishing. I felt touched: they are so innocently strong, these young women. They are so benign that we forget their strength.

"How's Melissa?" Lainie asked.

"Great. She just got here. She'd love to see you," I said, then wondered if she would: I'm no longer sure of what Melissa wants. To make up for my own uncertainty I added, "You look wonderful, Lainie," which was true.

"Thank you," Lainie said. Her smile was diffident but unsurprised, and I was glad that she'd heard this from others.

This transformation from girl into young woman is a miracle, like a flower revealing itself. I was glad it had happened to Lainie, glad it was being celebrated. I thought of Melissa, who was still struggling to free herself from the finespun cocoon of childhood.

When Lainie left, John asked, "Is she the same age as Melissa?" I nodded, and John looked down at his menu.

"Why do you ask?" I said, wary. "What are you thinking?" John only shook his head, without looking up.

"They aren't so different, Lainie and Melissa," I said, defensive. "I don't know how you imagine Melissa."

"I only know what you tell me about her," John said.

"And?" I said.

"You don't tell me the wonderful things about her," said John. "You tell me about the things that make you unhappy. That she came home for Thanksgiving and didn't speak to you for four days."

I was unprepared for this. Hearing John say it easily, out loud, was like a blow: the memory was terrible.

When Melissa arrived home, I had been waiting all day for her. That autumn was my first alone, and it had been hard. The air around me had been infected by misery, and I was looking forward to Melissa's warmth, her affection, to dispel it.

The hall in our townhouse goes straight through from the front door to the kitchen, where I was waiting. I heard Melissa's key in the lock, and I was at the door when it swung open. The late-afternoon chill swept in, and noises from the street. Melissa staggered in, dragging her blue-and-green duffel bag, her knapsack over her shoulder. My arms were open: I couldn't wait to hold her, my warm, sweet daughter.

"You're here!" I said joyfully.

Melissa was hunched over, sliding the duffel bag in through the door. She didn't answer. Her head was down, and there was no place for me to put my arms around her.

"Here," I said, reaching for the duffel, "let me help."

"No," Melissa said, her head still down. "I'm okay."

She slid the bag past me with her foot. She didn't look up or touch me. When I closed the door behind her she kept right on going, her head turned away, as though I weren't there. She slid the duffel along the floor to the bottom of the stairs. There she hefted it and started up, without a word.

"Hey, Liss!" I said. My voice was loud and cheerful, as though she had just forgotten, as though this was an oversight. *"Hello!"*

Melissa answered with her back to me. "Hello," she said, her voice without tone. She was at the landing and didn't turn.

I could see she needed time to herself, so I didn't answer, or follow her up. That evening I made her favorite dinner, homemade pasta and sausages. When Melissa came downstairs I was in the kitchen. The table was set for two, and at her place I'd put her mail and some packages—little things, funny striped tights, paperbacks, a pretty barrette.

Melissa appeared in the doorway, and I smiled at her.

"Hi, sweetie," I said. "Bangers and pasta, you're just in time."

But Melissa's coat was buttoned up to her chin, and her face was cold stone. "I'm having dinner with Dad," she said. She didn't come in. She didn't look at the table, at the packages by her plate. "I'm leaving now," she said. When she opened the door, she let in a great blast of cold air, and after she had gone I felt it in the kitchen, chilling my legs, my hands, my face.

Melissa blames me for the divorce. She believes that I have voluntarily destroyed her world. It's true that the divorce was my idea, but it didn't feel to me as though I had much choice about it, really, or any choice at all. Michael, of course, encourages Melissa to blame me. I know what he tells her.

Michael and I disagree: I think that only he and I should be witness to our failure. I think that only we should occupy the smooth and ghastly chamber we've created, the doorless cell that still rings with rage, disappointments, accusations. Michael feels that "in a spirit of fairness" he should tell Melissa his side of things. I don't call this fairness: his side of things is accusatory, informed by rage and hatred. I can't prevent this, but I won't contribute to it. I won't tell Melissa my side of it, I won't criticize her father to her, I won't ask her to hate him. I'm waiting for her to realize for herself that there might be another version of this story, that the person Michael describes is not the person Melissa knows. When this happens, Melissa and I will be friends again, and I hope it will happen soon.

That night when Melissa came home from seeing her father she walked loudly past my door. I called good night, but she didn't answer. I heard her door shut hard, like a blow.

The next day my parents, my sister, Gail, and her husband, Ted, and their twins were coming for Thanksgiving dinner. I let Melissa sleep late, and when I finally knocked on her door, there was just time for her to get up and set the table. I'd done everything else. When I called her name, she answered "Yes?" on a rising, formal note, as though she were in a hotel and I were the maid. I stood in the hall outside her closed door, my head bent. I didn't dare go in. I called out the plans to her. I knew she was there, alive, awake, listening to her mother's voice, but she didn't answer.

She came downstairs dressed for dinner, in a white high-necked blouse and a long skirt. Her hair was polished and shining, hanging down her back like a length of satin. She looked the way she used to: warm and sweet, radiant and responsive. She went straight in to the dining room and began setting the table, spreading out the big white linen cloth with my grandmother's initials on it, laying the places with my grandmother's heavy old-fashioned silver. She put out the crystal water goblets that she'd once been too small to hold upright; she folded the linen napkins in neat long triangles. At my mother's place she stood the little Chinese porcelain figure that we always put before the most honored guest. I felt calmed: no matter how she felt toward me, Melissa was taking her place in our family. She was performing our ritual with our familiar things—old silver, worn linen, and faded china. She was setting forth our symbols in a calligraphy that she knew well, a pattern that stood in our household for festivity and love, and she was honoring this.

"The table looks beautiful," I said, coming in to admire. But as I spoke, Melissa slipped past me, back into the kitchen. I followed her. "Thanks, Liss," I said, but she was standing at the open refrigerator, looking for something to eat for breakfast. Her back was to me, and she did not answer.

I could have said something sharp. I could have said Now-see-here, and You-listen-to-me-young-lady. There have been times when I've said those things, and maybe I should have then. But I didn't have the heart. All I could demand from Melissa was the form of love, only courtesy, its husk, and I didn't care about that. If Melissa hates me, I don't care if she's polite. Love is what I want from Melissa, and I won't ask for it. Asking for love is the saddest question in the world, and if you have to ask, the answer is too painful to hear. So I said nothing. It took the heart from me to see her so cold and distant, filled with animosity.

I just hoped that when the others came, Melissa would be nicer, and she was. She kissed my white-haired, straight-backed parents, and my gabby sister, Gail, and her family. She asked my father about his stargazing and my mother about her garden club. She sat on the rug with Gail's twins and played a clapping game that made them weak and floppy with laughter. I talked a lot, as though everything were fine, and I hoped that everything actually was. I hoped Melissa was beginning to relax, expand, like one of those folded-paper flowers you set into a glass of water— that she would feel herself cherished in this warm bath of family affection, and would gracefully unfurl, revealing her deep and vivid colors and the form of her lovely spirit. I hoped that she would remember who she was and who I was, why she was here.

At dinner Melissa was ebullient. She teased my father and asked the twins riddles. The sound of Melissa's laughter was wonderful to me, and the sight of her open smile. When I asked the girls to clear, after the turkey, Melissa stood up and looked sternly at the twins.

"Okay, you two," she said. "No giggling." Thrilled, they started giggling at once. I went out into the kitchen to scrape the plates, and Melissa followed me. As she came through the swinging door, I saw her face in the small glass window. She was laughing at something my father had said, and as she pushed the door with her shoulder, she called back to him.

"I'll bet you did," Melissa said loudly, grinning.

Her face, in the tiny window, was lit up with light from the kitchen. It was radiant, the face I loved, and I was so thankful. Here was Melissa, back at last, beautiful and candid, with her smooth pale cheeks, her wide cheerful mouth, her shining eyes. Seeing her own exuberant smile, I smiled myself.

The door swung through, and Melissa found herself in a different room, face to face—and alone—with her mother. At the sight of me her face was transformed, vividly, instantly, like a sheet of paper blackened by flame. Her laughter stopped and her mouth cramped and tightened. Her eyes went cold and angry. It was like a cruel magic trick, a bright vision of the past Melissa brutally erased by the way she was now. I stood in front of her, still smiling, as her face blackened with rage and contempt. As I watched, my own face stiffened, foolishly, painfully. It was like a splash of acid in my eyes. I turned back to the sink to hide my foolish face.

All winter Melissa made long-distance calls to Michael, from boarding school, and charged them to me. She wants me to pay, literally, for what I've done. But in the spring, things had improved, and I had hopes for the summer. After two months of being together, things will be better still.

"She was upset," I said now to John. "You can hardly blame her. That was our first Thanksgiving after Michael left."

"I know that," John said. "I just mean that's the kind of thing you tell me about her."

It hurt for John to mention this, so casually. And it also seemed that John was reminding me of my glaring flaws as a mother, and of Melissa's glaring flaws as a daughter. I felt that I was meant to compare Melissa with the docile and decorous Julia, properly raised by a Good Mother, and that I was meant to feel chastened.

"Well," I said firmly, "Melissa is wonderful. You'll see."

John smiled, raising his eyebrows. "I'm sure she is," he said gallantly. "She's your daughter."

I smiled back. We picked up our menus and John frowned as he scanned. "What are you going to have?" he asked.

"The duck," I said, "only is this the kind I like?" I can never remember if it's *magret* or *confit*.

"I don't know," John said affably. "Is it?"

I looked up, and from his expression I realized that John had no idea which kind of duck I like. It's Michael, my husband of twenty years, who knows this. I felt shocked and guilty, to have so easily confused my lover with my husband. It seemed both cavalier and chilling, a fatally telling slip that must show the superficiality of my feelings. And it grieved me: you know so much about your husband, you have such a vast collection of random and important facts about him—that he loves Melville and kidneys, that he hates sweetbreads and the ballet—and he knows these things about you. Jointly you own this secret, intimate, trivial knowledge. It's comforting, this charting of the particularities of your own existence on someone else's map.

But the shared knowledge between Michael and myself is now useless, poisoned. I relinquished my claim to it, as I gave up my claim to Michael's affection. Michael now detests his knowledge of me, and the knowledge John and I share is meager. We are still hardly visible to each other's eyes, we are still only silhouettes, barely defined by gleams on our rounded edges.

But forward is how you go, and John and I are learning each other. Each time we're together we chart unknown territory, exploring newfound lands through loving invasion. And as for the duck, it was time I remembered what I liked myself.

"*Magret,*" I said, at random. "That's the one I like."

"Good," said John peacefully. "Have it."

After we ordered, I asked, "Now tell me, how does Julia like it here?"

"I think she likes it all right," John said cautiously.

Julia is a frail, timid creature, with wispy hair and narrow shoulders. She seems disheartened by the world, as though she has tried it and found it too much for her.

"Is she in sailing class?" I asked. This is the core of childhood in this coastal community. It starts with rowing, for six-year-olds, and goes up to racing and overnight cruises for teenagers.

"She is. I think she likes it," said John.

"I hope so. Melissa loved it. *I* loved it," I said, and then wondered if I had. I think now that I loved it, but maybe this is nostalgia. Maybe at the time I hated it. Melissa tells me now that her childhood was miserable. Memory is kaleidoscopic: the slightest shift creates another picture, detailed, complete, convincing. Who can say what childhood was really like? We cling to the view we've chosen. But I think that I really did love sailing class: the cold, taut line against my strong hand, and the damp, fresh wind in my face. Hunkering down in the well of the little boat with my best friend, setting out across the choppy water toward Sutton Island as though it were the Peloponnese. There must have been cold weather and high winds, fights and feuds, but I don't remember them. Now those days seem full of exultation. I wondered what Melissa would say now, about sailing class. I wondered what she would say, years later, about her parents' divorce.

John looked judicious. "Well, Agnes isn't crazy about sailing. She may want Julia to do tennis instead."

"She can do both," I said officiously. "We all did. But why doesn't Agnes like sailing?"

"It's pretty strenuous. Four hours, out in the cold wind, three days a week. And what if she fell in?"

"But did Agnes just find out now that it was four hours, three days a week? Didn't you register Julia months ago?"

John took a drink of water. "I think Agnes just focused on it. She called this morning, and she was concerned. And I must say I think she has a point."

I raised my eyebrows. "Well, children have managed it somehow, for generations. With very few fatalities."

John sighed. "Sarah, Agnes is Julia's mother. I think she knows what's best for Julia. She is a very responsible mother, you know. She sees things differently from you."

It's true that Agnes sees things differently from the way I do. To start with, I would not call abandoning your child in favor of graduate school a demonstration of maternal responsibility. John, however, defends everything Agnes does. "She was unhappy," he explains, about her abandoning him and Julia. John defends Agnes because, though she has left him, she won't leave him alone. She won't let him be angry: she calls him her best friend. They talk every day, and she comes over to his house all the time. John calls this mature. I call it dishonest.

"Agnes and I see most things differently," I said. "Not only how to treat your daughter but also your ex-husband."

"First of all, Sarah, I am not Agnes's ex-husband. Agnes and I are not divorced," John said, precise. "And second of all, I must tell you that you sound just the faintest bit jealous. Agnes and I have been very fortunate, and we have worked very hard. We have managed to maintain our friendship despite our separation, which few people seem able to do. This makes things much easier on Julia, to say nothing of being easier on us. And I'll tell you that I'm very grateful to Agnes for making this possible." He sounded incredibly smug.

"I'm not jealous," I said, irritated. "What Agnes has made possible is the end of your marriage. Why are you grateful to her?"

John took a swallow of his drink. "I see this as a little more complex than that," he said primly.

"Agnes wants it both ways," I said. "She wants to leave her husband without accepting the consequences."

"I didn't realize you were an expert on what my wife wants," John said, cool. "And what are the consequences?"

"The consequences of divorce? How can you ask? Her guilt. Your anger."

"Well, but we aren't divorced. And I'm not angry at Agnes," John said, pleased.

"But why aren't you?" I asked.

John shook his head. "I understand her," he said, and smiled loftily, as though he were a philosopher and I were a hysterical shrew.

"She is selfish and cruel," I said. "What is there to understand?"

There was an angry silence. I was furious: Why did he keep calling Agnes his wife? Why did he defend her? But I said nothing more: For one thing, I know I shouldn't criticize Agnes to John, it's low-grade behavior. I have to trust John to make his own way through this, and I know he will. Besides, maybe I am jealous. And I also kept quiet because I particularly didn't want to quarrel that night. So I waited until I could smile at him.

"I'm sorry," I said. "That wasn't very nice."

John looked at me gravely and patted my hand. "Thank you."

In Philadelphia, at night, John and I always went to my house. We were alone there, with Melissa away. The first time he came was difficult for me: I felt invaded, John's footsteps in Michael's house, his strange new body in my marriage bed. I had to close my eyes to shut out the thoughts of invasion, to shut out those sickening thoughts of guilt and regret and nostalgia. But I had to, I had to let my house and marriage be invaded: my marriage was over, and both my house and I must receive my guests. I closed my eyes and hurled myself into the moment, into John, like a moth into a flame, hoping he was hot enough.

Afterward we lay peacefully tangled up in each other. I was proud of us both, for pushing past that anxiety, for insisting on happiness. I ran my hand up and down along John's shoulder. When I felt him sit up, I opened my eyes. His back was to me, and he was picking up his clothes.

"What are you doing?" I asked.

He didn't turn around. "Getting dressed."

"Are you leaving?"

"I'm afraid I have to," said John. I waited, and finally he said, "Julia wakes up in the night a lot. I don't want her to find me gone if she does."

I thought of Julia's frightened call in the empty hallway, the light shining on the polished floor, the silence of the late-night house. I thought of John's big, calming presence. I couldn't argue. Who would let a child cry alone?

Still. "What about Hannah?" I asked.

John's voice was now distant. "I don't want Julia to wake in the night and find me gone," he repeated, testy.

I said nothing: one more question and we would be fighting. I lay there, watching him dress and feeling abandoned. I pulled the sheet up over my nakedness so that if he turned, he would not find me unprotected.

Each time we made love I hoped that this time he would stay. I hoped he would feel so blissfully depleted, so cherished, so safe, that his reasons for leaving would dissolve. I hoped this time he would fall trustingly asleep in my arms, next to my beating heart, and I would have him with me all through the dark hours of the night.

Tonight, here, this would finally happen, and it was John himself who had planned it. Julia was staying with a friend, and John had boldly told the baby-sitter that he'd be back in the morning. My parents were gone, and Melissa doesn't appear before noon. I felt John was drawing himself up for that step into the spinning air, and I was proud.

That afternoon I had opened one of the guest rooms. It was a big square room, musty and silent, with slanting eaves and faded flower-sprigged wallpaper. I turned down the bedspread and plumped up the heavy pillows, which, in that house at the edge of the water, were always cool, always faintly damp. I pushed open the small diamond-paned windows and stood in the silent room while the soft air flowed in past me, lifting the white curtains and letting them drop. I thought of how it would be, later on, the two of us sinking into the softness of that strange bed. I closed my eyes: the faded Victorian room in the dim light, John looming over me, putting his hands where he pleased, the two of us skin to skin among those soft ancient sheets. I thought of seeing him in the early morning, in that muted light still empty of color. I thought of waking to find the warmth of his body, the rich smell of him, of us, all around me. That was what lay ahead of us, and I wouldn't let anything threaten it. I wouldn't argue now with anything John said.

When we left the restaurant I paused, balancing on the edge of the sidewalk, and took a deep, peaceful breath of the night air. The village was silent, and the great black sky went straight up forever. The world spread out around us, dark and rich, and the night that waited was sweet. We didn't talk on the way home; we didn't need to.

Melissa's window was dark as we drove past. John parked the car and turned off the engine but didn't move. I turned to him, but he was staring straight ahead. I knew what he was thinking about. "Did you leave this number with the baby-sitter, in case Julia calls?" I asked.

"Actually . . ." John said. He still was not looking at me, he was looking into the black thicket of pine trees. When I heard the tone of his voice, I closed my eyes: I didn't want to hear what he was going to say.

We sat in silence. The space in the car had turned cold and claustrophobic; there was no longer quite enough air for us both.

Finally I said, "Actually?"

"Actually," John repeated, "I meant to tell you before."

"About what?" I asked.

John turned to look at me. "Now, don't fly into a rage," he said, smiling. His voice was affectionate, paternal. He made rage sound absurd and childish, something I should be ashamed of flying into.

I said nothing.

John reached out and took my boneless hand. He patted it. "I'm sorry to let you down."

"What happened?" I kept my voice neutral and wondered why I was the only one to be let down.

John frowned and looked ahead again. "I just don't feel right about leaving for the night."

"But Julia's not even at home," I protested. "She's staying with a friend."

"Still," John said. "She may wake up and call home. I don't want her to feel she can't reach me."

"But you could give her this number."

John sighed again. "This is a small community," he said. "Everyone knows this number. I don't want to make a public announcement about where I'm spending the night. And I don't want Julia to have to call me at a stranger's."

"I'm not a stranger," I said, hurt. "Julia knows me. But okay, if you don't want to give her the number, give it to Hannah. If Julia calls home, Hannah can tell her to call here."

"Sarah, look," John said, his voice authoritative. He was getting down to it. "Julia is my daughter. I feel responsible for her. I know you feel differently about your daughter, but this is the way I feel. We do things differently: that's how it is."

John's tone was lofty. He was withdrawing to a higher elevation where the Good Parents were. I could see he thought that only he and Agnes belonged there, that I should be kept in the outer darkness with the rest of the Bad Parents. This enraged me, and I said something that surprised me.

"Is it really Julia you're expecting a call from in the middle of the night?" I asked.

John turned away at once, and his lips drew together dismissively. He pushed his tortoise-shell glasses farther up on his nose with a long finger.

"Sarah," he said, "my feelings for Agnes have nothing to do with my feelings for you."

"Oh, good," I said heatedly. "And what *are* your feelings for me?" I asked without thinking.

John paused, and cleared his throat. "Well," he said uneasily, "you know it's hard for me to say these things."

"Yes," I said. At first I had thought—I had hoped—that he would answer the way I had spoken, at once, and with feeling. But John said nothing, and the pause lengthened. Then dread began to rise up in me, and regret: I should never have asked.

John frowned, and then swallowed. I could see he was working. Finally he looked at me. "I feel, well, I feel very warm toward you." He paused. "At least, I feel very warm, myself, when I'm with you." He looked proud.

"Very warm," I repeated. I felt sick, shamed, and I turned my face away from him. John put his hand on my shoulder.

"Really, very warm," he said, earnestly.

I looked at him, speechless and despairing. I could see that we had not been exploring each other at all. We had been in different countries all along, speaking to each other in different languages. I could see that John was nowhere near the leap, and I was no longer sure he wanted to make it.

"Do you still want me to come up?" John asked. "I'd like to." He stroked my shoulder in a tentative way.

I stared at him. I waited for a moment before I spoke, choosing my words.

"Sarah?" he said, stroking my shoulder gently, tenderly.

His hand on me felt exquisite, and it distracted me from my pain. I sat still, and his hand moved from my shoulder to my neck. I felt so miserable that I closed my eyes. For a moment I let myself pretend that things were all right, that nothing had happened, and that we would go on and do what we both wanted. Feeling his hand on my bare skin, slow and possessive, knowing, gentle, I didn't want it to stop.

Maybe I was looking at this wrong. Maybe I was mistaken about John. Maybe this was the only way that he could move away from Agnes, obliquely, undeclared. Maybe he needed to make a safe place with me before he could break away from Agnes. Maybe this was the only way he could approach the leap. John's hand, moving so gently along my collar bone, with other parts of me longing for its arrival, made these thoughts seem sensible.

I thought of the room I'd gotten ready for us, the smooth worn sheets on the bed, the white curtains lifting in the breeze off the water. I had left a light on, its glow invisible in the afternoon sun but deepening and growing with the twilight, so that when we opened the door, our world would already be golden. I remembered the light left on. I thought of walking down that hall alone, entering the room alone, to turn off the light.

"Yes," I said, "come up."

The house above us was dark, and we climbed the steps quietly. Reaching the top, I pulled open the screen door and turned the handle of the glass-topped inner door. It resisted, and I peered into the dim living room, full of mysterious shadows. It was silent, and I tried again: the door had been locked. Of course I didn't have a key—no one here locks the door during the summer. There is only one key to our house, and it lives on a shelf in the pantry. Of course Melissa knows that. I thought of her face as she turned the key in the lock.

"Well," I said, making my voice cheerful, "this is a nuisance. Melissa must have watched a scary movie and she's locked the door. Let's try the kitchen."

But Melissa had thought of the kitchen, and she had thought of the side door. The last possibility was the door onto the front porch, which she might not have bothered with: the porch is self-contained, and no steps lead off it. To reach it I'd have to climb the stone foundation at its highest point, but with John's help I could do that.

We clambered down the steep, needle-covered slope in the dark, and the house rose high above us against the sky. John braced himself, bending his knees. He laced his fingers together, making me a stirrup. Gingerly I set my foot in it: feeling the small cradle of muscle and bone beneath me I felt suddenly heavy, excessive. This would never work, I thought. I could feel that I was too much for him, and I hopped apologetically on one foot.

"Go on," John urged, "go on."

I lunged up. I could feel John taking my weight, I felt his shoulders settle against the strain. I teetered in his hands, groping for a purchase against the cold rusticated stone. He didn't flinch, and I felt him solid and comforting beneath me. Perhaps it would work after all, I thought, and I pushed myself slowly erect against his cupped palms. I stood shakily upright and reached over the parapet. I felt the rough bark of the log railing above it as I searched for a grip. The railing itself was too high, but I set my hands around it and pulled, and I felt John pushing from below. My progress was uneven and wobbly, and I couldn't tell whether this was because of me or him. As I scrabbled, raising one knee against the rough surface, a light went on in the living room.

Melissa's silhouette appeared on the other side of the glass door. I tried frantically to drag my knee all the way up on the wall. Please, I thought, oh, please.

The door opened and Melissa stepped partway out onto the porch, holding the doorknob protectively so she could close herself in again.

"What are you doing out there, *Mother,*" she said, and the word in her mouth was a curse.

I pushed desperately against John's hands, trying to rise, but I felt his hands shaking. Now I could tell that the unevenness came from him. I could feel that this was too much for him, and he was giving way, giving up. As he wavered, I took a great breath, trying to fill myself with air, to make myself weightless. I tried to gather myself together and hurl myself up the wall. I tried for a wild, miraculous skyward leap.

But to leap, you need open air before you, and to spring, you need a solid place beneath your feet to start from, something stable, absolute. Before me was hard stone, and beneath me were John's trembling hands. I could feel his whole body trembling, wavering. I tried to pull myself up by my arms, but I found that I was starting to cry. The strength in my arms and hands was leaving me, and I was no longer sure of what I was able to do.

"What are you *doing* out there, *Mother?*" Melissa said again. Her voice was terrible, an accusation, a hiss. She asked the question as though she had no connection with what I was doing, with my struggle against that brutal stone.

Below me I felt John's shaking hands finally part. He stepped away, letting go of me entirely. My foot plunged down and I felt the chill air and the emptiness beneath me. I was only halfway up, and my arms weren't strong enough to pull me any farther. The heart seemed to have gone out of me. I had no answer for my daughter; there was no question I dared ask anyone.

Mr. Sumarsono

O h, Mr. Sumarsono, Mr. Sumarsono. We remember you so well. I wonder how you remember us?

The three of us met Mr. Sumarsono at the Trenton train station. The platform stretched down the tracks in both directions, long, half-roofed, and dirty. Beyond the tracks on either side were high corrugated-metal sidings, battered and patched. Above the sidings were the tops of weeds and the backs of ramshackle buildings, grimy and desolate. Stretching out above the tracks was an aerial grid of electrical power lines, their knotted, uneven rectangles connecting every city on the Eastern Corridor in a dismal industrial way.

My mother, my sister, Kate, and I stood waiting for Mr. Sumarsono at the foot of the escalator, which did not work. The escalator had worked once; I could remember it working, though Kate, who was younger, could not. Now the metal staircase towered over the platform, silent and immobile, giving the station a surreal air. If you used it as a staircase, which people often did, as you set your foot on each moveable, motionless step, you had an odd feeling of sensory dislocation, like watching a color movie in black and white. You knew something was wrong, though you couldn't put your finger on it.

Mr. Sumarsono got off his train at the other end of the platform from us. He stood still for a moment and looked hesitantly up and down. He didn't know which way to look, or who he was looking for. My mother lifted her arm and waved: we knew who he was, though we had never seen him before. It was 1961, and Mr. Sumarsono was the only Indonesian to get off the train in Trenton, New Jersey.

Mr. Sumarsono was wearing a neat suit and leather shoes, like an American businessman, but he did not look like an American. The suit was brown, not gray, and there was a slight sheen to it. And Mr. Sumarsono himself was built in a different way from Americans: he was slight and graceful, with narrow shoulders and an absence of strut. His movements were diffident, and there seemed to be extra curves in them. This was true even of simple movements, like picking up his suitcase and starting down the platform toward the three of us, standing by the escalator that didn't work.

Kate and I stood next to my mother as she waved and smiled. Kate and I did not wave and smile: this was all my mother's idea. Kate was seven and I was ten. We were not entirely sure what a diplomat was, and we were not at all sure that we wanted to be nice to one all weekend. I wondered why he didn't have friends his own age.

"Hoo-oo," my mother called, mortifyingly, even though Mr. Sumarsono had already seen us and was making his graceful way toward us. His steps were small and his movements modest. He smiled in a nonspecific way, to show that he had seen us, but my mother kept on waving and calling. It took a long time, this interlude; encouraging shouts and gestures from my mother, Mr. Sumarsono's unhurried approach. I wondered if he too was embarrassed by my mother; once he glanced swiftly around, as though he were looking for an alternative family to spend the weekend with. He had reason to be uneasy: the grimy Trenton platform with its corrugated sidings and aerial grid did not suggest a rural retreat. And when he saw us standing by the stationary escalator, my mother waving and calling, Kate and I sullenly silent, he may have felt that things were off to a poor start.

My mother was short, with big bones and a square face. She had thick dark hair and a wide, mobile mouth. She was a powerful woman. She used to be on the stage, and she still delivered to the back row. When she calls "Hoo-oo" at a train station, everyone at that station knows it.

"Mr. Su*mar*sono," she called out as he came up to us. The accent is on the second syllable. That's what the people at the U.N. had told her, and she made us practice, sighing and complaining, until we said it the way she wanted: Su*mar*sono.

Mr. Sumarsono gave a formal nod and a small smile. His face was oval, and his eyes were long. His skin was very pale brown, and smooth. His hair was shiny and black, and it was also very smooth. Everything about him seemed polished and smooth.

"Hello!" said my mother, seizing his hand and shaking it. "I'm Mrs. Riordan. And this is Kate, and this is Susan." Kate and I cautiously put out our hands, and Mr. Sumarsono took them limply, bowing at each of us.

My mother put out her own hand again. "Shall I take your bag?" But Mr. Sumarsono defended his suitcase. "We're just up here," said my mother, giving up on the bag and leading the way to the escalator.

We all began the climb, but after a few steps my mother looked back.

"This is an *esc*alator," she said loudly.

Mr. Sumarsono gave a short nod.

"It takes you *up*," my mother called, and pointed to the roof overhead. Mr. Sumarsono, holding his suitcase with both hands, looked at the ceiling.

"It doesn't work *right now*," my mother said illuminatingly, and turned back to her climb.

"No," I heard Mr. Sumarsono say. He glanced cautiously again at the ceiling.

Exactly parallel to the escalator was a broad concrete staircase, which another group of people were climbing. We were separated only by the handrail, so that for a disorienting second you felt you were looking at a mirror from which you were missing. It intensified the feeling you got from climbing the stopped escalator—dislocation, bewilderment, doubt at your own senses.

A woman on the real staircase looked over at us, and I could tell that my mother gave her a brilliant smile; the woman looked away at once. We were the only people on the escalator.

On the way home Kate and I sat in the back seat and watched our mother keep turning to speak to Mr. Sumarsono. She asked him long, complicated, cheerful questions. "Well, Mr. Sumarsono, had you been in this country at all before you came to the U.N. or is this your first visit? I know you've only been working at the U.N. for a short time."

Mr. Sumarsono answered everything with a polite unfinished nod. Then he would turn back and look out the window
again. I wondered if he was thinking about jumping out of the
car. I wondered what Mr. Sumarsono was expecting from a
weekend in the country. I hoped it was not a walk to the pond:
Kate and I had planned one for that afternoon. We were going
to watch the mallards nesting, and I hoped we wouldn't have
to include a middle-aged Indonesian in leather shoes.

When we got home my mother looked at me meaningfully.
"Susan, will you and Kate show Mr. Sumarsono to his room?"
Mr. Sumarsono looked politely at us, his head tilted slightly
sideways.

Gracelessly I leaned over to pick up Mr. Sumarsono's suitcase, as I had been told. He stopped me by putting his hand
out, palm front, in a traffic policeman's gesture.

"No, no," he said, with a small smile, and he took hold of
the suitcase himself. I fell back, pleased not to do as I'd been
told, but also I was impressed, almost awed, by Mr. Sumarsono.

What struck me was the grace of his gesture. His hand slid
easily out of its cuff and exposed a narrow brown wrist, much
narrower than my own. When he put his hand up in the *Stop!*
gesture his hand curved backward from the wrist, and his fingers bent backward from the palm. Instead of the stern and
flathanded *Stop!* that an American hand would make, this was
a polite, subtle, and yielding signal, quite beautiful and infinitely
sophisticated, a gesture that suggested a thousand reasons for
doing this, a thousand ways to go about it.

I let him take the suitcase and we climbed the front stairs,
me first, Kate next, and then Mr. Sumarsono, as though we
were playing a game. We marched solemnly, single file, through
the second-floor hall and up the back stairs to the third floor.
The guest room was small, with a bright hooked rug on the
wide old floorboards, white ruffled curtains at the windows,

and slanting eaves. There was a spool bed, a table next to it, a straight chair, and a chest of drawers. On the chest of drawers there was a photograph of my great-grandmother, her austere face framed by faded embroidery. On the bedspread was a large tan smudge, where our cat liked to spend the afternoons.

Mr. Sumarsono put his suitcase down and looked around the room. I looked around with him, and suddenly the guest room, and in fact our whole house, took on a new aspect. Until that moment I had thought our house was numbingly ordinary, that it represented the decorating norm: patchwork quilts, steep, narrow staircases, slanting ceilings, and spool beds. I assumed everyone had faded photographs of Victorian great-grandparents dotted mournfully around their rooms. Now it came to me that this was not the case. I wondered what houses were like in Indonesia, or apartments in New York. Somehow I knew: They were low, sleek, modern, all on one floor, with hard gleaming surfaces. They were full of right angles and empty of allusions to the past: they were the exact opposite of our house. Silently and fiercely I blamed my mother for our environment, which was, I now saw, eccentric, totally abnormal.

Mr. Sumarsono looked at me and nodded precisely again.

"Thank you," he said.

"Don't hit your head," Kate said.

Mr. Sumarsono bowed, closing his eyes.

"On the ceiling," Kate said, pointing to it.

"The ceiling," he repeated, looking up at it too.

"Don't hit your head on the ceiling," she said loudly, and Mr. Sumarsono looked at her and smiled.

"The bathroom's in here," I said, showing him.

"Thank you," he said.

"Susan," my mother called up the stairs, "tell Mr. Sumarsono to come downstairs when he's ready for lunch."

"Come-downstairs-when-you're-ready-for-lunch," I said unnecessarily. I pointed graphically into my open mouth and then bolted, clattering rapidly down both sets of stairs. Kate was right behind me, our knees banging in our rush to get away.

Mother had set four places for lunch, which was on the screened-in porch overlooking the lawn. The four places meant a battle.

"Mother," I said mutinously.

"What is it?" Mother said. "Would you fill a pitcher of water, Susan?"

"Kate and I are not *having* lunch," I said, running water into the big blue-and-white pottery pitcher.

"And get the butter dish. Of course you're having lunch," said my mother. She was standing at the old wooden kitchen table, making a plate of deviled eggs. She was messily filling the rubbery white hollows with dollops of yolk-and-mayonnaise mixture. The slippery egg-halves rocked unstably, and the mixture stuck to her spoon. She scraped it into the little boats with her finger. I watched with distaste. In a ranch house, I thought, or in New York, this would not happen. In New York, food would be prepared on polished man-made surfaces. It would be brought to you on gleaming platters by silent waiters.

"I told you Kate and I are *not* having lunch," I said. "We're taking a picnic to the pond." I put the pitcher on the table.

Mother turned to me. "We have been through this already, Susan. We have a guest for the weekend, and I want you girls to be polite to him. He is a stranger in this country, and I expect you to *extend* yourselves. Think how *you* would feel if *you* were in a strange land."

"*Extend* myself," I said rudely, under my breath, but loud enough so my mother could hear. This was exactly the sort of idiotic thing she said. "I certainly wouldn't go around hoping people would *extend* themselves." I thought of people stretched out horribly, their arms yearning in one direction, their feet in another, all for my benefit. "If I were in a strange country I'd like everyone to leave me alone."

"Ready for lunch?" my mother said brightly to Mr. Sumarsono, who stood diffidently in the doorway. "We're just about to sit down. Kate, will you bring out the butter."

"I did already," I said virtuously, and folded my arms in a hostile manner.

"We're having deviled eggs," Mother announced as we sat down. She picked up the plate of them and smiled humorously. "We call them 'deviled.' "

"De-vil," Kate said, speaking very loudly and slowly. She pointed at the eggs and then put two forked fingers behind her head, like horns. Mr. Sumarsono looked at her horns. He nodded pleasantly.

My mother talked all through lunch, asking Mr. Sumarsono mystifying questions and then answering them herself in case he couldn't. Mr. Sumarsono kept a polite half-smile on his face, sometimes repeating the last few words of her sentences. Even while he was eating, he seemed to be listening attentively. He ate very neatly, taking small bites, and laying his fork and knife precisely side by side when he was through. Kate and I pointedly said nothing. We were boycotting lunch, though we smiled horribly at Mr. Sumarsono if he caught our eyes.

After lunch my mother said she was going to take a nap. As she said this, she laid her head sideways on her folded hands and closed her eyes. Then she pointed upstairs. Mr. Sumarsono nodded. He rose from the table, pushed in his chair, and went meekly back to his room, his shoes creaking on the stairs.

Kate and I did the dishes in a slapdash way and took off for the pond. We spent the afternoon on a hill overlooking the marshy end, watching the mallards and arguing over the binoc-

ulars. We only had one pair. There had been a second pair once;
I could remember this, though Kate could not. Our father had
taken the other set with him.

Mother was already downstairs in the kitchen when we got
back. She was singing cheerfully, and wearing a pink dress with
puffy sleeves and a full skirt. The pink dress was a favorite of
Kate's and mine. It irritated me to see that she had put it on as
though she were at a party. This was not a party: she had merely
gotten hold of a captive guest, a complete stranger who understood nothing she said. This was not a cause for celebration.

She gave us a big smile when we came in.

"Any luck with the mallards?" she asked.

"Not really," I said coolly. A lie.

Kate and I set the table, and Mother asked Kate to pick
some flowers for the centerpiece. We were having dinner in
the dining room, my mother said, with the white plates with
gold rims from our grandmother. While we were setting the
table my mother called in from the kitchen, "Oh, Susan, put
out some wineglasses, too, for me and Mr. Sumarsono."

Kate and I looked at each other.

"*Wine*glasses?" Kate mouthed silently.

"Wineglasses?" I called back, my voice sober, for my
mother, my face wild, for Kate.

"That's right," said mother cheerfully. "We're going to be
festive."

"*Festive!*" I mouthed to Kate, and we doubled over, shaking
our heads and rolling our eyes.

We put out the wineglasses, handling them gingerly, as
though they gave off dangerous, unpredictable rays. The glasses,
standing boldly at the knife tips, altered the landscape of the
table. Kate and I felt as though we were in the presence of
something powerful and alien. We looked warningly at each
other, pointing at the glasses and frowning, nodding our heads

meaningfully. We picked them up and mimed drinking from them. We wiped our mouths and began to stagger, crossing our eyes and hiccuping. When mother appeared in the doorway we froze, and Kate, who was in the process of lurching sideways, turned her movement into a pirouette, her face clear, her eyes uncrossed.

"Be careful with those glasses," said my mother.

"We are," said Kate, striking a classical pose, the wine glass held worshipfully aloft, like a chalice.

When dinner was ready mother went to the foot of the stairs and called up, "Hoo-oo!" several times. There was no answer, and after a pause she called, "Mr. Sumarsono! Dinner. Come down for dinner!" We began to hear noises from over-head as Mr. Sumarsono rose obediently from his nap.

When we sat down I noticed that mother was not only in the festive pink dress but that she was bathed and particularly fresh-looking. She had done her hair in a special way, smoothing it back from her forehead. She was smiling a lot. When she had served the plates, my mother picked up the bottle of wine and offered Mr. Sumarsono a glass.

"Would you like a little *wine,* Mr. Sumarsono?" she asked, leaning forward, her head cocked. We were having the dish she always made for guests: baked chicken pieces in a sauce made of Campbell's cream of mushroom soup.

"Thank you." Mr. Sumarsono nodded and pushed forward his glass. My mother beamed and filled his glass. Kate and I watched her as we cut up our chicken. We watched her as we drank from our milk glasses, our eyes round and unblinking over the rims.

We ate in silence, a silence broken only by my mother. "Mr. Sumarsono," my mother said, having finished most of her chicken and most of her wine. "Do you have a *wife?* A *family?*" She gestured first at herself, then at us. Mr. Sumarsono looked searchingly across the table at Kate and me. We were chewing, and stared solemnly back.

Mr. Sumarsono nodded his half-nod, his head stopping at the bottom of the movement, without completing the second half of it.

"A wife?" said my mother, gratified. She pointed again at herself. She is not a wife and hasn't been for five years, but Mr. Sumarsono wouldn't know that. I wondered what he did know. I wondered if he wondered where my father was. Perhaps he thought that it was an American custom for the father to live in another house, spending his day apart from his wife and children, eating his dinner alone. Perhaps Mr. Sumarsono was expecting my father to arrive ceremoniously after dinner, dressed in silken robes and carrying a carved wooden writing case, ready to entertain his guest with tales of the hill people. What did Mr. Sumarsono expect of us? It was unimaginable.

Whatever Mr. Sumarsono was expecting, my mother was determined to deliver what she could of it. In the pink dress, full of red wine, she was changing before our very eyes. She was warming up, turning larger and grander, glowing and powerful.

"Mr. Sumarsono," said my mother happily, "do you have photographs of your family?"

There was a silence. My mother pointed again to her chest, plump and rosy above the pink dress. Then she held up an invisible camera. She closed one eye and clicked loudly at Mr. Sumarsono. He watched her carefully.

"Photo of wife?" she said again, loudly, and again pointed at herself. Then she pointed at him. Mr. Sumarsono gave his truncated nod and stood up. He bowed again and pointed to the ceiling. Then, with a complicated and unfinished look, loaded with meaning, he left the room.

Kate and I looked accusingly at our mother. Dinner would now be prolonged indefinitely, her fault.

"He's gone to get his photographs," Mother said. "The poor man, he must miss his wife and children. Don't you feel sorry for him, thousands of miles away from his family? Oh, thousands. He's here for six months, all alone. They told me that at the U.N. It's all very uncertain. He doesn't know when he gets leaves, how long after that he'll be here. Think of how his poor wife feels." She shook her head and took a long sip of her wine. She remembered us and added reprovingly, "And what about his poor children? Their father is thousands of miles away! They don't know when they'll see him!" Her voice was admonitory, suggesting that this was partly our fault.

Kate and I did not comment on Mr. Sumarsono's children. We ourselves did not know when we would see our father, and we did not want to discuss that either. What we longed for was for all this to be over, this endless, chaotic meal, full of incomprehensible exchanges.

Kate sighed discreetly, her mouth slightly open for silence, and she swung her legs under the table. I picked up a chicken thigh with my fingers and began to pick delicately at it with my teeth. This was forbidden, but I thought that the wine and excitement would distract my mother from my behavior. It did. She sighed deeply, shook her head, and picked up her fork. She began eating in a dreamy way.

"Oh, I'm glad we're having rice!" she said suddenly, gratified. "That must make Mr. Sumarsono feel at home." She looked at me. "You know that's all they have in Indonesia," she said in a teacherly sort of way. "Rice, bamboo, things like that. Lizard."

Another ridiculous statement. I knew such a place could not exist, but Kate was younger, and I pictured what she must imagine: thin stalks of rice struggling up through a dense and endless bamboo forest. People in brown suits pushing their way among the limber stalks, looking fruitlessly around for houses, telephones, something to eat besides lizard.

Mr. Sumarsono appeared again in the doorway. He was holding a large leather camera case. He had already begun to unbuckle and unsnap, to extricate the camera from it. He took out a light meter and held it up. My mother raised her fork at him.

"Rice!" she said enthusiastically. "That's familiar, isn't it? Does it remind you of *home*?" With her fork she gestured expansively at the dining room. Mr. Sumarsono looked obediently around, at the mahogany sideboard with its crystal decanters, the glass-fronted cabinet full of family china, the big, stern portrait of my grandfather in his pink hunting coat, holding his riding crop. Mr. Sumarsono looked back at my mother, who was still holding up her fork. He nodded.

"Yes?" my mother said, pleased.

"Yes," said Mr. Sumarsono.

My mother looked down again. Blinking in a satisfied way she said, "I'm glad I thought of it." I knew she hadn't thought of it until that moment. She always made rice with the chicken-and-Campbell's-cream-of-mushroom-soup dish. Having an Indonesian turn up to eat it was pure coincidence.

Mr. Sumarsono held up his camera. The light meter dangled from a strap, and the flash attachment projected from one corner. He put the camera up to his eye, and his face vanished altogether. My mother was looking down at her plate again, peaceful, absorbed, suffused with red wine and satisfaction.

I could see that my mother's view of all this—the meal, the visit, the weekend—was different from my own. I could see that she was pleased by everything about it. She was pleased by her polite and helpful daughters; she was pleased by her charming farmhouse with its stylish and original touches. She was pleased at her delicious and unusual meal, and, most important, she was pleased by her own generosity, by being able to offer this poor stranger her lavish bounty.

She was wrong, she was always wrong, my mother. She was wrong about everything. I was resigned to it: at ten you have no control over your mother. The evening would go on like this, endless, excruciating. My mother would act foolish, Kate and I would be mortified and Mr. Sumarsono would be mystified. It was no wonder my father had left: embarrassment.

Mr. Sumarsono was now ready, and he spoke. "Please!" he said politely. My mother looked up again and realized this time what he was doing. She shook her head, raising her hands in deprecation.

"No, no," she said, smiling, "not me. Don't take a picture of me. I wanted to see a picture of your wife." She pointed at Mr. Sumarsono. "Your wife," she said, "your children."

I was embarrassed not only for my mother but for poor Mr. Sumarsono. Whatever he had expected from a country weekend in America, it could not have been a cramped attic room, two sullen girls, a voluble and incomprehensible hostess. I felt we had failed him, we had betrayed his unruffled courtesy, by our bewildering commands, our waving forks, our irresponsible talk about lizards. I wanted to save him. I wanted to liberate poor Mr. Sumarsono from this aerial grid of misunderstandings. I wanted to cut the power lines, but I couldn't think of a way. I watched him despondently, waiting for him to subside at my mother's next order. Perhaps she would send him upstairs for another nap.

But things had changed. Mr. Sumarsono stood gracefully, firm and erect, in charge. Somehow he had performed a coup. He had seized power. The absence of strut did not mean an absence of command, and we now saw how an Indonesian diplomat behaved when he was in charge. Like the *Stop!* gesture, Mr. Sumarsono's reign was elegant and sophisticated, entirely convincing. It was suddenly clear that it was no longer possible to tell Mr. Sumarsono what to do.

"No," said Mr. Sumarsono clearly. "You wife." He bowed firmly at my mother. "You children." He bowed at us.

Mr. Sumarsono stood over us, his courtesy exquisite and unyielding. "Please," he said. "Now photograph." He held up the camera. It covered his face entirely, a strange mechanical mask. "My photograph," he said in a decisive tone.

He aimed the camera first at me. I produced a taut and artificial smile, and at once he reappeared from behind the camera. "No smile," he said firmly, shaking his head. "No smile." He himself produced a hideous smile, then shook his head and turned grave. "Ah!" he said, nodding, and pointed at me. Chastened, I sat solemn and rigid while he disappeared behind the camera again. I didn't move even when he had finished, after the flash and the clicks of lenses and winding sprockets.

Mr. Sumarsono turned to Kate, who had learned from me and offered up a smooth and serious face. Mr. Sumarsono nodded, but stepped toward her. "Hand!" he said, motioning toward it, and he made the gesture that he wanted. Kate stared but obediently did as he asked.

When Mr. Sumarsono turned to my mother, I worried again that she would stage a last-ditch attempt to take over, that she would insist on mortifying us all.

"Now!" said Mr. Sumarsono, bowing peremptorily at her. "Please." I looked at her, and to my amazement, relief, and delight, my mother did exactly the right thing. She smiled at Mr. Sumarsono in a normal and relaxed way, as though they were old friends. She leaned easily back in her chair, graceful— I could suddenly see—and poised. She smoothed the hair back from her forehead.

In Mr. Sumarsono's pictures, the images of us that he produced, this is how we look:

I am staring solemnly at the camera, dead serious, head-on. I look mystified, as though I am trying to understand something inexplicable: what the people around me mean when they talk, perhaps. I look as though I am in a foreign country, where I do not speak the language.

Kate looks both radiant and ethereal; her eyes are alight. Her mouth is puckered into a mirthful *V*: she is trying to suppress a smile. The *V* of her mouth is echoed above her face by her two forked fingers, poised airily behind her head.

But it is the picture of my mother that surprised me the most. Mr. Sumarsono's portrait was of someone entirely different from the person I knew, though the face was the same. Looking at it gave me the same feeling that the stopped escalator did: a sense of dislocation, a sudden uncertainty about my own beliefs. In the photograph my mother leans back against her chair like a queen, all her power evident, and at rest. Her face is turned slightly away: she is guarding her privacy. Her nose, her cheeks, her eyes, are bright with wine and excitement, but she is calm and amused. A mother cannot be beautiful, because she is so much more a mother than a woman, but in this picture, it struck me, my mother looked, in an odd way, beautiful. I could see for the first time that other people might think she actually was beautiful.

Mr. Sumarsono's view of my mother was of a glowing, self-assured, generous woman. And Mr. Sumarsono himself was a real person, despite his meekness. I knew that: I had seen him take control. His view meant something; I could not ignore it. And I began to wonder.

We still have the pictures. Mr. Sumarsono brought them with him the next time he came out for the weekend.

Halloween

I was alone in the house.

Usually I take Kate trick-or-treating myself, but this year she had been invited to go with a friend. Kate was, as always, a fairy queen, with rouge-pink cheeks and an aluminum-foil-covered cardboard crown. She wore a white lacy blouse and a long, tiered skirt of mine. Over her shoulders and clasped at her throat was a cape, made from another of my skirts, this one striped and ruffled taffeta.

When Kate was ready I knelt down in front of her, pulling up her lacy collar and settling the cape around her neck. She was excited and would not meet my eye. She waved her wand back and forth in an imperious figure eight.

"Palambanami," she said mysteriously, making a dot in the air with the wand.

"You look beautiful," I told her.

"Mananunu," she said, fixing me with a cold, queenly gaze.

"I hope you have a lovely time," I offered, but she turned away. She looked out the window into the darkness, seeing things that mortals could not, and making cabalistic signs in the air.

A car drove up the driveway, and I heard Stephanie give a brief, courteous honk. Kate, like a stately sleepwalker, stepped to the door and waited regally for me to open it. Her face was remote, and she was casting spells under her breath.

I took her out into the driveway and stood, shivering, while I admired Amanda's ballerina costume.

"Oh, beautiful," I said to her.

"And slippers," Amanda replied, pointing her toe in the air. "*Ballet*," she added severely.

The back seat was filled with the rustle and flounce of little girls in crowns and crinolines, their black-rimmed glances charged with mystery. Another mother was in the front with Stephanie. I went around to the driver's side and Stephanie opened the window.

"Have fun," I said to Stephanie, and she smiled.

"Don't worry," she said.

"Be careful," I added.

Stephanie smiled again. "Don't worry."

There are dangers peculiar to Halloween. There are grown-ups who use this night to play their own sinister tricks; there are horror stories about drug-injected candy, razors inside apples. But we can't avoid risks, can't keep our children safe at home forever. We send our children—spangled with excitement, alight with hope—out into this dark, unknown world, where strangers wait. We must.

I waved good-bye to Kate, where she was deep among crowns and wands in the back seat, but she had already left me. She looked directly at me, but her gaze was cool and enigmatic. She would not wave or smile, or even nod. She would not acknowledge that I was there waving good-bye. Majestic in her ornate robes, head held high beneath her glittering silver crown, Kate spurned me as an empress would a beggar. Usually Kate is shy and dutiful, and I liked seeing her like this, so powerful, so splendid.

As Stephanie drove off, I stood in the dining-room window of the silent house. I watched the car slide slowly down the driveway; I watched its red taillights move away up our dirt road and vanish around the next corner. Without those lights the landscape was entirely dark. We are in the country, half a mile from another house, and when there is no moon there is nothing to relieve the blackness of our nights.

On that night, of course, there was an extra light outside. Kate and I had spent a chilly brilliant afternoon with our pumpkin, sitting on the wide stone back step. We scooped from its inside messy handfuls of pale slimy seeds; we dragged out wet clinging tresses, like orange seaweed. Then we took a paring knife to the grooved outer surface, jerkily carving out damp, angular morsels, the jagged negatives of eyes, mouth, nose. That night our jack-o'-lantern sat outside the front door, its fierce and fiery smile vivid in the October dark.

In the front hall, I had set out a bowl of candy corn and one of apples. I was pleased with the look of them, the rich complicated white-and-orange pattern of the triangular kernels, the deep shining scarlet of the apples. I always have something ready to give them, but we get few trick-or-treaters. Our house is too solitary, set back from our empty road. The children prefer the developments, where the houses are companionably close together, and where each little drive ends in a hospitable ring of rooftops.

A few neighbors' children came by early in the evening, but after that I was alone, the house quiet and unvisited. My husband was away, and I had nothing to do but wait for Kate. Stephanie had promised to have her back at nine-thirty. Nine-thirty is late for a school night, but Halloween is the greatest day in the year for an eight-year-old, better, even, than Christmas. Fantasy is where they live, these children, and on Halloween the grown-ups' rules fall away. On that night the rest of the year—the rest of the world—falls away. That night the children's souls darken and enlarge. They take on their real identities, chanting magic spells, revealing royal bloodlines, and laying claim to their true, immense, arcane, unknowable powers.

I was reading in the library, at the back of the house, when I heard the front doorbell. I was surprised: I'd heard no car. Whoever was there had come on foot, up the dark dirt road through the woods for half a mile before our house appeared. It was past nine o'clock. I walked through the silent rooms, and looked out at the driveway on my way: it was empty. There were no headlights outlining our garage, no patient parent sitting in a car.

I opened the front door. A boy was standing outside, against the night. He was unexpectedly tall: his eyes were level with mine, and for some reason this was unnerving. He wore jeans and a sweater—no costume, no mask—but he was completely disguised. His face was divided straight down the middle. One half was painted densely and entirely white, gleaming and opaque. The other side was shining, oily black. Every inch was meticulously covered, even his eyelids. His eyes, surrounded by the artificial gloss of the paint, looked strange, unnaturally mobile and liquid. His lips, and the inside of his mouth, were a shocking rubber-pink. His features were visible but completely unrecognizable. I kept trying to read his face, to know it, but it resisted.

"Trick or treat," said the boy, but he spoke flatly, without excitement. His voice suggested adolescence: it had changed, but was not yet deep. I looked behind him into the night, expecting friends, a boisterous group of them out together, but there was nothing there but the big sugar maples on the slop-ing lawn, and far below them the murmuring black wall of rhododendrons.

Still I smiled at him: we were acting out a ritual. I would furnish enthusiasm if he did not. "Happy Halloween," I said. I held out my two bowls. "Here you are."

The boy did not answer and stood looking down at the bowls.

Holding them out, looking down with him, in silence, at the apples and candy corn, I felt dismay. I had meant to offer something healthy and simple. Now, in our shared silence, as both of us looked down from our adult height, the contents of the bowls looked suddenly mean-spirited and uninteresting.

"No, thanks," the boy said calmly.

This was wrong. I had never seen a trick-or-treater refuse the treats. It was not part of the ritual. Looking down, I saw that the boy carried nothing in his hands. There was no sack to put anything into, even if he had wanted something.

The boy looked back at me. "Actually," he said, "I'd like to make a phone call."

I hesitated: this too was not part of the ritual. And there were things that had happened that year, near us, out in the country. These were truly terrible events, things that everyone, the whole community, had kept from all the children. The things began with strangers who came to the door at night, claiming car trouble and asking to make a phone call. After we had heard the stories and knew what had then happened, it was hard for us to believe that these women had let these strangers into their houses, alone, at night.

I stood in the hall, hesitating.

"I need to call my mother," the boy said.

The magic word, the password. I was a mother, and he was a child. He had reminded me of my role, my responsibility, my duty to children.

"I'll show you the phone," I said, and stepped back into the hall, letting him in. He did not smile or say thank you, just followed me. We walked through the unlit dining room, through the pantry and into the kitchen. We passed by the mudroom, and the boy noticed our tennis racquets.

"Oh, do you play tennis?" he asked easily. He sounded relaxed and offhand, as though he and I were good friends, as though this kind of social inquiry were appropriate. It was unsettling.

"Yes," I said shortly, then wished I had said no. For some reason I wanted to give away nothing to him; I wanted him to have no knowledge of me.

"So do I," said the boy. "Where do you play?"

"At a club," I said forbiddingly, then asked, "Where do you?" I was proud of my craftiness; this would give me a clue to his identity.

"Nowhere," said the boy. I felt chilled.

In the kitchen, at the telephone table, the boy stopped. Instead of picking up the telephone, he stood looking around the room: my kitchen, the heart of my house. He surveyed it coolly, appraisingly, as though he were planning to take it over. In the light I could see him more clearly, though his face was still unreadable. He was about five feet eight, slight, with narrow shoulders. He had not yet filled out into manhood, had not taken on adult bulk. I found myself wondering how strong he was, and if I was as strong as he.

"Here's the phone," I said loudly and accusingly, to remind him why he was here.

He looked at me for a second and then picked up the phone. He dialed a number and waited.

"Mother?" he said, and my heart froze.

No sixteen-year-old boy calls his mother Mother to her face. He calls her Mom, or Mum, or Ma, or something else, but not Mother. Especially not a boy with his face painted in this eerie, threatening way. Hearing him say that word, I admitted to myself that I was frightened. I moved away from him, over to the kitchen island, near the drawers that held my paring knives. My heart was pounding.

The boy spoke bending over. His face was lowered, his gaze fixed on the telephone. "I'm ready to be picked up," he said neutrally. "I'll tell you where I am." Without looking at me, he gave directions to the person on the other end of the line. I listened as he did this, I waited, passive, polite, as he told someone how to reach my driveway, my house.

This is how it happens, I thought, by steps, in stages, through courtesy. This is how we are tied up and murdered: We are too polite to mention what is about to happen. When they ask us for a rope, we go off and rummage for one in the cellar.

When the boy hung up I stared at him accusingly, trying to let him know I understood his plan. I kept the kitchen island between us, and my hand close to the knife drawer. I hoped that whatever was going to happen would be over by the time Stephanie got back with Kate. I hoped Stephanie wouldn't stay out in the car. I hoped she wouldn't just let Kate run inside, alone, and find me.

The boy looked curiously around the kitchen again, his glance casual, assured. I held him angrily in my gaze as he watched. There was nothing worth stealing in here, and I would not let him go into another room.

"How long will she take to get here?" I asked.

"Who?" the boy said.

"Your 'mother,' " I said coldly.

"Oh, not long," he said easily, and again I was frightened. It was his ease.

I kept my gaze on him, trying to memorize his features, trying to penetrate his disguise, to see his face. But the black and white division, central, dislocating, masked him altogether. He was perfectly disguised as his own halved and doubled self, his identity concealed by its division. I would never know him if I saw him again, undisguised. This too was frightening. The knife drawer, for some reason, now seemed little help.

"I think I'll wait outside," the boy said. He seemed to make decisions easily, he seemed to be in charge.

"All right," I said. I wondered what this meant as he walked coolly past me. In the shadowy dining room he turned suddenly black, becoming his own negative. I followed his silent silhouette around the table and out to the front hall. I opened the door for him and stepped back. He glanced at me sideways as he stepped past me, and I felt myself shivering at his nearness.

"Thanks," he said, his courtesy chilling. He smiled, his open mouth a strange rubber-pink crevice in his black-and-white cheeks.

He stepped out into the dark. Beside him the jack-o'-lantern flared evilly, and beyond him the lawn sloped down to the silent, invisible road. There was no moon.

Impulsively, I leaned out after him. "You're sure you'll be all right out here?" I asked suddenly.

Why did I ask? Hearing myself ask such a question frightened me even more: it was a fool's question, a victim's.

But I had to ask it. I was desperate. I was trying to transform us, to make us parent and child. I was asking the boy if he was not someone's son. I was reminding him that I was someone's mother. My question was a plea, a reminder of who we were.

"Yeah," the boy said, his voice indifferent. He did not bother to look at me again. He stepped onto the lawn and was taken at once by the shadows.

He had turned me down, as easily as turning out a light. Every murderer is some mother's child, he had replied.

I stood in the doorway for a moment, looking out after the boy. There was a night wind high up in the sugar maples, and small bare branches brushed confidentially against each other. I couldn't hear the boy's footsteps on the lawn. My heart was still pounding, loud, and I closed the door.

I went into the dark dining room and stood in the window. I was invisible now myself. I stood looking out onto the lawn, watching for him to leave. As he walked toward the driveway, the boy would have to pass in front of the dining-room windows. In the light from the front door, in the flare of the jack-o'-lantern, I would see his outline, I would see his silhouette pass me by.

There was nothing. No movement, no shape. I stood in the dark window, staring out into the night, straining to see him. I wondered if he had slipped along the side of the house, hugging it. I wondered if he was now crouching soundlessly beneath me against the wall, where he would wait, without moving, until the car that he had summoned arrived.

I stood waiting, seeing nothing moving on the lawn, knowing the boy was there. Terror took over, then. My heart clamored, hurtling, out of control, like a runaway horse. I didn't know what to do. Without moving I waited for the next thing to happen.

I stayed by the window for a long time, but I didn't see the boy again. I didn't hear his footsteps on the flagstone path, or see his silhouette pass on the way to the driveway, didn't see the headlights of a car, coming to pick him up.

Finally I turned away from the cold black glass. I went through the darkened downstairs rooms, locking up. I turned on no lights, and I moved quietly, quietly, as though there were someone in the house with me, listening. I hardly breathed: fear had entered into me, like a disease into my system.

I thought of calling the police, but what would I tell them? Nothing had happened. And even if they came—loud, ponderous, reassuring—they would leave again, their taillights would vanish into the dark. Kate and I would be alone afterward, that night, and others: my husband travels often.

I went back to the kitchen to wait. My heart had slowed, but the silent house seemed surrounded still by danger. Watching the driveway for Stephanie's car, I remembered asking her, earlier, to be careful, setting off. I had talked as though I were a safe place, and the only dangers lay elsewhere. I had thought the layer of safety that surrounded us was dense, impenetrable, hard as horn. Now I could see that here was as dangerous as anywhere, that safety was a fragile membrane, trembling and permeable.

I watched from the kitchen window, but I saw nothing of the boy, no shadow, no car. When headlights finally flared onto the garage and a car pulled into the driveway, it was Stephanie, returning. Kate climbed out at once, and shouted good-bye. Swinging her big shopping bag of booty, she ran across the driveway. She burst into the kitchen and slammed the door behind her.

"I'm back," she announced.

The real Kate was back. She still wore her cape and crown, her eyes were still rimmed with black, but she had cast off her Halloween persona. She was no longer a queen, but a child, and she began eagerly to talk about her evening.

Listening, I thought of her as she'd been earlier—the chill imperial power she had assumed with her costume. I thought of the cool unknowable boy, with his painted face. I wondered if he was now at home, standing before the bathroom mirror, taking off the concealing grease with wads of Kleenex, shouting to his mother that he would not make a mess. Maybe. Maybe he was still out, in the countryside, or in someone else's house, doing things I did not want to contemplate.

Kate slept in my bed that night. Her Halloween was over, and she sank easily into sleep. Her head was thrown back among the pillows, her arms flung out on either side; her whole body declared that she was safe.

My Halloween was not over, and I did not sink easily into sleep. I lay listening to the noises of the house around me, staring into the darkness. I watched the bedroom door, which stood open onto the lighted hall. I watched it for movement, and sometimes, staring at it, I thought I saw the door shift slightly. I watched the steady red eye of the alarm system: sometimes it seemed to wink, falter. I listened to the subtle shiftings of the old house; sometimes I thought I heard a human step, the thud of a shoulder against clapboard.

I lay there through the black silent part of the night, motionless. My eyes grew dry and strained from staring, but I hardly dared blink. It was as though some mysterious law of physics held that the more intently I waited for an intruder, the less there would be one. It was as though I thought my wakeful consciousness would spread a protective glow, like lamplight.

In the morning, early gray light revealed empty lawns, un-invaded territory, the absence of intruders. My fear, as fear does in daylight, faded, leaving only a shadowy essence.

The boy never came back. I never saw him again, and I never forgot him. I never forgot what he had taught me: that here is as dangerous as anywhere, that safety is a fragile membrane, easily pierced. Maybe I was wrong, that night, maybe I misread that masked, divided face. Maybe I was wrong to be alarmed. Maybe the boy was merely a boy, feeling, like Kate, daring, in his Halloween disguise, out in the wild black night.

Or maybe I was lucky.

The Reign of Arlette

When I pulled into the driveway on Friday afternoon I was relieved, as always, to see that our house was still standing. There it was: a gray-shingled, weather-beaten farmhouse, its chimneys still upright. What I worry about each week, while I'm in the city, is not arson or hurricanes but the fact that my two children are spending the summer here, parentless.

I parked the car and walked up the uneven flagstone path, across the scrubby lawn. Huge old lilac bushes crowded in shifting green masses beside the doorways, and the ancient sugar maples stood around the house like peaceful giants. I went in the back door and into the big sunny kitchen. It was empty and silent.

I love this house. I think of it as mine, though it actually belongs to Willis. He bought it when we were married, six years ago. During his first marriage everything was owned jointly, and during his divorce he regretted it. This time, everything is in his name. I don't care. I work for a foundation. I've never made much money and I never will. My first husband, Walter, was not generous, and the children and I went through some hard times when I was single. I am lucky to be married to someone who is generous, and I don't care whose name the house is in. Willis gives us a good life, and I'm grateful, on any terms, because of Nicko and Belinda.

In past years, the children went to summer camp, and their father and I split the rest of their vacation time between us. But this year Nicko is sixteen and too old for camp, and Belinda is twelve and has discovered horses. Nicko found a job out here, and Belinda found a stable. Nicko is really too old for a babysitter, but he's a lot too young to be left alone with Belinda all week in Bridgehampton. So I hired someone to be me—someone to buy the groceries, do the laundry, drive the children where they needed to go, and call the repairman when the dishwasher broke. I wasn't worried about rules; my children aren't rebellious. Nicko's shy and hasn't many friends. He's never had a girlfriend; he's never even had a date. Belinda hasn't hit adolescence yet, and she loves everyone. So I didn't want a policeman, I wanted a mother. I wanted someone who would keep the house sailing peacefully along before the wind, with Nicko and Belinda safely inside it.

I looked around the kitchen: it was clean and serene. The gray-and-white checkerboard floor was swept, the butcher-block counters were smooth and empty, the geraniums in the bay window had been watered. I felt a sense of great peace and relief: today was the start of my own vacation, and for the next two weeks I'd be here full-time. I felt as though I'd completed some arduous task and was receiving my reward.

I went to the back stairs and called up. "Nicko? Belinda?"

There was no answer, and the house felt empty. I went out to the tiny cottage where Arlette lives. This is just two small rooms, side by side, looking straight out onto the back lawn. It has no privacy, and I called, to let Arlette know I was coming. When I reached it she was standing at the screen door.

I had imagined very clearly the person I would find to look after the children: a woman in her thirties or forties, maybe a teacher, with the summer free. Maybe divorced, a little down on her luck. Someone like that would be appreciative of the job, even grateful to be there, and her gratitude would spill over onto my beloved children. Maybe she'd be plump and messy-haired, indifferent to appearances, someone with a great sense of humor and a great heart. Someone who would think it a pleasure to live in our pretty house in Bridgehampton, with my two wonderful children, for the summer.

I didn't find anyone like that. For months I couldn't find anyone at all, and by the time I found Arlette it was only two weeks before vacation began, and I was desperate. The idea of gratitude had somehow shifted, and it seemed by then as though she were doing me a favor.

Arlette is twenty-five and French. She has short dark hair, a pointed nose, and a heavy accent. She is thin, chic, and alarmingly cool. When she answers a question her eyebrows rise disdainfully, as though she can't imagine why you had to ask. I find her unsettling, but she does everything I ask. The larder is always full, the laundry hamper always empty, the children are taken where they need to go. I can't complain, but she wasn't what I'd had in mind.

"'Ello, Jan, how was your trip?" asked Arlette politely. She was wearing two very thin gold bracelets and a bikini.

"Not too bad, actually," I said. I was still in my office clothes, now hot and grubby after the drive. Arlette looked cool and sleek, as though she'd done nothing all week but lie out at the pool.

"Good," Arlette said, and waited, her head cocked. She gives out nothing, Arlette, she answers only the question. This makes it hard for me to feel that we are friends.

"Well, what's been going on all week," I asked. "Did the repairman ever come?"

"The repairman came yesterday," she said. "The deesh-washer works."

"Amazing," I said.

Arlette nodded. "Amazeeng, but true."

I am never quite sure when Arlette is being funny. I smiled now, in case she was, and asked what I really wanted to know. "And where are the kids?"

"Belinda's at the barn, an' Nicko 'as gone to the 'ardware store wis Willis."

"I'll pick up Belinda," I said. "What are Nick and Willis doing at the hardware store?"

"I seenk Willis want' some new cleepers for the 'edge. I told him to take Nicko, Nicko would know which are the best."

Nicko has been working at a garden center, so he ought to know about clippers. Still, Willis has never asked his advice about anything before. I tried to picture the two of them standing at the counter, companionably side by side, discussing heft and calibration, blades. I was pleased and touched to hear that it had been Arlette's idea. Maybe I had misunderstood her, I thought, maybe I wasn't giving her enough credit.

When you're a single parent, you feel solely and wholly responsible for your children, as though you were refugees, making your way through a war-torn landscape. You feel protective in a fierce, constant way. A relentless vigilance lives in you like a heartbeat. You are never not aware of where your children are, or of the dangers that surround them. You feel that you are your children's carapace, their shield against the world.

I've worked full-time ever since Nicko started school. And whatever the arrangements were, whoever was looking after him and Belinda, however carefully I'd planned, I've always worried, from the very beginning. How could you not? And when you come home and find your child happy, bathed, asleep, you feel awash with gratitude to the baby-sitter. You also feel, secretly and uncharitably, resentful of her for doing such a good job. For the better she is, the less he needs you. So, as you take the sleeping baby, you notice that his pajama top is on inside out, and you purse your lips in annoyance. You make a small noise of irritation to let her know about her mistake.

This response is unkind, but so are some of hers. Sometimes, when your son begins to whimper in your arms, the baby-sitter says ingenuously, "Oh, that's the first time he's cried all day." You say nothing, but you hate her. She says, "Here, let me take him," but you turn away, with him in your arms. Her words send a dagger deep into your heart, reminding you that you have been absent for your son, and perhaps your presence is no longer what he needs.

But if I had been absent, now I was back. The reign of Arlette was over, and my own had begun. I felt relieved and, now that I was taking the throne, magnanimous. I was ready to forgive Arlette her coolness, to believe I had misjudged her. I was happy, and in this mood I asked her to come to dinner with us that night.

"We're taking the kids to Pete's," I said. "Would you like to come along?"

As I spoke, I wondered about Willis.

He has a horror of invasion, and at the start of the summer he had gloomily predicted that Arlette would appear at breakfast every morning full of loud Gallic chat, and a horde of her radio-playing friends would hang around our pool. So I had carefully explained the rules to Arlette: she was always welcome at the pool, but her friends were not. No loud radios, and so on. As it turned out, all that was unnecessary. In the mornings, when we were there, Arlette took her mug of breakfast coffee back out to her house. We saw very little of her, in any case: a large group of blond friends with sunglasses picked her up and brought her home from wherever it was they went.

I thought Willis wouldn't mind, now—the danger of invasion was past. It was the end of the summer, and too late for anything to go wrong. And anyway, Arlette would probably refuse—she'd have plans with the blond people.

But to my surprise, she nodded composedly and said she'd love to 'ave deener wis us. I felt rather flattered that she would choose us over the blonds.

I changed my clothes and went off to pick up Belinda. I found her in the deep summer gloom of the barn. She was standing on a box, brushing a big chestnut horse on cross-ties. Another girl was on the other side of the horse, brushing it too. I called out to Belinda. She stepped off the box, set it carefully by the wall, picked up her dusty black hard hat, and came out. She's skinny, now, growing, with long spindly legs, and was wearing the tan jodhpurs she's worn every day this summer. She has freckles, short brown hair, absolutely straight, and a quiet, abstracted manner.

"Hi, Bell," I said, and kissed her. She let me, and smiled sweetly: she's still unselfconscious, and I don't embarrass her yet. I'm grateful for this.

Driving home I asked her how the week had been.

"Okay," she said. "We did cavalletti today, which is *so boring.* And I still haven't got my diagonals right. But Ann said I was doing much better at the canter."

"Good," I said equably. "And how about at home? With Arlette?"

"Okay," said Belinda, looking out the window.

"Do you like her?" I asked baldly.

"She's fine," Belinda said, shrugging. "She's kind of weird, actually."

"How do you mean?" I asked.

"Oh, I don't know. She's just so, you know, like . . ." Belinda lost interest and trailed off.

"So what?" I said.

"Oh, fussy about everything. Everything has to be, like, just exact. And the way she talks! Nicko and I call her Lee Fwog." She turned back to me. "Not in front of her," she reassured me.

I laughed. It was what I had hoped would happen: Nicko and Bell had looked after each other, and Arlette had looked after the house. My children were safe, and I was happy. I was happy to be back, happy that Bell was doing better at the canter, and happy about Willis and Nicko.

Willis and I have been married for six years, but Willis and Nicko are not yet friends. One Saturday morning in June, Willis and I sat in the kitchen over coffee and the *Times.* In the silence, the first noises from upstairs were conspicuously audible: the creakings of the floorboards and the heavy footsteps overhead as Nicko got up. Finally he came thundering down the steep back stairs and appeared in the doorway. He was barefoot, in faded blue jeans with the inevitable rip across the knee. He had on a wrinkled football jersey, too big, from a school he does not attend. In spite of his noisy descent, he came into the kitchen quietly, his eyes covered by his dark-blond bangs, and his shoulders hunched. He moved gently, his eyes lowered, as though he were trying to escape attention.

"Good morning, Nicko," I said, loud and cheerful. Partly, I wanted to establish the tone, and partly, I truly was delighted to see him. I am delighted every time that I see Nicko, now that his life is so divergent from ours, now that he has left home forever. They never really live at home again, after fourteen. First it's boarding school, then it's college, then it's Life. So I treasure the times I have with Nicko, and each morning my heart lifts, the way it did years ago, when he was tiny.

In those years, I used to come in to Nicko's room early, as soon as I woke up. I'd push the door open silently, in case he was still asleep. But Nicko was already awake, always, waiting for me to start his world. He'd be already up, standing in his crib in his pale-blue footed pajamas, his diapered rump plump and bunchy. He'd tiptoe bouncily along the mattress, talking earnestly to himself in rapid and fluent Baby, peering alertly around his room. When he caught sight of me, his face would light up. He'd lunge toward me, grab the crib railing, and give a long indrawn gurgle, a backwards crow, like a tiny exuberant cockerel. I'd feel the same way, a crowding excitement in my throat, at the sight of this creature whom, at that moment, I longed for physically, desperately, as though we had been separated for years.

Things were different now, of course.

"Morning, Mom, morning, Willis," he said, not looking at us. He slid into a chair without pulling it out from the table, as though he were barely there. He brushed his hair out of his eyes and it fell back at once. Willis looked up from his paper and smiled majestically.

"Good morning, Nicholas," he said. Willis is a splendid-looking man, with wide shoulders and a thatch of glossy dark brown hair, which is turning gray in a distinguished manner. He speaks slowly and very precisely, almost theatrically, carefully articulating each word. He looked at his watch. "Not quite the record, this morning," he said. "But still in training, I see."

Nicko smiled without looking up. He didn't answer.

"Well, yes, we're still working on it," I said, sprightly, trying to counteract the edge in Willis's voice. "We're trying for a solid thirteen hours." Actually, I don't see why Nicko shouldn't sleep late on weekends. "Now, what would you like, Nicko? Cereal? Eggs?" I went to the stove, ready to cook up a storm.

Willis spoke before Nicko answered. "What are your plans for the weekend, Nicholas?" he said, still with his calm half-smile. "Besides training for the Olympic Sleep-Ins? Any 'job interviews' lined up?" He put the words in quotes, as though this was an absurd concept.

"Actually, you do have an interview, don't you?" I said to Nicko. He was silent, looking at his plate, so I turned to Willis. "He has an interview at the Green Thumb Nursery. They told him they need someone full-time, for the whole summer."

"Ah," said Willis. "Do they need someone on the electric guitar, or are we branching out into other fields of endeavor?"

"Not electric guitar," I said quickly, putting butter into the frying pan. "I think they said they needed a bass, but Nicko's really nearly as good on bass as he is on guitar, aren't you, sweetheart?" There was a pause, and when I saw Nicko wasn't going to answer, I said, "You do want eggs, don't you, Nicko? Fried or scrambled?"

Nicko finally spoke. "Scrambled," he said. He didn't look at me.

I hope things will get better between them, and this summer I've been hoping it especially. Nicko is taller each weekend. He is taking on the height and the silhouette of a young man, but his fresh skin, his silky hair, his bashful sweetness, his awkwardness, all remind you where he still is: boyhood. He is on the edge of manhood, on the cusp, but he is not there yet. He is still tender and vulnerable, and I would like to protect him forever, from everything.

I can't, of course, protect Nicko from much of anything, not from the edge in Willis's voice, nor even from his own father. Nicko's father, Walter, hasn't spoken to him since February, when Nicko had lunch at Walter's apartment. Walter has remarried, and he and his new wife, Marilyn, have a new baby. Nicko was excited about having another sister, and he smiled whenever he talked about Vanessa. The lunch was to celebrate her birthday, and he bought her a present. It was a bear in a flowered sundress, quite expensive, and he chose it himself, and paid for it. Belinda had gone to stay with a friend that weekend, and Nicko went to his father's alone.

After the lunch, Nick came back earlier than I'd expected. I heard the front door slam, and I listened for him to come along the hall. I didn't hear him so I called out.

"Nicko?" There was no answer, and I went to find him. He was in his room; he must have tiptoed past our door. He was on his bed with his shoes on, lying on his back and staring at the ceiling.

"Hi, Nicko. I didn't hear you go by. How was the lunch?"

"Okay." He didn't look at me.

"What went on?" I asked cheerfully. "Was it a birthday party, with Vanessa's friends? Or just the four of you?"

"Just the four of us." He still didn't look at me.

"And?" I said. "Was it fun?"

"No," said Nicko. "It was shitty."

I waited for a moment. "What happened?"

Nicko turned his face toward the wall and made his hand into a fist. He pressed his fist against the wall. "Just shitty."

I waited again. Nicko is not a talker. "Want to tell me about it?" I asked.

"No," he said, pushing his fist against the wall again.

I waited, but he didn't say anything more, so I said, "Well, I'm sorry," and turned to go. When I was in the doorway, Nicko spoke.

"I guess I won't be seeing Dad anymore."

"You mean for a while? Why? Are they going away?"

"No. I mean I guess I won't see him at all."

This time I walked over to the bed and sat down. I didn't say anything, I just waited. Nicko rolled over on his side, away from me, and began picking at the quilt, pulling at the tufts on it.

"At the beginning it was fine," he said. "I got there, and Vanessa was running all over the place like crazy. She was all dressed up and she looked really cute. She had a pink ribbon tied in her hair, and it made her hair stand up like a little water-fall. When I came in she shouted 'Nicko! Nicko!' and she made this gurgling noise in her throat, she was so excited. I carried her around and we chased the cat. She liked that, and she waved her arms all around and laughed and yelled." Nicko paused, pulling at the tufts.

"And how was Marilyn?" I asked.

"She was okay. She was nice when I was carrying Vanessa around. She was smiling a lot. But she doesn't usually look at me. She looks at Dad, or she looks at Vanessa. She doesn't look at me."

I hated Marilyn for this. "So then what happened?"

"So then we had lunch. By then Vanessa was tired, I guess, and she started whining and kind of whimpering. She sat in her high chair and spat out her food and waved her hands like no, no, every time Marilyn tried to give her something. Marilyn stopped talking to anyone, she just kept wiping the spit off

Vanessa's chin and bringing the spoon up again with more, and Vanessa would start to cry and put her lips in a pout and spit it out again. The food was getting on her dress, even though she was wearing this bib." Nicko paused again. Now he was stabbing at the quilt with his finger, over and over.

"I thought I'd try to help out. I'd been such a big hit before, carrying her around and chasing the cat, and I thought I could cheer her up again. I hadn't given her the present yet. It was in the front hall with my coat. I thought it was for after lunch, with the cake. So I leaned forward and said, 'Vanessa, I have a surprise for you.' She opened her eyes, and I leaned really close to her and I made a face, to make her laugh. She smiled, so I went on making these faces and then she started to laugh. I thought Marilyn liked it. She didn't say anything, but she scraped some more food out of the jar and Vanessa had her mouth open because she was smiling and the spoon went right in. And instead of crying and spitting it out, Vanessa laughed, and then started to chew and swallow. I thought Marilyn and Dad liked what I was doing. I stood up and made more faces, and Marilyn fed Vanessa. When I saw the jar was empty I thought Vanessa was through, so I stood up and reached across the table and picked her up right out of her high chair.

"But I didn't know she was sort of strapped into it, there was this, like, harness, underneath the bib, that attached her to the chair. I was leaning over, trying to swoop her across the table, and the chair was pulled over. It fell into the table and knocked over the water pitcher, and Vanessa started to cry because the harness was hurting her shoulders, and she was kicking her feet in among the plates and all the food, and she knocked over everything else, the plates and her milk glass and my Coke. It was a mess."

Nicko stopped again. I put my hand on his shoulder and rubbed it a bit.

"But everyone could see it was all just a mistake?" I said.

"Marilyn looked at me like I had gone after the baby with an ax. She grabbed Vanessa out of my hands and said, 'Nicholas, that is enough. I've had it with you. All you've done since you arrived is upset Vanessa. You nearly had her in hysterics over the cat, then you upset her so much that she wouldn't eat, and now you've destroyed everything on the table. Just leave Vanessa alone. Don't touch her. Don't even talk to her.' "

"She couldn't have said that," I said.

"Then Dad said, 'Nicholas, would you come into the library with me for a minute.' So I went in there and he said all this stuff about how I wasn't considerate to Marilyn, and I only used their house in Southampton like a hotel, and how I only thought of myself, and I never offered to help or anything, and how it was Vanessa's birthday and I hadn't even brought her a present."

There was another long pause. I went on rubbing Nicko's shoulder. I could see his face in profile. He has long, straight eyelashes, and they brushed his cheek each time he blinked.

"And so?" I said.

"So I left," said Nicko. "I left the present in the hall."

Since then, Nicko hasn't heard from his father. I called, of course, to tell him what I thought of his behavior, but Walter hung up on me.

There's nothing I can do; it drives me wild. All I want to do is make my son happy, keep him from pain, and I can't even do it at home, in the most private part of his life. Willis says I'm overprotective, and maybe I am. But it was my idea to get divorced; it's because of me that Nicko doesn't live with his father, that he lives with Willis, and that Walter takes out his rage at me on Nick. All I can do is try to make things go well for Nicko however I can. How could I not be overprotective?

But that evening in late August I felt normal, I even felt successful, as a mother. I felt the summer had gone well for Nicko and Bell.

Standing in the crowded doorway at Pete's, I felt proud of all of us: Willis, solid and dignified, his blue eyes gleaming under his flamboyant graying eyebrows. Nicko, clean and tanned and wonderful, his blond hair freshly washed, his jeans miraculously holeless. Belinda was wearing faded but clean jeans and a loose cotton sweater. Arlette, of course, dressed up the rest of us: cool and elegant in a very short, very tight jersey dress and her gold bracelets. And I felt light and happy that we had at least managed this peculiar sort of family group, all of us bound to each other by these odd strands of commitment, affection, and good will.

At the table, I leaned back in my chair, relaxed and happy, and turned to Nicko.

"So," I said. "Tell me about the week. What's been going on?"

Nicko looked out from under his bangs and smiled. "Oh, yeah. It's been a pretty exciting time out here."

"Yes?" I said.

"Well, the high point was really Thursday."

"Thursday?"

"The repairman came," Nicko said. "He fixed the dishwasher."

Everyone laughed. "Very funny," I said, laughing too.

"I had a better time than Nicko," Bell said. "I jumped three feet two. And I was the only one Ann let do it."

"You didn't tell me that, Bellie," I said, pleased.

"I forgot," said Bell, smiling into her glass.

"That's terrific," I said, and then I pushed at Nick's shoulder. "And what about you? Come on, Nicko. Give me the scoop. Tell me things I want to know."

"What do you want to know?" Nicko asked. He was grinning, we all were.

I knew better than to ask about Nicko's job, which is a touchy subject, and I had alternate questions ready.

"Well," I said, "did you see Harry?"

Harry is a schoolfriend from New York whom Nicko never sees. I keep hoping that Nicko will acquire friends. I want him to be part of a big, roving herd of kids, boys and girls, rowdy and cheerful and warmhearted, surging in and out of one another's houses, shouting and thrashing in the pool, tracking water through the kitchen, going out for pizza and on to the movies. This is my dream.

"No, Ma, didn't see Harry," Nicko said, shaking his head. "Sorry. Didn't see Harry, again. *Another* bad week for me and Harry."

"Nicholas, you're torturing your poor mother," Willis said, jocular. "Call Harry, and put her out of her misery."

Nicko grinned. "Sorry, Ma. Maybe *you* should call Harry," he offered.

"Right," I said. "I'll call him right now. Give me a quarter," I said to Willis, and everyone laughed.

But in the end, of course, I couldn't help myself.

"So how are things going at the nursery?" I asked, very casually, and Nicko stopped smiling and looked down at his beer.

"Okay," he said.

"Did you work every day?" I asked.

Nicko shook his head, not looking at me.

Arlette spoke up. "Oh," she said contemptuously, "they are no good, at that nursery." Her mouth was pursed critically. "They do not tell the truth. They tell Nicko to come in, yes, we need you, then they say to go 'ome, we don' need you. Sometime' Nicko go in at ten, 'e come 'ome at two. Sometime' they say no, don' come in at all." She shook her head.

"Puh," she exhaled dismissively, and with one disdainful breath she banished the nursery forever from her universe.

I don't know what's going on at the nursery. I don't know whether Nicko isn't working hard enough, or whether they lied to him to begin with, but it hasn't gone well. I was struck by Arlette's contempt for the nursery and her loyalty to Nicko. Her attitude infected Willis, who ordinarily sides genially against Nicko, whatever the issue.

Now Willis said, "You know, that really is rather shocking," as though that were the first he'd heard of it. "Didn't they *say* they wanted you full-time?"

Nicko shrugged his shoulders and nodded. "That's what they said, all right," he said.

Willis shook his head. "Shocking," he said again, setting the weight of his disapproval against the enemy.

"Shockeeng," Arlette echoed primly.

"Shockeeng," Belinda said, grinning in a nice way, and we all laughed, including Arlette.

Dinner was a success, and by the end of it I was feeling even more affectionate toward everyone, particularly Arlette. I forgave her everything—her coolness, her near-insolence, her bikini—for her defense of Nicko. Now I was glad she'd been there with him all summer: if Nicko didn't have a big, loose group of friends, at least he had one fiercely loyal one.

When we stood up to leave, someone called from another table. "Arlette!" It was a girl with very red lipstick and long blond hair, very straight.

Arlette looked around and gave a brief neutral wave.

"That was a great party!" called the girl.

Arlette said, "Ah," noncommittally, and kept moving.

"Moonlight swimming! Love it! Thanks!" called the girl, but this time Arlette just waved, like a queen signaling the end of an interview.

When we were outside I asked, "Who was that?"

"Jus' a girl from out 'ere," Arlette said vaguely, shrugging. "I don' really know 'er very well."

"What's her name?" I asked.

"I seenk Susan," Arlette said, remote, as though Susan were from another universe. Arlette got in the back with Nicko and Belinda. I got in front with Willis. I said nothing more. I didn't want to question Arlette now, in front of everyone. In fact, I didn't want to question her later. Whatever had happened had happened, and now I was here it wouldn't happen again. There's no such thing as a perfect au pair, and there were worse things than one moonlight swimming party. I didn't want to make retroactive accusations: Arlette's reign was over. She had done her job, and the summer was ending.

At home, I got out of the car and stood still for a moment, basking in the summer darkness and the full moon. Arlette climbed out noisily behind me and slammed the door.

"We're going to the movies," she announced, and added insultingly, "if zat's all right."

"The movies?" I said. I felt ambushed, flattened. I had thought the evening was over, for one thing: it was quarter of ten. I thought that Arlette would say good night, and go off to her house. I thought that Willis and I and the children would mooch around for a while, reading or talking or listening to music, inside, in the library, or out on the porch. And then we would all go to bed. Arlette made me feel as though I had just given a dinner party and then been told that everyone was going on afterward to a restaurant.

I also felt hurt that Willis and I were not included: I had thought we were friends. I had felt, at dinner, as though we— Willis and Nicko and Bell and I—were opening our circle to Arlette. I thought that the five of us had established a core of friendship, acknowledging that we took pleasure in one another's company. And I even felt rather generous about this, as though we were offering Arlette something special. Now it turned out that she and my children had their own circle, and that it was even smaller and more exclusive than ours.

"Oh," I said brightly, trying to conceal all this. "All right." I turned to Nicko. "What are you going to see?"

But Arlette answered. "*Lace Two,*" she said, or maybe it was "*Lay Stew,*" or maybe "*Les Stoux.*"

I looked again at Arlette. Her face was closed and expressionless, and she seemed now hostile and alien. The name of the movie hung in the air between us like a coded challenge that she had thrown out contemptuously, knowing that I dared not answer it. The incomprehensible words seemed proof of my ignorance, my exclusion from their world.

"Fine," I said, more brightly, nodding, cowardly. "Don't stay out too late," I added, and then wished I hadn't.

"Don' worry," said Arlette condescendingly. They all climbed at once into my car, as though this had been planned. As she drove out the driveway Arlette waved, the gold bracelets sending a brief scornful gleam into the night.

I went to bed at once, feeling forlorn, and fell asleep even before Willis came in. I woke up later, in the dark room, full of urgent certainty: I knew at once that it was very late, and that the children weren't back. Willis was solidly asleep, and I got quietly out of bed and tiptoed down the hall in my nightgown.

Nicko's room was silent and empty. The bed was flat, unoccupied, untouched, the pillow still covered by the patterned bedspread. Nicko's muddy leather boots lay on their sides by the closet door, where he had kicked them off after work. The clock by his bed said twenty past four.

I looked into Belinda's room. She lay in her bed, her face set deep into her pillow. I turned on the light.

"Where's Nicko?" I asked. Her face was crumpled furiously against awakening, and she rubbed her hand hard against her mouth. She shook her head.

"I don't know," she got out.

"Did he come home from the movies with you?"

She stared at me. "The movies?" She was blinking, hard.

"Did Nick come home from the movies with you?"

"Yes," she said, and set her face back deep into the pillow again.

I went downstairs. My car stood in the driveway, innocent, shining faintly in the moonlight. Unaccountably, my heart began to pound. There was no wind, and the maples towered overhead, black and remote. Barefoot, I tiptoed gimpily across the gravel, wincing at the sharp stones. The noise I made seemed deafening: the gravel crunching, and my own breathing. At Arlette's door I knocked firmly. The raps were horrifically loud, like rifle shots in the stillness.

"Arlette," I said, speaking quieter than in a daytime voice, but not in a whisper, "Arlette."

At once she was there, on the other side of the screen door. I could see her white robe, a pale glimmer in the dimness.

"Yes?" she said rudely. "What ees eet?"

"Where is Nicko?"

"I don' know," she said.

"Did you bring him home?"

"I brought 'eem 'ome. I di'n tuck 'eem eento *bed*." Her tone was like a slap in the face.

"Well, maybe you should have," I said, furious, "because he's gone. He's not in his room."

Arlette shrugged her shoulders.

"If you don't know where he is I'm going to call the police," I said.

"Did you look in ze bassroom?" Arlette asked coolly. "Why don' you look in ze bassroom."

I hesitated, and Arlette pressed her advantage. "Go an' look, why don' you," she urged. "Probably 'e ees jus' zere."

I went back to the house and pounded upstairs. Nicko was not, of course, in the bathroom, but when I went back downstairs I found him standing in the driveway. He was wearing only his jeans. It was cold, and he was shivering, his arms crossed on his chest.

"Nicholas," I said, stiffly. "Where have you been?"

Nicko put up his hand, palm flat, as though to keep me from charging. "Mom," he said, awkward, preliminary.

"What?" I said.

"Look," he said, "I have something to tell you."

"Here I am," I said. "Tell me."

Nicko hesitated and swallowed, and shifted his bare feet on the stones. He crossed his arms on his chest again and tucked his hands underneath his armpits, for warmth. I didn't move or suggest that we go inside. I didn't say a word.

"Mom, I know you've been looking for me."

I didn't answer.

"Well, I was here all along." He paused. "I'm sorry to have to tell you this. Because I know it will disappoint you. The thing is, I was up in the top of the garage," he said. "I was smoking." His voice dropped awkwardly.

"Smoking." I stared at him. "You were up in the top of the garage smoking," I repeated.

Nicko nodded hopefully.

"In the middle of the night," I said. "All alone. For four and a half hours."

He nodded again, less hopefully.

"And that's where your shirt is, and your shoes," I said, merciless. "If we go up there right now we'll find them."

Nicko didn't answer, and dropped his eyes.

I was filled with fury. I was outraged at Arlette, this arrogant, mendacious young woman, this duplicitous hussy. She had coolly used my life for her purposes: my car for her friends, my pool for her parties, my son for her sex. I had hired her to look after my children, and she had taken my money and corrupted my son. She had stolen the body of my child.

I was even angrier at Nick, my flesh and blood. He was lying to me, to his mother, his greatest ally, his partner against the whole world. All his life I have taken his side. I thought of him coming downstairs at breakfast, seeing Willis check his watch.

Now Nicko stood on the cold gravel, curling one bare foot over the other for warmth. He looked down at the ground, his shoulders hunched. He was shivering, waiting for me to answer his lie, waiting for the wave of my rage to break over him.

But I was too angry to speak. Fury had taken me over: I was ready to kill Nicko. I wanted to attack him physically. I could understand, right then, in the cold wild center of that wave, how mothers could kill their children, how they could go on and on hitting.

I stood there, blazing, murderous. I could hear my own breathing, the passage of air into my nostrils. I swelled with my own power, I could feel it gather inside me. Over us the maples moved in the darkness, murmuring. Around us the night was cold and dark, and I could feel something in me rising.

Nicko's arms were crossed on his chest. The moonlight struck the top of his head and his shoulders, but his face was dark. Only his silhouette was clear, the shape and size of his body. In the shadows he looked much larger, taller than I thought he should. His silhouette looked like a man's, which angered me more, since I knew he was not.

"Mom," Nicko said, "I'm sorry."

His voice was gentle, and that sound—gentleness—was terrible. It was like a wave breaking over my own head; it quenched my rage and turned it to cold dread. For gentleness is what you hear in a lover's voice when he tells you he is leaving, gentleness is what you are offered when there is nothing else left. When you hear it, you know the worst has come, and in Nick's voice I could hear that it was not Arlette's reign that had ended.

Breaking
the
Rules

O n Thursday, Anna was awakened by the thump on the
bedroom door, the firm knuckle on hard oak. The
brisk announcement "Morning!" was followed by
footsteps receding down the carpeted hall and another, fainter,
knock, on the next door. At the sound, Anna rose up into consciousness to find herself next to her husband in a high carved
Victorian bed, in a shooting lodge in the Scottish borders, on
the first anniversary of her father's death.

Under the covers Tim put his arms closely around her. His
skin was warm and faintly moist against her. He kissed her.

"Are you okay?" he asked. His face was close, his high smooth forehead, his wide patient mouth, his kind eyes.

"Yes," she said. "I love you."

"I love you, too." Tim hugged her again, but now briefly. She felt him moving toward his day.

"I'm up," he said, and was gone.

When he went into the bathroom, Anna threw back the heavy bedclothes. Barefoot, shivering, she walked to the window and drew open the long gray-green brocade curtains. It was still dark outside; the day before her was impenetrable. The windowpanes were black, their lower edges thickly ferned with white frost. Anna pulled the window shut and stood for a moment, huddled over the old iron radiator. Warmth was starting noisily up inside it, flooding into the room. Anna, always cold, leaned into the invisible flow of comfort, trying to store up the feeling of warmth for later. She wanted to prepare herself.

Downstairs, breakfast was laid out on the big mahogany sideboard in the dining room: platters of glistening russet bacon, a basin of rumpled gray porridge, round cottage loaves of bread, stiff golden kippers. Silver racks of cold toast were flanked by clusters of jams and marmalades. Thermoses of tea and coffee stood on a tray. People served themselves and sat down anywhere at the long table.

Tim was already sitting between two of the other men, Otto Carpenter and an older man, Edward Drover. Otto was Tim's college roommate, and the trip had been his idea. There were eight "guns" altogether, all Americans, all businessmen, all here with their wives for a week's shooting. Tim and Otto were in their fifties, but most of the others were in their sixties—graying, heavyset, ponderously good-natured. All but Tim and Otto were strangers to one another, but they all seemed members of the same prosperous, comfortable tribe.

After breakfast everyone assembled in the gun room. This was small, low-ceilinged, and stone-damp, dense with the smells of oil, dog, and gunshot. The men clumped heavily across the flagged floor in their high rubber boots. Tweed caps were settled firmly onto heads, gloves tucked carefully into pockets. Beneath the hanging brass lamp, Tim carefully hefted his newly cleaned gun. He squinted narrowly up at the barrel, his face intent. Otto, florid and fair-haired, stood by the bins, scooping handfuls of green shells into his pouch. The men were quiet, frowning in concentration: the serious day lay ahead of them, death held in their hands.

Outside in the courtyard stood the muddy Land Rovers, square-nosed and powerful, with a military air. Field boys, with bright pink cheeks, wearing green quilted jackets, walked briskly back and forth, loading gear. Springer spaniels, with white cotton-fringed legs, whined with excitement. Their hazel eyes pleaded, their stumpy tails quivered. They leapt keenly in and out of the Land Rovers, and were sworn at.

At nine the Land Rovers drove off. The men were packed solidly inside, brown shoulder to brown shoulder. As the cars turned the corner of the stone lodge, the husbands looked back, waving. Anna stood among the other wives on the damp cobblestones, arms folded tightly against the Scottish chill, calling out good-byes. Anna waved to Tim as he vanished around the corner, and felt his warmth suddenly withdrawn from her landscape.

Two of the other wives had gone out with the guns, to watch. Some were going to Edinburgh; others had hired a car, to see the Border Country and to shop for cashmere in the Georgian villages. Anna had been twice to sooty, handsome Edinburgh and had bought several cashmere scarves for Christmas presents. She refused to go out on the shoot.

The other wives gone, the lodge was empty except for Anna and the kitchen girls. In her room, Anna curled up with a book. She sat in an armchair by the window, a plaid blanket over her legs. As the morning waned, the big house turned slowly chill: the heat was turned off when the guns left. Inside, it was entirely silent, and outside there was only the faint brushing sound of the wind.

All morning Anna read, blocking out everything but Trollope. Since they had arrived, on Sunday, Anna had felt the week steadily darkening toward this day. She had a sense of doubled time: the days here in Scotland seemed to be moving, side by side, next to the days of that other week, in America, one year ago. It was as though one week lay somehow inside the other, transparent but still present, the hours in that week giving troubling color to this one. As the hours went by dread pooled inside her like rising black water. Anna felt it approaching and struggled to keep herself above it, out of reach.

After lunch Anna set out across the fields. The house was down in a glen, and the surrounding hills rose sharply up from it, close together, their curves echoing each other. Narrow streambeds, now dry, hurtled down between the hills, into the burn, as they called it here. A wide stretch of shallow black water, cold and wild, it chattered through the flat bottomland and across the shepherd's wintry fields.

The shepherd wore the hues of the landscape: dull green, brown. His rose-colored cheeks were the only bright spots in the afternoon. Anna stopped to watch his black and white Border collie, bushy-coated, small-boned, quick, bring a herd of mud-colored sheep up the paddock. The sheep, broad-bummed and stiff-legged, jostled wildly up the meadow. The dog shifted like water from side to side. Holding them in a tight, hurtling bunch, he wove himself into a flying fence around them. When a sheep bolted, the dog turned wolflike:

ears cruelly flat, a black velvet lip lifted to reveal an ivory fang. His blue gaze was annihilating; he ruled by terror. This surprised Anna. She had imagined a sheepdog to be like a father, wise, tender, kind, but stern. The dog was not like a father but a fanatic.

Anna waved; the shepherd gave her a cheerful jerk of his chin. Anna went on, setting her shoulders against the cold and pushing her gloved hands into her pockets. The wind, even down here, was bitter. This cold was like nothing Anna had known before: deep, ancient, punitive. Anna wore layers for warmth—silk, cashmere, down—but even so, she shivered. It would be not layers but movement, her own blood rising, that would finally warm her.

The path led past the flat-roofed sheep shed and the shepherd's stone cottage, following the burn's glittering ribbon upstream. Anna crossed the water on teetering black rocks, then set off on the rutted trail that slanted up Ladyside Hill, passing a solitary tree. These Scottish trees were black and bare-branched, their limbs a fierce, chaotic tangle. The trees in America seemed more orderly.

Anna had grown up in the country, but not country like this. In Connecticut there were rolling fields, boggy cow pastures, scattered woods: mild farmland, not a dour ascetic emptiness like this. Anna had learned the Connecticut landscape with her father. Together they had skirted the plowed fields, laboring along the weedy hedgerows, through the thin scrubby woods. They walked silently and carried binoculars. They were stalking.

"Listen!" her father would whisper, urgent, his forefinger raised. "Hear that?" He would fix Anna in his blue gaze, not seeing her. "Hear it? Hear it? Wood thrush." He would stay motionless, listening, vibrating with intensity. Anna often missed the birdsong, tangled as it was with wind, leaves, the creaks of branches, their own soft rustlings. She stood silent and watched her father listen. She watched the long, rocky cliff of his profile, his pale, radiant skin, the liquid gleam in his narrow blue eyes. The clean fold of white skin along his eyelid, his small, fine mouth, pursed in concentration. His authoritative finger still aloft, rigid. He was never wrong, her father, not about birdsong or about anything else.

Anna began the long steep struggle up Ladyside. There were no trees at all up here, and the wind was soundless. She began to hear her own breathing; the cold began loosening its grip. The track led through thick ferny bracken, waist-high, rust-colored. She trudged steadily toward the sky, her blood beginning to stir. She took deep breaths; the air was pure and sweet. Vast somber patches of heather spread across the flanks of the hills like the shadows of clouds.

A movement caught her eye on the next hill: a covey of partridge rocketed into the distance. The kitchen girls had instructed Anna to report any game birds she saw, for the shoot. Anna had nodded gravely; she would never dream of doing this. Now she looked away, so as not to see where the partridges had landed. Anna felt guilty merely being here. Her father would never have come to this place, where they killed living creatures for pleasure.

Anna's father would not shoot birds or any other living creature, not even enemy soldiers, not even to save Western civilization, not even during World War II, a time when enemy soldiers seemed not human but like fiends from hell. His stance had made Anna's father both famous and infamous—pacifists were widely held in contempt. He had broken the rules of the community; he had outraged his friends, his family. He didn't care.

All that had happened before Anna was born, but her father's ferocious pacifism had not ended with the war. As she was growing up, Anna had often heard him holding forth, his neat mouth tight, his pale blue eyes incandescent—dangerously bright, like burning phosphorus. He raised a warning forefinger. "I believe," he would say, and then pause, for impact. "That killing," he would say, and pause again, for drama. "Is wrong." Triumphant, he would fold his lips together, his eyes aglitter, like the sheepdog's.

Her father was a man of principle; he never wavered. He seized the moral high ground and held it, spurning the gentler slopes of compromise. Nothing swayed him, no argument made him doubt. His blue stare was lofty, implacable.

On Ladyside's broad crest Anna struck out cross-country, leaving the rutted trail. The vast rounded top of the hill felt like the curvature of the earth. There was nothing now around Anna but sky. The air was still, and each cold breath stung sweetly, deep inside her chest. The hills spread out, repeating themselves into the clear blue distance. She was alone up there. Anna was warm now, from climbing. Her chest rose and fell steadily in the warm cave of her clothes. This was exhilarating: the height, the solitude, the ringing, limitless distances. The austere and glowing day.

On the far side of Ladyside, Anna started down, though she could not find the trail. The ground was rough, the heather dry and springy underfoot. The colorless tussocks of wiry grass showed no usage, no footsteps of any sort. Still, Anna thought she recognized the flat-roofed sheep shed below and began to make her way down the vertical plunge of a dry streambed.

Her father had died of a stroke, one year ago today. The hospital in Hartford had called her at ten o'clock that night. There was no one else to call: Anna was an only child, and her mother had died six years earlier. There had only been herself and her father in all the world, it seemed right then. The nurse said brusquely that it was bad, that he might not last until she arrived. Tim was away, and Anna put on her coat and walked straight out of their apartment.

During the solitary nighttime drive up from New York, with the dead roar of high speed steadily in her ears, Anna began to cry. Tears rose up in smooth swells, over and over, covering her cheeks, sliding down her neck. She was afraid that she would be too late, that her father would be gone when she got there. She was even more afraid that she would be there in time. She was afraid that when he saw her, her father would set his small, fine mouth and, without speaking, turn his face away to the wall.

The streambed went straight down Ladyside. As Anna descended, its slanting walls drew in and it steepened. Anna clambered down clumsily, finally using her gloved hands, gripping the cold turf with her cold fingers. She was no longer sure of the sheep shed. Nothing seemed familiar now, but she continued; she had come too far to go back.

At the time of his death, Anna had not spoken to her father for over a year. She could hardly now remember how their quarrel had begun, but she remembered exactly how it had ended. After her father's shouting, her own furious stammering response, her father's imperious gesture, Anna left his living room. She strode across the front hall, grabbing the heavy newel post at the bottom of the stairs, yanking it so hard that she felt the solid shaft give, creaking. She marched upstairs, her blood pounding, and packed.

When Anna came down, her father was still standing in the living room. He was motionless, the newspaper in one hand, trailing on the carpet, the other hand upraised, his finger pointing like a prophet's at the sky. His blue eyes glittered, triumphant. Anna saw him from the corner of her eye as she went through the front hall. Her coat was on, her suitcase in her hand. Neither spoke. Anna, her face burning, strode out the front door, slamming it behind her.

As Anna climbed awkwardly down the hill, the glen below grew dimmer and dimmer. There were no lights anywhere. The hill became steeper and steeper, nearly vertical. Anna's footsteps turned cautious and she stepped twice on each hummock, testing it for strength. She could no longer see her way down.

On this night a year ago, Anna arrived at the hospital, her heart racing. After speeding wildly along the highways, she found the slow pace of the local roads intolerable. Each minute was crucial and endless. When she reached the hospital complex she turned frantic, trying to find her way through the maze, searching for the right entrances, the right buildings, the right parking lot. She found, at last, the parking lot, then a space in it, in the last row. The entrances were not marked, the arrows not clear. She entered finally through a service door and discovered inside that it was the wrong building. Minute after minute was lost. She blamed herself. Her panicky heart raced at the delays: she might miss him by a few minutes, by seconds.

Anna reached the bottom of the hill and saw, through the dimness, the burn. She was not lost, then, though dusk was rising fast, and the lodge was still distant. She picked her way quickly across the black, teetering stones, through the fierce dark water. Shadows were filling up the narrow valley. The remaining light, vast and vague, came from high above the hills. The hills themselves now towered above her, black and unknown. The cold had set in with a passion, and Anna could feel it creeping again inside her layers, though she was walking fast. Night was closing in.

At the hospital, swearing and crying out loud, Anna found at last the right building, the right entrance, the right bank of elevators, the right floor, and when she found the right ward, she began to run. She ran down the long, tiled hall, her feet pounding, loud and undignified, past more decorous people. She saw that her father had been right: She was disorganized, ineffectual. But it had seemed, right then, that this was all that was left for her to do for him. This was the last thing she could do: run to him through the tiled hospital halls.

In the darkness, Anna hurried across the rough bottom-land, stumbling. She could see the lights of the lodge, but in the dark the way seemed longer. She quickened her steps, the vast cold empty landscape behind her. She kept her eyes fixed on the lights, and gradually they grew brighter. Finally the small steep bank rose in front of her, and with her heart pounding, she clambered at last up out of the fields, onto the paved road in front of the lodge, as though she had made a narrow escape.

Anna pushed open the hall door and stepped inside. Every-thing was different. The lodge was now expansive, alive. Every-one was back, the heat was on, there was noise and movement in the halls. In their bedroom, Tim's muddy clothes lay on the floor. He was in the bath down the hall, leaving their own tub for her. She felt a pang of gratitude as she leaned over and turned on the taps. The water began to thunder in, steaming, important. Anna was in the deep claw-footed tub when Tim returned.

"Are you there?" He peered around the door. He was wrapped in a terry-cloth robe, and his hair was plastered untidily against his forehead.

"I'm here," she said. "Thanks for leaving me the tub. How was your day?"

"The best," Tim said fervently. His skin was pink, glowing.

"Where did you go? I've forgotten."

"Bow Hill, at the Duke of Buccleuch's. The country is just ravishing," said Tim. "The hills go on and on."

"Lovely," said Anna. "And the birds?"

"The birds went on and on too," said Tim ruefully. "Regardless of my efforts. Though I had a couple of good shots, good or lucky."

"I'm sure it wasn't luck," Anna said, sloshing slowly in the tub, basking in the heat.

Tim picked up a towel and began working on his hair, rubbing vigorously. "Oh, right, of course," he said. "I'm sure it was skill."

"I'm sure it was," Anna said, smiling up at her glowing husband.

Tim's shooting had troubled Anna at first. It would not have troubled her father: he'd have seen it very simply. Killing for pleasure is brutal and wrong, he'd have declared. But Anna knew that Tim wasn't brutal, and that the point of shooting wasn't killing, for him. What Tim loved was being in the landscape, just as her father had. As to the killing, the birds shot here ended up on the table. Unless you were a vegetarian, which Anna was not, how could you condemn killing for food? And this system was more humane than meat factories and abattoirs.

Anna had reached this conclusion with relief. It would not have satisfied her father, though, and knowing this, Anna felt proudly rebellious. She had escaped the peaks of her father's convictions. She had abandoned his grim, cold landscape and found her way down to warmth and comfort, accommodation, other people. Here she was, luxuriating in the hot water, smiling at her husband, who had spent the day shooting. She felt daring and successful.

Every evening at the lodge everyone gathered for drinks in the sitting room before dinner. A fire in the iron grate lit up the heavy curtains, the faded rugs, the Scottish landscapes on the walls. For dinner the men wore gray flannel trousers and tweed jackets, the women, ruffled silk blouses and velvet pants. A silver tray on a sideboard held bottles, an ice bucket, heavy crystal glasses. People fixed drinks and then settled onto the vast faded sofas, against the soft, collapsing pillows. It was exactly like an English house party, except that they were all Americans, all paying guests, and almost all strangers.

Still, it was like a house party in that everyone understood the rules. They were all from similar backgrounds; they all knew the dances that allowed them to move easily, without a stumble, through an evening with a stranger. For a woman, it was simple: You followed your partner's lead. You yielded to his pressure; you slid smoothly away from the risk of collision.

That night Anna was seated for the first time next to Edward Drover. He was a favorite in the group, Tim had told her. The oldest gun, in his late seventies, he was staunch in the field. He labored gallantly up the long hillsides, trudging through the heavy plowed furrows without complaint. Everyone liked him.

Edward drew Anna's chair out for her, his manner courtly.

"What a pleasure, Anna, to sit next to you," he said, half-bowing over her chair as he pushed it in.

"Thank you," Anna said, sitting down, smiling at Edward. His gesture made her feel comforted, cherished.

Edward smiled back. He was a handsome man, with smooth pink cheeks and a long, fine profile. His hair was bright white and was parted cleanly on the side. His lips were blunt, like a sheep's.

Anna began the first steps of the dance. "Now, tell me, Edward, is this your first time here?"

"This is my first time *here,*" Edward answered. "But it's not my first time shooting. I've been on many shoots, on many, many shoots." He said this smiling, forgiving Anna her ignorance of his vast experience. He took the next step, offering Anna the silver basket of rolls.

"I won't have one myself," Edward said. "I'm on a diet."
He looked sideways at Anna, for her response. He was not
plump; in fact he was quite trim. He was rather dandyish, in a
pale yellow cashmere sweater, a polka-dotted silk ascot. His
tweed jacket had an eccentric stitched-down self-belt in the
back. He thought himself a bit rakish, Anna saw.

"Goodness," Anna said politely, "why on earth are you on
a diet? You don't need it."

Pleased, Edward held up his index finger. "That's just why,
you see. I don't need it because I'm always on it. My doctor
told me, years ago: 'Never finish the food on your plate. Leave
a third, and you'll never worry about your weight.'" Edward
smiled again. A profound satisfaction surrounded him like a
halo. He was pleased by everything he said. "And he's right. I
never have."

"What a good idea," said Anna, as she was meant to do. She
waited, but he said nothing more.

"Have you been shooting all your life?" she asked, setting
out again.

"Practically speaking, yes," said Edward, his manner now
pompous. "My father taught me when I was very young. It's a
great education, I promise you. You learn safety and respect. For
the birds, for the guns, for the environment. All hunters are
environmentalists, you know. We care very much about wildlife.
That's something many people don't realize."

The kitchen girl set down soup plates before them.

"Of course that's true, isn't it," said Anna.

"Hunters are very strong lobbyists for the preservation of
open land," Edward said. He raised a spoonful of clear broth
and blew on it carefully. "Hunters are often unfairly maligned,
you know." His manner was wise and kindly.

"Yes, I suppose they must be," Anna said peaceably.
Edward's instruction was somehow soothing and comforting.

She raised her own spoon to her mouth. "And tell me what it was like, learning to hunt from your father?"

Edward smiled confidingly at her. "It was a great experience. It was the way I got to know my father. He was a rather distant man, and I think I might never have known him at all if it hadn't been for shooting. On the days that we went out together, he would come to wake me up, very early. It would still be dark, and I knew everyone else in the house was asleep. I would see my father standing over my bed, and it would come to me that my father was waking me up because he wanted me to go with him, he wanted me beside him in the woods. He had chosen me. It meant a lot to me. I think I would never have known my father loved me if it weren't for hunting."

Touched, Anna smiled at him. "It must have been wonderful." She had not expected this candor, vulnerability.

Edward, taking another spoonful, blinked and smiled back. "It was the only thing he taught me. He was a distant man. You learn what someone is like by having them as a teacher. And that was the way I learned my father."

"How lucky you are," Anna said, "to have had that. And did you teach your son to shoot?"

Edward raised his forefinger. "Now I believe you're being what's called sexist," he said, ponderously jocular. "I have no son, but I've taught my *daughter* to shoot."

"Oh, you're right, I am," Anna said, charmed. "I apologize. And does your daughter love to shoot?"

Edward beamed. "She *loves* it. She's a wonderful shot, and a wonderful companion. She's been hunting with me ever since she was twelve. I take the greatest pleasure in hunting with her. I invited her to come here this week, but she couldn't. She's a judge, you know, in Massachusetts."

"A judge?" said Anna, impressed.

Edward nodded, proud. "U. S. district court."

"How very distinguished," said Anna.

She had expected something more conventional from Edward's daughter, not something so bold and powerful. Clearly he had encouraged his daughter to excel, and in difficult territory. She had underestimated Edward. She had assumed that all these portly jocular businessmen were conservative, chauvinist, reactionary. Anna, who was very liberal, had carefully avoided dangerous subjects with them all week. Now she thought her assumptions were unfair: Tim, after all, looked like a member of this tribe, and he was a moderate. And now here was Edward: maybe she was wrong about them all. Chastened by her error, curious about its extent, and comforted by Edward's calm sensibility, Anna took a risk. She stepped outside the decorous line of dancers.

"It must be very satisfying to learn from your father how to handle a gun, the way you did," she said. "But how do you feel about these boys in the inner city with guns? How do you feel about gun control?"

But she had made a mistake: Edward's face darkened at once. "Guns don't kill people, people do," he said abruptly. "Gun control is a terrible idea. Any restrictions will set a dangerous precedent." He wiped his mouth with his napkin, prim and final.

"Even in the inner city?" Anna asked. She kept her voice neutral. "Even handguns and assault weapons?"

"Those are just the thin edge of the wedge." Edward spoke loudly, with authority. "There should be no gun control in the United States." He turned and stared at her, his blue eyes now hooded. The corners of his mouth twitched.

"But children are killing each other in the streets," Anna protested, her voice still mild.

Edward set down his soup spoon and looked at her. "Any 'child' who kills another should be put in the electric chair," he said with angry satisfaction. "That should slow them down."

Angry now herself, Anna said nothing. Her empty soup bowl was replaced by a dinner plate rimmed with blue and gold. "Thank you," Anna said to the kitchen girl, her voice full of rebuke, for Edward.

Edward did not hear it. "I'll tell you what," he said, friendly again, instructive. "The real problem, you see, is not the guns. The real problem is the equatorial types." He looked at her, proud, his mouth ready to smile. "That's the problem."

" 'The equatorial types'?" Anna repeated. The kitchen girl held out a platter of sliced lamb. The slices lay in overlapping waves, like soft pink scales.

"If you look at the problems we're having today, around the globe, you'll find it's all caused by the people who live along the equator, or who come from there." Edward raised his finger again, teacherly. "They make the problems. All of the problems: inner city violence, civil war, invasions. That's the root of the problem, you see."

"Really?" said Anna. She began to cut up her lamb carefully and slowly, to avoid looking up at him. She should not go on with this, she knew. It would only end in an argument, anger. She should shift gracefully and steer them in a new direction.

Edward nodded solemnly. "For responsible behavior, you must look to the northern peoples, the northern Europeans."

"Two world wars in this century?" asked Anna pleasantly. She was unable to resist. "I'm not sure I'd call that responsible behavior. Those weren't started by the equatorial types."

Edward frowned. "The equatorial types don't have the *initiative* to start world wars. They're too lazy!" He looked to see Anna's response. "I know about them. I used to work in Caracas, for many years. Those people are lazy, and deceitful. They have no sense of responsibility."

"That's not my experience of them," said Anna. She was being inflammatory, but she could not stop. "The Latinos I know, the ones in New York, are hardworking. They're incredibly brave, to have come there. The ones I know are polite and diligent." Now she must stop. She must change the subject. She would, right after Edward answered.

"The Latinos you know?" Edward repeated, his tone insulting. "Who are the Latinos you know?"

"Just, just the ones in New York," said Anna. At his contemptuous tone, she felt the familiar infuriating stutter begin. She felt anxiety rise. "The men who run the garages, the delivery men. The cleaning women."

Edward smiled loftily. "Anecdotal, I'm afraid," he said dismissively. "That's like saying 'Some of my best friends are Jews.'"

Anna felt luminous with rage. She concentrated on her food, on the blue-and-gold-rimmed plate. She cut meticulous bites and placed them carefully in her mouth. She chewed soberly, not talking.

Men like Edward, she thought angrily, were like loose cannons, spraying their loathsome opinions all over the field, heedless of whom they hit, whom they disgusted. No one held them to account.

But she was also angry at herself. She had broken all the rules by raising this dangerous subject, challenging Edward's views. What would she accomplish, fighting like a child at the dinner table? Nothing. And what had she expected, bringing up gun control to a rich old man who loved to shoot? What had she expected him to be? A liberal pacifist, like her father?

She was angry at herself and at Edward, and beneath that was the sense of something else, some other emotion, rising within her. Whatever had been gathering itself, all week, was imminent. She had thought she had escaped when she got back to the lodge, but she found now it was still there, waiting for this final dark evening to fill slowly inside her. Now it was beginning to move, rising and expanding without her permission, taking over.

"No," said Edward, "let me tell you." He smiled again, ready to forgive her if she behaved. "I lived in Caracas. I know those people. Latinos are lazy and deceitful. They have no idea of fiscal responsibility, for example."

Up and down the long table, glittering with silver, glinting with crystal, the others were deep in agreeable conversation. They were interesting each other. Across the table, Edward's wife, Nina, sat next to Tim. Nina was small and neat, her short blondish hair in stiff whorls. She had a pleasant, doggy face, with a pointed nose and bright dark eyes. She and Tim were smiling, and as Anna watched, Tim leaned back to laugh comfortably. Nina, feeling Edward's eye on her, looked over and smiled at him.

Edward set his knife and fork down on his plate and went on. "When I was in Caracas," he said, "I worked in a beautiful brand-new office building. Clean, dazzling white. And you want to know something?" He paused, but Anna refused to commit herself. "By noon of every day," said Edward. He paused again and lifted his index finger authoritatively. "By noon of every day those bathrooms were filthy. Filthy," he repeated with satisfaction. He nodded, looking at Anna. "It's their culture. They don't care about the same things that we do: morality, cleanliness, order. You have to go to the Nordic peoples for those things."

It was too much. "Oh, I see," said Anna, nodding. "You think dirty bathrooms are worse than Hitler? Dirty bathrooms are worse than the Holocaust? I have to say I disagree with you."

Edward's face changed again, closing down completely. Anna had broken the rules again, this time unforgivably. She had been hostile and challenging; she had directly attacked him. He faced her, drawing his fine white eyebrows together. His eyes were tightly pouched with anger.

"Why don't you talk to the person on your other side," Edward said roughly, his own manners now gone. "You don't seem to want to have a conversation with me. I think you'll do better on that side." He turned away from her, his head high. He drank aggrievedly from his wineglass.

Furious and mortified—Edward had now broken the rules as well—Anna turned away from him. The man on her other side, of course, was deep in conversation with the woman on his left. Anna was spurned, wallflowered, alone and silent among the brisk and animated voices. The kitchen girls glanced curiously at her as they passed. Tim looked up and caught her eye. He raised an eyebrow interrogatively at her and she smiled fiercely. Nina looked up too, sensing something. Edward, like Anna, was sitting stony-faced, staring across the table. Nina, automatically solicitous of her elderly husband, mouthed at him, "Cover up." She mimed pulling a scarf closely around her own throat; she smiled, and went back to Tim.

Anna looked back at Edward, who had spurned her so publicly. Humiliated, she let herself hate him. He was chewing grimly, staring straight ahead, revealing his chilly handsome profile, his long, distinguished nose. The plump little hammock of flesh beneath his chin, the hoary crumpled ear, a tiny spray of white hair at its core. From this close, Anna could see the intricate webbing on his pink cheeks, the ancient delta of small rosy veins. His old skin was clean, soft, used, like kid gloves. His neat white hair was thin, she could now see; it was only a fragile veil over his spotted scalp. And his skull stood out beneath his skin. The bones were clean and visible: year by year, the flesh had been leached away by age. His dry pink hand, the fingers shrunken, shook as he picked up his wineglass.

Anna sat, burning with shame, filled with anger. And whatever was stirring inside her rose to meet her shame and anger: she felt in full spate, as though something she could not control was taking over. Struggling for control, she stared furiously at Edward's long, jagged profile. She found another image intruding, overlaying Edward's, like double vision.

Another twinning, transparent world was set confusingly on the one she saw. The vivid shape of her father's profile, the rosy skin of her father's cheek, seemed like an afterimage, an echo of Edward's, haunting his face. The querulous voice, the frail, translucent skin, the clean, scrubbed old man's look, pink and tender-skinned as an infant: the more she looked, the less Anna could quit herself of this other presence. Edward's raised forefinger, rigid, tyrannical, as though he quoted God. The implacable blue stare, like the fanatical sheepdog's.

In the hospital, panting, her blood pounding in her ears, her face now slick with sweat, Anna had paused at the nurses' station to ask for her father's room. At his name, the nurse's round pasty face changed: a crumple of concern appeared between the brows, the skin around the eyes tightened, and the mouth compressed. Anna did not want to see this. She wanted to shout, *Just the room number, don't tell me anything more.* That was all she wanted to know, only the room number. But the nurse's face had changed, and she had seen it.

"Which room number?" Anna repeated, angry. The nurse, inside the square well of the station, had looked across it for help, but the other nurse was on the phone.

"What *number?*" Anna asked again, now loud and accusatory, as though she might bully things into being better.

"Five seventy-two," the nurse said, looking at a chart. She picked up a clipboard and headed for the gate to let herself out and come with Anna, but Anna, desperate to escape the nurse and whatever dreadful knowledge she now held, went on alone.

In her father's room she found what the nurse's face had warned her of: the end of everything. The end of all her anger, all her strong, pulsing indignation, the urgency of her run. This, what she saw there, was the whole and only point of the blood pounding in her ears, the tears now rising endlessly up in her eyes. It was the end of that long, vital cord she had thought would connect her to her father forever. Anna had thought she had the rest of her life to make up their quarrel, but she had only had the rest of his.

On the bed lay her father, an old man gone. Only his body was left. His beautiful white hair, now limp and thin, was ruffled. The skull was now strong; the buried bone had risen like a boulder through earth; it had outlasted the flesh. The fold of immaculate white skin along her father's eyelid, the pale lashes fretted modestly against the withered cheek: each detail of his body seemed now miraculous and heartbreaking, like those of a newborn.

Anna put up her hand to stroke her father's head, a gesture unthinkable while he had been alive. His temple was cool, hard against her fingertips. The pale skin had a bluish cast, like modeling clay. The long hollow of his cheek was slack and terrible. He was gone. Anna looked up at the room with its pale green walls, the visitor's chair where she had never sat. The glazed gray eye of the television hung huge and bulbous in a corner. Angled toward her father's face, poised, it waited for him to summon up its gaudy blare. This would never happen. Her father was gone.

If she had known, if she had known, she could have called him. If she had called, even yesterday morning, she could have prevented this terrible moment. She could have called him to say things to him, things that were now clear in her mind, so clear she could not imagine that they had not been said. They rang now in her head. She had not said them, had not called him. She could have called her father at any time, to apologize, to end their quarrel, and she had not. She had let him die unforgiven, her heart still set hard against him. What she had thought she'd felt for him was rage, but she was wrong. There was no rage left, she now knew, only something else, much stronger.

Anna glanced sideways at Edward. He was chewing steadily, his eyes fixed unforgivingly away from her, his expression angry. He set his knife and fork to one side with a final gesture. He had not finished what was on his plate. Anna, looking down, saw the tidy heap of food that he denied himself. He folded his hands meekly on the table.

Anna looked down at her own plate, the slivers of soft pink meat. What she was eating was lamb, killed for her dinner. What right had she to judge anyone?

Anna thought of Edward in the silent woods with his father, Edward setting out in the early morning with his small daughter. She thought of him now, out in the field, toiling up the long, deadly hillsides, struggling upward against the heavy earth, his breath unsteady, his heart knocking ominously. Each thump inside the cavern of his chest like that brisk morning knock, loud, alarming, reminding him relentlessly of the time.

Looking now directly at Edward, his craggy profile, his pink skin, Anna saw again the image of the other man. Opinions, the tyrannical raised finger, the outrage: all that was only part of the man. There were other parts, and she, Anna, was not his judge. Now the thing she'd been dreading, this rising feeling, had caught up with her at last, it rose up to her throat. Here she was, with another old man, fragile, soon to die. Here she was beside him, angry, arrogant, judgmental. Here she was, rigid and intolerant, shameful, worse than he.

Edward's speckled hand rested, next to Anna, in a loose fist on the linen tablecloth. For the third time that evening, Anna broke the rules, this time the worst of all. Embarrassing Tim, Nina, everyone who watched, most of all Edward, Anna placed her hand on top of his, pressing the frail breadth of it beneath her palm, feeling its warmth, covering his dry, wrinkled fingers with her own.

"Forgive me," she said.

Family
Restaurant

S usan pushed open the door to the restaurant and stepped into its steamy warmth, Vanessa close behind her. The big windows made the room bright with winter sun, and the air was dense with the cheerful smoke of grilling hamburgers. The brisk teenage waitresses wore blue-and-white-checked uniforms and carried jaunty white handkerchiefs in their breast pockets.

"Hello." A red-haired girl in rubber-soled nurse's shoes squeaked up to them. She held two big plastic-covered menus and smiled at Susan. She smiled more widely when she saw

Vanessa, who was five. "Hi there!" she said. Vanessa shrank behind her mother's coat and did not answer.

"Can I seat you?" the waitress asked Susan.

But Susan had caught sight of Matthew, his hand raised in a slow wave, in a booth at the back of the room.

"Thanks, we'll sit with our friends," she said, smiling first politely at the waitress and then, differently, truly, at Matthew. She took Vanessa's hand and began threading her way through the tables. They edged along slowly, encumbered by their puffy winter coats. Their coats matched—bright blue quilted down parkas, three-quarter length, with hoods. Their faces matched too—long-jawed and thin, with dark eyes framed by straight brown hair.

"Who are our friends, Mommy?" Vanessa asked in a clear voice. "Mommy, who are our friends?"

"I told you, Nessie. Matthew, Mr. Sloan, and his daughter, Hilary. Those are our friends."

"But *are* they our friends?" Vanessa asked, conscientious. "Is Hilary my friend, Mommy? I don't know Hilary."

"But after today you'll know her," said Susan, "and then you'll be friends."

Matthew smiled as they approached. He had hooded blue eyes, long, lined cheeks, and a fading hairline. One eyebrow was arched, the other straight; there was something crooked about the set of his jaw. His blue plaid flannel shirt was open at the neck, the sleeves rolled up to his elbows.

Sitting next to him was a little girl, older than Vanessa. She looked not at all like Matthew; her face was round, and her light brown hair was curly. She wore red pants and a dark blue turtle-neck sweater. Her hands were quiet in her lap, but under the table her legs were swinging. Her heels thudded against the padded base. Expressionless, she watched Susan and Vanessa approach.

Susan and Vanessa reached the booth and stopped. "Hi there," Susan said to Matthew. She started to lean across Hilary to kiss Matthew but checked herself and gave him a wave instead.

"Hi, lovey," Matthew said. He blew Susan a friendly kiss.

Susan looked down at Hilary, still smiling, and put out her hand. "Hello, Hilary," she said. "I'm Susan Walker."

Hilary looked up at Susan. She had slid her hands beneath her thighs, and her legs were still swinging. Hilary said nothing; there was a pause. Hilary's feet thudded raggedly against the padded base. Susan stood, smiling, waiting, her hand still outstretched. The pause grew.

Finally Matthew spoke. "Hilary, say hello to Mrs. Walker, please."

"Hello," Hilary said, neutral. She looked away at once and rocked sideways, shifting her weight from one hand to the other.

"Hilary. Say, 'Hello, Mrs. Walker,' please," Matthew said, irritated. "Shake Mrs. Walker's hand."

Hilary drew her shoulders up sharply to her ears and ducked her head. She blinked and did not answer. Matthew waited, his mouth tightening. He drew in his breath to speak, but as he did, Susan shook her head at him quickly and drew back her hand.

"This is Vanessa, Hilary," Susan said, still cheerful. She put her hands on Vanessa's small shoulders and moved her like an obedient doll, shuffling her sideways until Vanessa was squarely in front of the girl who might become her sister. "Vanessa, this is Hilary Sloan."

The two girls looked at each other. Vanessa's gaze was bold and unblinking, Hilary's wary, reserved. Hilary turned away from the younger girl and picked up her water glass. She began to drink from it.

"Hello," Vanessa said bravely. Hilary closed her eyes, deeply absorbed in swallowing. She made tiny, audible pumping noises.

"Hi, Vanessa," Matthew said. He winked, and gave her a long arcing wave. She smiled.

"Vanessa, you remember Matthew, Mr. Sloan," Susan said.

"Hello," Vanessa said again, her voice high as a bird's. She looked back at Hilary. Hilary set her glass down and intently considered it. She did not look at Vanessa.

"Okay, Nessie, let's take off our things," Susan said, brisk. She shrugged herself out of her own coat and set its bulky presence in the corner of the booth. Stooping, she unzipped Vanessa's coat. Under it was a white cotton jersey with a scalloped neck, which covered the brief, innocent slope of the chest, and worn pink corduroy overalls, which presided over the long, rounded belly. Susan turned Vanessa gently from side to side as she pulled off the coatsleeves. As her shoulders twisted, Vanessa's head stayed fixed, uninvolved with the movement, like a marionette. She stared steadily and silently at Hilary.

Susan slid first across the seat, settling into the corner, against her coat. Matthew, opposite her, held out both his hands. Susan took them: his hands were warm, and gripped hers hard. She smiled at him and tightened her own grip. She withdrew her hands and turned to Vanessa.

Vanessa was sliding slowly sideways along the seat after her mother. In the steamy warmth of the restaurant her skin had begun to glisten faintly, and the fine hair at her temples broke into tiny fragile ringlets. Her head stayed level as she moved, like a snake charmer's, and she did not blink. She stared at Hilary. Hilary set her chin on her fists and looked at the next booth.

Vanessa leaned forward over the tabletop, toward the older girl. "I can zipper my hood," she announced confidently, as though she had performed a miraculous trick.

Hilary's face changed from blank to condescending. She gave Vanessa a faint, superior smile and turned to look up at her father. But Matthew would not meet her gaze and looked instead at Vanessa.

"Can you?" he asked encouragingly. "Zipper it right up?"

Vanessa nodded slowly. "All the way," she said, proud.

Hilary stopped smiling and looked back at her water glass. She frowned at it with concentration, and rubbed her finger around its rim. Matthew patted her knee under the table and smiled at her, but she did not look up.

Hilary looked back at Vanessa and finally spoke, her tone hostile. "How old are you?"

Instantly Vanessa held up a wide open hand, palm front, like a traffic policeman's. The small pointed fingers spread out like a moist pink star.

"She's five," Susan explained. Vanessa gave her a stern look. "*I'm* telling, Mommy."

"Okay, Nessa," Susan said, and she smiled complicitly at Hilary.

But Hilary did not acknowledge the smile. She drank again from her water glass, her face aloof.

Vanessa, emboldened by Hilary's question, leaned forward. "How old are *you*?" she asked Hilary. "Put out your hand. You can put out your hand to show."

Hilary tucked her hands beneath her thighs. Her eyes were hooded, her brows lofty. "I'm eight," she said, reproving, and Vanessa stared respectfully.

Their waitress arrived. She was short, with a round flat face and a wild froth of brown hair. She gave them a professional smile and pulled her pad out of her apron pocket. She held her pencil hovering over the pad.

"Are we all ready to order?" she asked. Her voice was full of false solicitude, like a nurse's.

They were not ready. Their menus were still flat in front of them, the heavy plastic covers bonding stickily with the table-top. Susan picked hers up and held it so that Vanessa could see it—out of courtesy, as Vanessa could not read.

"Do you need some help," Matthew asked Hilary, "or do you know what you want?"

Hilary gave him a withering look and turned to the waitress.

"Grilled-cheese-and-tomato sandwich, french fries, and vanilla milkshake," she rattled off. The waitress wrote, nodding.

"What about you, Ness?" Susan said, scanning the menu. "Do you know what you want?"

Vanessa spoke with her eyes fixed on Hilary. "Grilled cheese and sandwich tomato, french fries, and—what?" Unable to fin-ish, she turned to her mother.

"Vanilla milkshake?" Susan suggested.

Vanessa nodded, pleased. She leaned onto the table and raised herself up, leaning on her elbows, kneeling on the seat.

"Are you sure that's what you want?" Susan asked doubt-fully. "Remember, you had a milkshake before and it was too sweet? What if you have a glass of milk instead, and you can try some of Hilary's milkshake." Susan smiled at Hilary, who did not smile back.

"*No,*" Vanessa said indignantly. She straightened, crossing her arms on her chest. As she spoke she nodded hard and definitively on each word. "No, Mommy. I, want, a, vanilla, milkshake." Her voice was loud.

"Don't raise your voice, please," said Susan, irritated. She looked at the menu again. "All right," she said, looking up at the waitress, "And a vanilla milkshake too."

When they had all chosen, the waitress stuck her pad and pencil in her shiny apron pocket and squeaked off. Matthew leaned back in his corner, his legs crossed easily under the table. He sighed comfortably and smiled at Susan.

"So," he said, "how are you?"

Susan smiled. "A bit frazzled."

"You don't look frazzled," he said. He reached out and stroked the hair away from her forehead, following the line of her face and briefly cupping the curve of her chin. "Actually, you look very nice."

Susan smiled but moved her chin out of his hand. Vanessa, watching, pushed closer to her mother. She kneeled sideways on the seat and patted her mother's shoulder with both hands. Still talking to Matthew, Susan patted Vanessa's knee.

"And how are you?" Susan asked him. "How did the meeting go? Did they like the plans?"

"The wife did," Matthew said. "The husband didn't."

Vanessa went on patting her mother's shoulder, the urgency increasing. "Mom-my, Mom-my," she said in a singsong voice. Susan flashed a smile toward her and patted her knee again, before turning back to Matthew.

"Again?" Susan said. "Do you think the husband likes the wife?"

"I'm beginning to wonder," Matthew said. "This house may not get built."

Vanessa breathed urgently into her mother's ear. "Mom-my, Mom-my, Mom-my." Her voice grew louder with each word.

"What *is* it, sweetie?" Susan turned to her. There was annoyance in her voice, and Vanessa looked abashed. She dropped her head at once on Susan's shoulder. Susan put her hand under Vanessa's chin, cupping it, lifting her daughter's head. "What is it? Don't interrupt, sweetie, unless it's important." Vanessa ducked her head again, hiding her mouth against the inside of her arm. She stared silently at her mother. "Vanessa, what *is* it? If you have something to ask me, then ask me."

There was a pause. Vanessa's face was aggrieved, and she said nothing until Susan turned away and started again to speak to Matthew. Then Vanessa leaned over and put her mouth to Susan's ear. Susan tilted her head, listening. She patted Vanessa's shoulder and smiled at her sideways.

"That's right," she said gently. "Vanilla is the white one. Chocolate is the brown. Vanilla is the one you like. Okay?"

Vanessa nodded. She sat down on the seat again, facing front, and turned back to Hilary.

Hilary was now leaning forward nonchalantly, her elbows on the table, her chin in her hands. She was watching a couple at the table across the aisle. Vanessa, following her gaze, settled herself in the same pose. She stared sternly at the other couple, periodically glancing sideways at Hilary.

Across the aisle was a table for two, with a man and a woman at it. They were vast, mountainous, with cascading chins. The slopes of their bellies echoed one another on each side of the table. Their feet planted solidly on the floor, they ate steadily, not talking. As the girls watched, the man paused, his fork still in one hand. With the other hand he lifted his glass of foaming milkshake. He held the glass up daintily, his little finger raised in a fastidious, arrogant gesture.

Vanessa watched, fascinated.

"Don't stare," Susan said to her quietly. Vanessa ignored her, and Susan touched the small shoulder. "Don't stare, Vanessa," she repeated. "It's not polite."

Vanessa's look did not waver, but her small index finger stabbed briefly in Hilary's direction. "*She* is," she said irrefutably.

Susan turned to Matthew, but he was absorbed in reading his place mat. Susan hesitated and then said briskly, "Hilary, please don't stare. It's not polite."

Hilary did not answer. She gave Susan a long, speculative look, then turned back to the fat man. She gazed steadily and openly at him, glancing sideways from time to time at Susan.

Susan did not look at Hilary again. She cleared the silverware off her own place mat. It was paper, with scalloped edges and a host of cartoon images of planets. Susan scanned a swarm of facts about Mars. Ceremonially, Vanessa picked up her water glass in both hands. Raising it solemnly to her mouth, she began to gulp; the half-melted ice cubes kissed randomly at her lips. Both her little fingers stuck out grandly, at right angles, into the air.

"Don't do that, Vanessa," Susan said quietly. Vanessa turned, looking at her through the bottom of the glass. She raised her eyebrows in a question. "With your little fingers. Don't do that," Susan repeated.

Vanessa lowered her glass. "Why not?" she asked. "Why can't I?"

"It just isn't—it's not something we do. I don't do it. I don't want you to do it," Susan said.

"He does it," Vanessa said reasonably, pointing at the mountainous man.

"Don't point," Susan said sharply, and Vanessa drew her hand back. "I know he does it, but we don't. It's not something I want you to do." She kept her voice down, but the man, sensing their attention, turned toward them. Chewing steadily, he gave them a hostile look. Susan turned on him a brief and inauthentic smile, and dropped her eyes to her place mat.

Hilary spoke, looking directly at Susan. "My mother does it," she said clearly. "She puts her little finger out when she drinks."

"Does she?" said Susan. She looked over at Matthew, who raised his head from the place mat.

"She holds her little finger like this," said Hilary, demonstrating.

Matthew said nothing, and finally Susan answered, her voice altered, suddenly loud, bright. "You see, Vanessa, everyone does different things." She pointed at her place mat, and the drawing of Mars—huge, pocked, grim. "Do you know what this says, Ness? This tells you about Mars. Do you know what Mars is?"

Vanessa, annoyed, said, "I know what Mars is. It's a planet."

Susan smiled at her. "That's right. Mars is a planet." Her voice was falsely sweet, teacherly.

Hilary, torn between lofty silence and the temptation to display her knowledge, yielded to the latter.

"But the sun is not a planet," she said, admonitory. "The sun is a star."

"That's right," said Susan, nodding her head. "Good for you, Hilary. The sun is a star."

"But I knew Mars was a planet," Vanessa reminded her, alarmed.

"Right," Susan said, nodding again. "You both know a lot, both you girls."

"Here's something else," Matthew said, looking from daughter to daughter. "Saturn, which is also a planet, another planet, has rings that float around it in the sky. Do you know how many rings it has?"

"Seven," Hilary said at once, smug. She closed her lips tightly on the word. "Seven rings."

"Wow," Susan said. "Hilary, you're a whiz on this stuff."

"But *I know* some too," Vanessa said, her voice rising. "We learned about Mars at school."

"Kindergarten," Hilary said, to herself.

"That's my school," said Vanessa, turning back to Hilary, wary, yearning.

"I know," said Hilary. She looked down at her mat and yawned suddenly.

Matthew smiled at Vanessa. "What's your teacher's name at school, Vanessa?"

Vanessa, distracted, still looking at Hilary, said loudly, "Her name is Miss Teacher."

Hilary smiled unkindly and put her hand over her mouth.

Susan shook her head involuntarily. "Not Miss Teacher," she said gently. "What is her name? Miss Wolf?"

Vanessa realized her mistake but refused to retreat. "Not Miss Wolf," she said, shaking her head slowly, "Miss *Teacher*."

"And do you like her?" Matthew asked. "Is Miss Teacher a good teacher?"

Vanessa nodded grandly.

"Tell Matthew"—Hilary's eyes flicked up at her at the word—"what you asked your teacher. About her name," she prompted. Vanessa stared at her mother, and Susan said again, "About her name. Miss Wolf."

Suddenly Vanessa smiled radiantly, remembering. "I said, 'Miss Wolf, Miss Wolf, if you're a wolf, then where's your bushy tail?'"

Matthew laughed. "And what did she say back?" Matthew asked.

"She said, 'I keep it tucked inside my underpants,'" Vanessa said, triumphant. She folded her lips into a proud smile, and looked around the table, beaming.

Matthew and Susan laughed irrepressibly, but Hilary looked away, her eyebrows lifted, aggrieved, elaborately unconcerned. She frowned suddenly and scratched her neck. She turned to Matthew, who was still laughing.

"Mom is taking me to the movies tonight," she said.

Matthew's face drained of mirth. He looked at her, his expression entirely, deliberately, neutral, as though he were waiting politely for her to finish the sentence. Hilary hesitated.

Then when she saw he was not going to answer, she shook her head briefly, as though brushing something away.

"She's going to take me to a movie about skaters," Hilary said. Her voice was now loud, boastful. "And then out to dinner after."

"Skaters," said Susan encouragingly. "That's nice."

Hilary did not answer.

"Could I go?" Vanessa asked, bold, hopeful.

For a moment, no one answered.

"You *said* Hilary was my friend," Vanessa reminded her mother.

Still no one spoke, and Vanessa looked from face to face around the table, trying to learn these new rules.

The
Nightmare

W hen Lewis and I left the restaurant it was raining
lightly, a mild, benevolent patter that fluttered gently
on our heads. The evening air was soft. A tingling
mist rose up from the damp pavement, and the cars drove past
slowly on West Eighty-second Street. My raincoat, which
was shiny gray, light and floaty, rustled against Lewis's, which
was oatmeal-colored, thick. Lewis is only slightly taller than
me, and when we walk side by side it feels as though we're
twins.

Out on the sidewalk I turned right, toward Broadway,
where we would find a cab. Unexpectedly, Lewis put his hands

on my shoulders and swiveled me firmly around so that I was walking in the other direction.

"What?" I asked.

"Surprise," said Lewis. "We're going to my place."

We were walking in front of a big grimy Italianate building, vaguely theological. Its entrance was halfway down the block. I waited until we had reached this, until we were under a hissing lamp, before I answered Lewis, as though I needed illumination before I could speak.

I had never been inside Lewis's house. Right now he's living with his daughter, Samantha, who is eight. I live with my son, Nicholas, who is sixteen. Nicholas is away at boarding school, so in the evenings, to be alone together, Lewis and I have always gone to my apartment, instead of to Lewis's brownstone. My apartment is new to me; I moved there after my divorce, two years ago. Its rooms are neutral; they carry no reproach. My husband and I never sat in that kitchen, reading the Sunday paper together, we never had Thanksgiving dinner in that dining room, we never made love in that bedroom. My apartment has held only me, and Nicholas, when he's there, and Lewis, when Nicholas isn't.

But Lewis still lives in the house he and Patricia shared. Since Patricia moved out, a year ago, Lewis has changed nothing.

"Didn't you even put up new curtains?" I asked.

"Why?" Lewis answered, puzzled. "The curtains are fine. Anyway, it's Samantha's house, too. She doesn't want anything changed."

I said nothing. I don't talk to Lewis about Patricia, because I loathe the idea of her. Everything about her seems absurd and contemptible, starting with her name. Those mincing, prissy syllables, full of lisps and ruffles: Paah-trish-ah! And she's a decorator; she spends her days looking for heavy gold braid and great damasks. The reason Samantha is living with Lewis right now is that Pah-trish-ah is doing someone's house in Jamaica.

Lewis doesn't talk much about her either, but one time I asked what happened between them. We were lying in bed, and when I brought it up, his face went closed. Lewis's face is lined and pleasant; he has small blue eyes, very kind, and very high arched eyebrows, as though he's always listening.

"Well," he said, not looking at me, "it was her idea."

"But why?" I asked.

He shrugged his shoulders. "It's not entirely clear to me."

"She must have said something," I said.

"She said it's not working out," Lewis said.

"And was it?" I asked.

"I thought it was," Lewis said. "It wasn't perfect, but I thought that was normal, that was the way marriage was. How do you know if your marriage is unacceptable or not? You don't know what anyone else's marriage is really like, when they're alone. I thought we were pretty normal. Then one time we were spending the weekend with some friends in East Hampton. I woke up on Saturday morning and she was lying next to me, staring up at the ceiling. Without looking at me she said she wanted a divorce."

"And that was it?"

"We spent the rest of the weekend as though nothing had happened. She didn't mention it again, and I thought maybe she'd changed her mind. She seemed happy enough. Then when we got back on Sunday night, she packed up with Samantha and they moved in with her sister."

"That was all she said?"

"She said she wasn't happy."

"Were you?" I asked.

"I thought I was," Lewis said. "Seven years." He looked at me. "She said I was a cold person."

"Cold?" I repeated. I stroked his bare shoulder and he turned and put his arms around me. If there's one thing Lewis isn't, it's cold, but of course temperature depends on chemistry. I could imagine him being cold to Pah-trish-ah. In fact, I liked him for being cold with her. He was saving himself for me.

I haven't met Patricia, but I have the feeling she's a nightmare: brainless, vain, and selfish. I picture her beautiful and spoiled. I'm also certain that she has terrible taste, and that the house is charmless and pretentious.

I haven't met Samantha either, though I know I will. I am trying to prepare myself. I want to like her, but it's hard to like the idea of her. She's living proof that Lewis and Patricia were married, that they loved each other, that they made a family. And then, Samantha represents Patricia. She's a biological message from her mother, written in genetic code, to me.

"Samantha looks exactly like Patricia as a child, exactly," Lewis told me once. "It's eerie. They could be twins."

"Really?" I answered, my heart sinking. Would I have to learn to love Patricia's face?

Lewis's brownstone, filled with Patricia's dreadful taste, inhabited by her living, breathing image, holds a dark fascination for me. I've walked past it more than once, out of unhealthy curiosity, hurrying and furtive, hoping that Lewis wouldn't suddenly emerge. There's not much to see, though, from the outside: it's a dark, unpainted brown building, its lower windows always shuttered from inside, its front door always locked against the street.

I said to Lewis, "We're going to your house?" I felt an odd thrill.

Stopping beneath the lamp Lewis put his arm around me. "I thought it was time," he said. "I've seen your place. I want you to see my place."

"And Samantha?" I asked.

"Well, no," Lewis said. "She'll be asleep. The baby-sitter, wants to go to a rock concert tonight, so I told her she could leave as soon as I come home. She's going on to spend the night with a friend. I know that means she doesn't want me to know how late she's coming in. Which means that I can have a friend over to spend the night with me."

I could see he had thought this all out very carefully. "And what about the morning?" I asked.

"I thought," said Lewis gently, "that you might be gone before Sam wakes up."

"What time is that?" I asked, uneasy. Would I have to sneak out in the dark, like a burglar, like an illicit teenager?

"Seven-thirty." Lewis looked at me anxiously. "Is that all right with you?"

"It's all right," I said, and smiled at him: he was taking this so seriously, being so careful of everyone. Then I pushed at his arm. "Are you nervous?"

He snorted. "Of what? That you won't like my wallpaper?"

I laughed. "I might not," I warned; it was true.

Lewis didn't bother to answer. He kissed the side of my head in a determined way, and squeezed my shoulder, and we kept walking. We were the only people on the block, and our footsteps tocked slowly, irregularly, against the stone faces of the houses. I took a little half step so that we were walking in the same rhythm, and when we reached the stairs to Lewis's house, we climbed them together, sounding like one person.

The front hall was dark when Lewis opened the door. At once he turned preoccupied and quiet, his mouth tense, and I realized that he didn't want the baby-sitter to know I was there. I had become, suddenly, a liability instead of a welcome guest. Without speaking he took me by the hand and led me into a small library, where he turned on a standing lamp.

"Be right back," he said, very quietly, and he left, closing the door behind him.

The room, with only one light in it, was shadowy. Gloomy bookshelves went up to the ceiling, and there were heavy, dark curtains pulled across the window. All the oak woodwork had been stripped and stained a somber brown and then varnished. There were deadly fishing prints on the wall. The room felt stuffy and oppressive. I was pleased to see the ghastly wood-work: I had been right. I stood in the middle of the room, wait-ing for Lewis to return.

"No, no," I heard him say, loud and jovial. "Don't be silly. It's no trouble to me. And you'll be back tomorrow when she gets home from school?" A girl's voice answered, high and pla-catory. "Right. Fine," Lewis said. "Have a good time, Joyce. Fine. Good night."

I wondered if Lewis was always so effusive when the baby-sitter left for the evening. I wondered if Joyce wondered if someone was standing behind the closed door of the library, holding her breath.

The front door finally clicked, and I heard Lewis locking it. As I stood there, holding my breath, my heart had begun to pound, as though Lewis and I were planning a robbery. I waited for a few moments, in case Joyce had forgotten something, and to let the echoes of her presence die away. Then I stepped out into the hall.

Lewis came toward me at once, apologetic. He put his arms around me and wrapped his body around mine.

"I'm sorry to have to do that," he said. "To hide you."

"Why did you?" I asked. "Why couldn't I have just been here for a drink?"

Lewis shook his head. "I don't want Joyce snickering about you to her friends. And I don't want her to say anything about this to Samantha. And I don't want to have to *ask* her not to say anything to Samantha."

He had thought about all this.

"It's all right," I said, "really."

And it was, it had to be. There are no rules, once you're divorced. The patterns are disrupted. You've had your moment, in the white dress, the veil, when everything was orderly, and understood: there was the bride's side, the groom's. After a divorce, everything is askew, uncharted. Now there are times when you stand behind a closed door, holding your breath so the baby-sitter will not hear you.

"So," Lewis said, beginning to relax, "what do you think?"

"Of the house? Or your baby-sitter? I've seen both equally," I said.

"Of my *library*," he said plaintively, and took me back to peer inside the little room. "Isn't this woodwork great?" he asked proudly. "Patricia wanted to paint it all white, but I put my foot down. Oh, no, I said. This woodwork is spectacular, I told her. We're just going to stain it and varnish it."

"Good for you," I said, nodding judiciously. This was a blow.

Lewis drew me out into the hall and put his arms around me again. He leaned back and looked into my face, and I could see anxiety beginning again. I was touched by this, that he had planned this so carefully, that he so wanted it to go well. He was so eager for me to like what he was offering: part of his life. It was a risky business, and I realized I was nervous too. I wondered if Lewis had felt this way when he first came to my apartment: uncertain at swimming in such alien and uncharted waters, unsure of the currents, the tides. But even though these waters were unknown, they were warm, and I trusted my pilot.

"Are you all right?" he asked, looking at me earnestly. "Really?"

I nodded. "I'm fine," I said, "really."

Then Lewis kissed me, on the mouth, and things changed. When Lewis kisses me on the mouth, I understand what the word "swoon" means, and why women do it. I know how it feels when your strength ebbs out of you, when it drains entirely away, and your body surrenders to this strange flood tide. I've never actually fallen to the floor, but I can imagine it easily: rapture drains you of your strength, and you are filled with something else.

"Let's go up," Lewis whispered, and he took my hand, with kindness and passion. He led me up the stairs, and I followed as though I were under a spell. The staircase was dark, with a somber leafy wallpaper and a murky patterned carpet. The upstairs hall was dimly lit, with only one light burning, at the farther end. It was like an illustration from a Victorian children's book, dusky and mysterious, rich with the promise of things not yet revealed.

Lewis opened the nearest door, his bedroom. I stepped inside, and at once Lewis took hold of me again. He pulled me over next to the bed, and put his arms around me, and put his mouth on my mouth. I had a brief impression of the room—dark and cluttered—but it no longer mattered. Patricia herself could have been standing there, watching and making comments, for all I cared. What mattered now was Lewis, and how it felt to have his hands on me. I stepped out of my high heels and stood in my stockinged feet, on tiptoe, so I could reach up and wrap myself around the part of Lewis that I wanted, his wide shoulders and his lovely broad chest. Lewis put his arms around me very tightly, and I felt as though I couldn't wait for this any longer, not one more moment, no matter how soon it was going to happen. It was as though each minute from now on would be unbearable, ecstatic.

We stood there, sinking into the embrace. Lewis put his hand down inside the back of my dress, and I began to shiver. Then he buried his face in my neck and began whispering my name. I couldn't stop shivering, and I wondered how long we were going to stand there. I wanted to be in bed with him, with nothing between us, nothing but our smooth, electric skins.

Lewis pulled his face away from me. I waited blissfully, my eyes closed, for him to touch me, to kiss my mouth again, but he didn't, and I realized he was leaning away from me. I opened my eyes: he was turned toward the door, listening, his face full of concentration. I heard it too.

"Daddy? Daddy?" The voice was frail and trembling, full of middle-of-the-night quaver. "Daddy," she said again, whimpering. She was near tears, maybe half-asleep. She was coming nearer, down the hall toward us. Lewis turned from me, without speaking, and left, pulling the door shut behind him.

I stood in his bedroom, waiting. I folded my arms on my chest and tried to calm myself. I was glad the door was shut. My face was flaming, and my hair was wild. My body was full of heat, and my heart was pounding. If Samantha had come in, I'd have ducked into the closet, gone under the bed. I radiated guilt: how could I not? I was standing in another woman's bedroom, my blood roused by her husband, their child standing outside in the hall.

I took a deep breath and tried to compose myself, to recover some dignity. I looked around the room. A huge mahogany four-poster dominated the space. Over the headboard were draped folds of flowered chintz, a sort of full skirt that rose to a circlet on the ceiling. At the windows were long curtains of the same chintz. On each side of the bed was a mahogany bureau, and over each of the bureaus hung a carved mahogany mirror. On each bureau was a pair of small lamps made from wooden candlesticks, carved in a spiral. Everything matched. It was all conventional and a bit pretentious, just as I had expected, but now, trying to quiet my galloping pulse, I no longer felt so superior, so contemptuous of this. Now things had altered, and this order seemed sensible, somehow, reassuring.

In my stockinged feet I walked across the needlepoint rug to one of the bureaus. It was bare except for a white linen runner and a porcelain jug holding a ragged bouquet of dried flowers. There was nothing else. On the other bureau there were things set out on the linen: a man's set of silver-backed hairbrushes, photographs in silver frames, a stack of books, a man's small leather jewelry case. It was a casual set of signals, semaphoring life.

I looked back at the bare bureau. There was a photograph stuck into the mirror frame, its edge curled over. I slid it out from the frame and spread it down flat. There they were, The Family. The three of them, Lewis, Patricia, and Samantha, stood smiling beneath a leafy tree. There were daffodils around their feet. Samantha, in a ruffled white pinafore over a pale blue dress, held a basket of jewel-bright Easter eggs. Lewis's arm was around Patricia, who wore a virginal pink suit. They all looked tidy and hopeful, as though they had just come from church.

I leaned over to examine Patricia's face. It was a surprise: for one thing, she wasn't beautiful. She had a pleasant face, squarish, with narrow smiling eyes. Her hair was light brown, frizzy, and boring. Her mouth was too low in her face somehow, like a baboon's. But the main thing was how nice she looked. Her mouth was humorous and her expression sunny: she looked, really, like someone it would be a pleasure to know, to have as a friend. She looked warm and solid and full of life, not at all like a nightmare.

Seeing them like this, in those bright colors, tidy and hopeful, was another blow. It did nothing to restore my dignity or make me feel more legitimate. Bent over the photograph, standing at Patricia's bureau, I felt worse, more furtive and illicit than before. Holding this proof of their family in my hands, I felt my touch was profane, and that I held something sacred. This was an icon, a symbol of their life. There were things in their life that were closed to me, secret, that I would never know, that I would never understand, no matter how much Lewis told me. I stood without moving, holding my breath, minimizing my presence. Why was I here?

I looked into the mirror for reassurance, to remind myself that I existed, that my face was real. But it only made things worse. Here, in this mirror, I was boldly setting my features on the space meant to hold Patricia's. My own face stared back at me, pink, alarmed, huge-eyed. The mascara had begun its inevitable treachery, and there were smudges below my eyes. My hair was messy, frizzy on top and in gauche hanks about my face. I looked like a study in chaos and guilt; they glowed around me like a halo.

In the hall, Lewis had been talking quietly to Samantha. Her answer now rose into a whine, high and irrational, nerve-racking.

"No, Daddy, no!" There was sobbing just beneath the words. "I want to sleep with you! I want to sleep in your room! Joyce isn't here. I'm scared, Daddy!"

"Now, stop it," Lewis said. He was getting angry, and his voice was stern. "Just stop this, Samantha." His voice dropped again and began to recede: he was taking her back down the hall to her room. I remembered the dark hallway, the one light at the end.

I stepped closer to the door, listening. I wondered what they would do now. Maybe Lewis would tuck her carefully back into bed, turn on her light, sit down on her quilt, and read to her, his voice rising and falling until the monster in her room had vanished. I hoped he would do that. I hoped he knew that I wasn't impatient. I thought of the little girl in the photograph, her straight dark eyebrows, her pale cheeks. I thought of her, frightened, trotting down the dark hallway in her thin cotton pajamas, her bare feet.

I turned away from the door. *Take your time,* I urged Lewis, *don't hurry.* I moved to the window and pulled the chintz curtain aside. The street outside was deep in black shadows, and the rain had stopped. A police siren raised its officious wail in the distance. The curtain in my hand was heavy and soft, printed in deep red blowsy roses. I thought of Patricia choosing this material, of her proudly showing it to her husband and daughter. I thought of Samantha watching, adoring her mother's face, admiring her mother's choice. Patricia's faith—in symmetry, convention—now seemed touching. And how could I criticize her? Why was I so scornful of her lack of imagination? Being conventional hadn't saved her marriage, but being unconventional hadn't saved mine. We were both divorced women; we had both failed at what we'd tried. I felt ashamed of my easy criticisms: her name, her curtains.

The door opened, sooner than I'd expected, and Lewis came back in.

"I'm sorry for that," he said. "Are you all right?"

I nodded, and he shook his head unhappily. He said again, "I'm sorry. I'm sorry about all this. I'm back now."

But he didn't seem to be. He stood with his hands deep in his pockets, his face was distracted. I wondered if things had gone too wrong now for him to fix them. I wondered if the strain of all this—the whispering and hiding, the undignified mendacity, and now Samantha's unexpected appearance and her rebelliousness—was too much for him, for us. I wondered if this had ruined our chance for tonight.

Lewis and I hadn't felt these strains before. We had only seen each other alone. We'd only listened to each other, only watched each other's eyes, only cared about each other's thoughts. We had thought it was essential, but I could see now it had been a luxury. We had allowed ourselves to believe that what we saw in each other's eyes was all there was. Now we had to look away from each other, we had to acknowledge the rest of the world.

I could see Lewis's distress.

"Are you sure you still want me to stay?" I asked. "Maybe I should go. We can see each other tomorrow. It doesn't matter about tonight."

But it did matter to Lewis. He had planned this. He was determined that the things he planned would work the way he wanted. He doesn't like change; I could see that if this didn't work, it would count for him as a failure, his failure.

"I'm sure," he said firmly. "I don't want you to go home. Stay." He pulled me into his arms again, and obediently I closed my eyes. When I felt his hand move across my back again, I moved beneath his hand, as though from passion, but passion had receded. My head was filled with thoughts, not feelings. I thought of Samantha in the dark hallway. I thought of her own room full of darkness and fear, monsters. I thought about the room around me, of Patricia's careful, conscientious choices.

The voice came again. This time Samantha must have been standing right outside the door. Now she was awake, eager, hesitant.

"Daddy?" she whispered, hopeful. "Can I come in?"

Lewis lunged away from me at once.

"No!" he shouted. "I have already taken you to bed. Now go back to your room, Samantha, right now. Do you hear me?" Lewis waited, his face clenched. There was a silence: she had not left. "Samantha?" he repeated. She said nothing. "I want you to go right to bed, right this minute." Silence. "Or I'm going to have to come out and spank you."

Lewis's voice rose angrily as he spoke. I closed my eyes. I could hear that he was desperate with frustration. He was going to force things to go right, he was going to bully them into going right. I knew he couldn't; they had gone too wrong. There are things that can't be forced, and children and passion are among them. I stood there listening, my eyes shut so as not to see his angry face, trying to think what I should do.

His last command was shouted at his daughter, and in the silence after it we heard her breath, a small broken one. She had begun to cry.

"Do you hear me, Samantha?" he said loudly, more distraught, furious.

Samantha couldn't answer. She was really crying now, and a series of small despairing gusts emptied her small lungs.

I knew now what she looked like, and I could see her standing outside the door. I could see her thin shoulders hunched over, her arms crossed tightly across her chest, one bare foot covering the other, for warmth. The dark hall behind her. Her baby-sitter gone, her room full of monsters.

What I wanted to do was to push Lewis gently away from me and go to her myself. I wanted to stoop down and talk quietly to her, smoothing the hair back off her face. I wanted to take her by the hand and lead her back to her own room, turning on first the big overhead light and then the one by her bed. I wanted to pull the sheet down for her to climb in, and then to tuck it tightly up around her as she lay against the pillow. I wanted to sit down on the edge of her bed and read slowly to her, looking up from time to time, to see if she was sleepy yet. I wanted to sit there until she fell asleep, and then I wanted to tiptoe, myself, back down the hall to my own bedroom, my own warm bed, my own husband.

I wanted to reassure her, but of course I could not. That was the one thing it would be impossible for me to do. I wasn't in this house as a mother, I was there as something else, something much less likeable. I had seen what I looked like, reflected in her mother's mirror: my eyes smudged with black, my cheeks fiery, my hair lank and wild, like a nightmare.

White Boys in Their Teens

T hat summer, on Saturday evenings, I would show up at what Harlem called the hotel. It was not a hotel but a rooming house on a side street in White Plains. Long, feathery grass grew casually along the cracked sidewalk there, and the clapboard houses were painted unexpected colors: yellow with brown trim, or dark green with white.

At around nine o'clock I arrived at Harlem's hotel and opened the wooden front door. There was no lobby, just a stairwell, and on each floor a narrow hall led from front to back. The walls were plaster along one side, and exposed brick against the stairwell. Harlem's room was on the third floor, and

I went up the two flights at a quick, silent jog: I was climbing into another world.

Harlem's door was the last on his hallway, which meant he had a window overlooking the backyard. I don't know what the backyard looked like because I was never there in the daytime. Six days a week, Harlem and I were at work in the daytime, caddying at the Westchester Country Club. There were thirty-two caddies at the club, and most of them were like Harlem: black men in their forties and fifties. The rest were like me: white boys in their teens.

I knocked on Harlem's door, and he answered from inside.

"Hold on," he said. In a moment the door opened, and he stood in front of me. Harlem was my height, not tall, but massive, with a broad face and hooded eyes, a flat nose and a powerful jaw. His hair was fine and grizzled, gray beginning to spread through it like dust. He stood very straight, and when he saw me he gave me a slow half-smile.

"Billy, my man," he said, and stepped back to let me in. He was wearing only his underwear: old clean white boxer shorts and a white cotton undershirt, its low scoop showing the arc of Harlem's big chest, a furling of gray hairs in its center.

"Harlem," I said, as if it were a password. I stepped inside.

"Okay, now," Harlem said, shutting the door behind me. "So, Billy. We gone to have a good time tonight."

"That's why I'm here," I said, and settled down on Harlem's bed. This part of the evening was always the same: I sat on Harlem's bed and watched him dress for the evening.

The room was small and simple. There was an iron bedstead, neatly made up with a red-striped bedspread, which was where I sat. There was a small table and chair, and a clothes cupboard with peeling veneer and a mirrored door. The bathroom was down the hall, and there was no closet. Harlem's pants, sharp-creased and immaculate, hung upside down from the top of the clothes cupboard.

Harlem took his time getting dressed. He slid his arms deliberately into the sleeves of his clean white shirt; he shot his cuffs with dignity. Harlem's moves were majestic; his body was rounded and solid, like a monumental sculpture. His huge chest extended downward into his muscular belly and swelled out from his trunk like the hard burl of a tree. As he dressed, Harlem checked himself from time to time in the mirror. The face he showed himself was closed and impassive.

When Harlem was finished he looked complete. His shirt was buttoned precisely up to his chin, his satiny tie, with its broad diagonal stripes, was knotted into a smooth triangle between the points of his collar. His narrow leather belt was buckled solidly underneath the noble belly. His socks were pale brown, and his shoes showed rich uneven striations from hard polishing.

Then Harlem turned and said, "One mo thing, Billy, fore we get on our way."

The first time he said this I nodded, and waited to see what would happen next.

Harlem stepped unhurriedly out into the hall and moved a few steps away from his doorway. Standing before the un-painted wall, he pulled a brick out from its crumbly mortar. Behind this was a cavity, and from inside it Harlem took out a small paper bag, folded over on itself. He worked the brick neatly back into its slot, where it merged once more into the wall. Harlem stepped back into the room and shut the door behind him with composure.

I watched all this, respectful, mystified, thrilled. The concealed chamber, the hidden cache, the unexplained code of secrecy—all this was marvelous to me. That summer I was eighteen, and what I wanted was a world full of richness and

excitement. I felt myself expanding, and I wanted to be surrounded by possibility, I wanted a world that would make me
quicken. But it seemed as though all the grown-ups around
me—my parents, the priests at school, everyone I knew—were
insisting on a world that was relentlessly sober, airless, hum-
drum.

Harlem and his mystery offered me something altogether
different: I felt I had climbed those wooden stairs into the Ara-
bian Nights. It was as though Harlem had pulled aside a spangled curtain, revealing a vast and starry space, full of strange
constellations. Anything might happen now, anything might
come from out of that crumpled brown bag.

Harlem sat down beside me on the bed and unrolled the
bag. Inside was a packet of fine white papers and a smaller bag
of loose dry brown leaves, flaking and shredding to an insub-
stantial powder. Harlem rolled us a lean, bumpy cigarette with
tightly furled ends, the frail paper twisted into tiny cornets. He
held it up and looked at me.

"You know this stuff?" he asked, raising a heavy eyebrow.

"Yeah," I said, not naming it: I was afraid I'd use the wrong
word.

"This weed, Billy," he said, taking a heavy metal lighter
from the bedside table. "Make you feel good."

I nodded again. To say that I knew the stuff was stretching
the truth. I'd heard of it, but I had never seen it, and I knew no
one who used it. In the late fifties, marijuana was not only
against the law, it was dangerously against it, in a way that
speeding, or using fake IDs to buy beer was not. Marijuana was
something else altogether—serious, consequential. I would
never have dared it alone, or with someone from my own
world. But with Harlem I was in a different universe, larger,
more expansive than my own, governed by another code. My
throat narrowing, I watched him draw on the tiny cigarette, his

eyes closing against the pungent smoke. I held out my hand, breathless with anticipation.

The Eagle Arms had a neon sign in the window that said steadily "Rheingold," in deep pink letters against the dark interior. Inside was a long, narrow room, dark and smoky. There was always music playing in the background, a jazz saxophone, or an organ working its way slowly through the blues. On the right was an old wooden bar, with swiveling stools, and a mirror behind it. When Harlem and I came in the crowd was already there: Cash Money, The Crawl, Nighttime Paul, Eddie the Fish, Shirt Walter.

When we arrived, Harlem walked at speed down the length of the bar. He looked straight ahead, purposeful, as if he had an appointment with someone in the next room. At the far end he turned deliberately and stood for a moment, his hands on his hips, his jacket pulled back to expose the pointed end of his shiny tie. His head was tilted slightly, as though he was ready for a challenge. Not making one, but ready for one if it appeared.

Then Harlem turned and greeted the bartender.

"Shirt Walter," he said formally, with a neat nod.

Shirt Walter was a solid, slow man in his fifties, with heavy eyes and a gray mustache. He wore a white shirt with the sleeves rolled up. There was a toothpick in the corner of his mouth. Shirt Walter nodded back at Harlem, his hands busy.

"Evening, Harlem," he said, and after I had been coming long enough, he began adding, "Billy."

"Evening, Shirt Walter," I said.

I liked Shirt Walter, as I liked most of the men at the Eagle. I liked the solid gleaming darkness of their skins, the deep bass of their voices, and especially I liked their laughs. At the country club, out on the golf course carrying the heavy bags and "making the loop" with the members, these men were distant and subdued. Here at the Eagle Arms they were living their real lives, and I could see them in all their powerful splendor. I felt that they had some dark and glowing secret. I couldn't share it, but I felt its heat.

I liked being here with them. I liked the things they said and the things they did. Every Friday afternoon Cash Money took his paycheck and turned it into bills, which he brought in a fat, folded wad to the Eagle. That night he bought his friends drinks. He spent every single dollar in his pocket, and every Saturday morning he was dead flat broke. The rest of the week his friends bought him drinks. I never knew how he paid his rent.

I stood next to Harlem at the bar. He drank scotch and milk, and I drank Red Cap Ale. Nighttime Paul stood next to me. He was a tall, stringy man, jittery, with ashy-black skin and a bumpy nose. He liked to talk politics, and we were in an election year.

"That Nixon is a man don't know how to speak the trufe," Paul announced to Shirt Walter.

Shirt Walter cocked his toothpick.

"Fact," said Nighttime Paul, nodding. "Wouldn't know how to let the trufe out if it swelled up inside him and boiled out his nose."

"An you think Kennedy different," said Cash Money, on the other side of Paul. Cash Money grinned derisively.

"You show me a politician tell the truth, I'll vote for him," Harlem announced. Harlem was older than the others, and his manner magisterial. He took a swallow of his drink; no one answered. I had nothing to say about politics; they seemed immeasurably distant from my life. At school, the priests never discussed them: we were meant to think only about our schoolwork and our immortal souls. At home, every night during the news I heard my father's familiar and good-natured complaints over the way everyone handled everything. It seemed to me that politics went on and on and never changed. It seemed that other people took it all seriously, which meant I didn't need to. I thought I would sometime, but not yet.

Down the bar there was a scuffle. Two men I didn't know were jostling each other and laughing, loud, ebullient.

"I seen you with her, last week," one of the men crowed. "I seen you, sneakin round." He punched the other man on the shoulder. "I know twas you."

The other man laughed, pleased. "Yeah, that was me," he answered. "I seen her, once, twice."

"Ahhh," said the first man. "You sholy *seen* her. *At least,* you *seen* her." More laughter, more jostling.

"What her name?" The first man jerked his chin up interrogatively.

The second looked at himself in the mirror behind the bar. He was round-faced, and the whites of his eyes and his teeth were rich yellow. He smiled at his reflection.

"Her name Ruby," he said, and paused. "She know me as Sweet Daddy."

"Sweet Daddy! Sweet *Daddy!*"

The two men scuffled again, hooting and slapping at each other's hands. Up and down the bar there was laughter, a rich and exultant chortling, as though something plentiful and delicious were being passed among the men, and tasted.

Those nights in the bar were like nights spent in a foreign country, a place I loved and tried to learn. I learned as best I could. Some things I learned myself, by watching: I saw that you never drained your glass of beer. Always a small measure was left at the bottom, out of courtesy. Other things I was taught. Sitting on my stool one night, I swiveled around to talk to someone behind me. I sat leaning back, talking and laughing, my spine resting easily against the bar. I felt a hard finger drill into my shoulder blade. I sat up and turned to find Shirt Walter's long black face thrust next to mine, stern, admonitory.

"Never turn your back to the bar, Billy," he said severely, as though he were reciting a law.

I swiveled meekly back around, shaken by Shirt Walter's face, his tone of voice. He now ignored me, moving farther down the bar without a glance. I sat silent, chastened. I was also baffled: I didn't understand the rule, but Shirt Walter's glare prohibited questions. I was chastened, but also grateful to know that Shirt Walter was watching over me. He wanted me to know the rules. I felt surrounded by the powerful presence of my friends.

One night I noticed a man I didn't know, craning his neck to look at me from halfway down the bar. He glowered at me, muttering, turning away, then peering back. Finally he set down his drink and headed toward me. He was heavy-set and very dark, with wide-apart eyes and a small flat nose. I saw him coming and put my drink down. I could feel my heart pounding: I was scared.

When he reached me he grabbed my shoulder, pulling me away from the bar.

"What you doin in here, white boy?" he demanded. He pushed my shoulder away contemptuously and set his hands on his hips. He cocked his head. "Dis no place f' you." He reached out again, maybe to grab me, maybe to push me.

His hand never reached me. Harlem and Nighttime Paul stood on either side of him. They took him under the elbows, not gently, lifting him off his feet in a bundling rush all the way down the bar and out the door.

When Harlem and Paul came back, they were without the man. Harlem sat down again next to me. He picked up his drink, calm, unhurried.

"Don't pay no attention to him, Billy," Harlem said. "He nothing but a fool."

I felt safe with Harlem. I trusted him.

That summer I spent my Saturday nights with Harlem whenever he asked me, climbing the wooden stairs up into his dark, spangled world, saying the password at his closed door. I never told my parents where I was going: my mother would have worried, my father disapproved. My parents wanted to keep me tucked safely in their world—white, dry, cautious—but I had found somewhere new: Harlem's hotel and the Eagle Arms, Shirt Walter and Cash Money; the suddenness and vehemence of the talk, the laughter, the intimacy, the vividness. Mysterious, immensely glamorous, it was like a secret chamber, a vast nighttime cave I had been granted permission to enter. And no matter what dangers presented themselves, I was protected there, by my wise and powerful friends.

At the end of the summer, Harlem and I said good-bye. We shook hands slowly, clasping each other's elbows and smiling.

"So, Billy," Harlem said, "you off to college."

"That's right," I said, shaking my head. "Four years of books and winter, man, hard work and bad weather. Pretty bad. Not like you: you're going down South to lie around in the sun, you dog."

Harlem and the other caddies lived in Westchester only in the summer; the rest of the year they lived in West Palm Beach. They owned no winter clothes, and I admired this. They seemed to have outsmarted winter, to have simply made a decision to avoid, smoothly and without effort, the bleaker part of life.

"That's right," Harlem said equably. He smiled. "No winter for me, no sir. Sunshine every day, that's right."

"You dog," I said again, grinning back.

It seemed to me then that our destinations were roughly equivalent. Harlem had another life, elsewhere, and so did I. We were both moving on. Harlem's life was different from mine, but then, so were all the adult lives I knew. The choices made by grown-ups were incomprehensible to me. My father's life seemed grim and pointless: the tedious commute in to New York and the insurance company each day, the exhausted return to our small house in Port Chester each night. I didn't plan to live my father's life any more than I planned to live Harlem's. I felt no pity for either of them, only the vast difference between our generations. My sight was clearer than theirs. My own choices would be simpler than theirs, my decisions wiser. My own life lay ahead of me, glorious and unknowable.

That fall I went to a Catholic men's college outside Boston. It was the first time I had ever lived away from home, away from my parents' anxious eyes, and it felt wonderful. I could see that this was how it would be from now on, an increasingly expansive universe, giving me more and more room. My own achievement and advance seemed effortless, as though I were riding a wave, a long, slow, endless surge, on which I rose and rose. Simply by virtue of my age and my existence, it seemed, I was rising into power.

That first year, I went South at spring vacation. I was going to a place my parents had never been, had never even dreamed of going. It was easy for me to go there; I felt it was my right. I felt it was my right to do anything I wanted.

Florida wasn't crowded and built up then, it wasn't a place for old people in air-conditioned condominiums. In the late fifties, Florida was a romantic place, tropical and opulent. Along its edges were wide beaches, and deep in its interior were mysterious swamps. Florida lay dreamily right at the very bottom of the country, stretching down a long, elegant leg from the rest of the continent, dipping a toe excitingly into foreign currents, warm turquoise waters.

Seven of us drove down, in two cars. We drove straight through, taking turns at the wheel, snoring and sweating in the back seat. When we finally arrived in Delray we cheered. Our motel was a terrible place, a low, unpainted concrete bunker. Still, we cheered because we had arrived: we had escaped from our school, our parents, and winter. We didn't care how awful the motel was, because we would hardly be there. We were going to sleep on the broad, endless beach, or in the flowery, sweet-smelling beds of the beautiful girls we were going to meet. We didn't care about squalor. All that was temporary, we would be rich later, and we were powerful now. The possibilities of our world were limitless.

We did most of the things we had hoped to do. During the day we played volleyball on the sand and swam in the surf, wrestling with the long, relentless rollers. We turned browner and browner, mysterious proof of our excellence, our manhood. We talked to the girls who walked past us, up and down the beach. The girls had bouncy hair and they wore two-piece bathing suits: a heavy bra-like top and an exciting underpants-like bottom, tight around the crotch. A virgin territory was revealed: soft white midriffs, supple and untouched, unbearably smooth. We longed for the girls, we longed to have them. At night we drank cheap beer in crowded bars and talked to the girls. Afterward, when they would let us, we took the girls with us and stretched out next to them on the sand, in the wide night. None of us actually had sex—it was the fifties still—but we got drunk every night. There was no one to stop us. There was almost nothing we could not do.

I had brought Harlem's phone number down with me, and after a few days I called him.

"Harlem?" I said.

"Who this?" he answered. His voice was cool.

"It's me, Billy," I said. At his voice I felt, unexpectedly, elated. But there was silence from him.

"It's me, Billy, from Westchester," I said.

"Billy," said Harlem, completely there. "My man. How you doing?"

"I'm down here, man," I told him, "in Delray."

"Got to get together," Harlem said. He and Cash Money were going to be out flying around that night, he said. They would fly by and pick me up around ten. They would take me back with them to West Palm Beach, to their dark, powerful, spangled world.

That night I stayed in our room when the others went out to get drunk. I told them who I was going out with, but they pretended not to believe me.

"Oh, very *sly*, Ryan," Coccaro said, and punched my shoulder. "Some guy you used to *caddy* with, of course. Right. We believe that." He looked around our dank, low-ceilinged room: it was hideous. The beds were seas of rumpled sheets; the floor was strewn with dirty clothes and filthy towels.

"Who is it? She'll be very impressed by your handsome *quarters*," Coccaro said.

"Ryan isn't going to impress her with his *quarters*," Sullivan shouted. "He's planning to show her something *else*, right, Ryan? You're planning to impress her with that!"

"Shut up, Sullivan," I said, and thumped him on the arm, hard.

They were right to think that I was deserting them, though wrong about where I was going. For some reason I didn't want to tell them about Harlem's world. I didn't invite anyone along with me. This was my secret.

Around ten-thirty I heard a low throbbing outside, an engine that sounded like an outboard motor. I looked out into the parking lot: there was an old two-toned Buick Roadmaster, green with a white top, polished and shining. It had white sidewalls and little chrome portholes along the front fender.

I went outside and Harlem climbed from behind the wheel. He came over to me, grinning.

"Harlem," I said.

"Billy," he said. We shook hands slowly, smiling at each other. Harlem gripped my arm as though we were old friends, and I thumped him, in a respectful way, on his massive shoulder. He looked even nattier down here than he had up North. He was wearing a light brown suit and a patterned brown tie. His white shirt glowed, and in the tropical twilight of the parking lot lights his eyes were liquid and gleaming.

"Get in, Billy," he said, opening the door. In the back seat there were two other men. "Look who's here, Cash." Cash, who was in the front seat, cocked his index finger in the air and nodded at me in a friendly way.

"Cash Money," I said, "how you doing?"

"Billy," he said, smiling and closing his eyes. "Good to see you."

"This Fred," Harlem said, pointing toward the man in back, "and you know your man Nighttime Paul. Billy, you get in back wid Paul."

The car was low-slung, and I bent over. Paul slid over to make room. He was smiling, his face nearly invisible in the dark.

"Hey, Paul," I said.

"Billy," he said, and we shook hands. Fred and I nodded, and we set off. I leaned back against the seat. The car was big and had a good, solid feel.

"Hey, Harlem," I called, "nice car."

"Oh, yeah," Harlem said. I could hear him smiling. "Had her awhile now. Beats walking."

"So, Paul," I said. "How's it going? How's the club down here?"

"Club fine," Paul said, nodding. There was a pause, and we waited for him to finish. "Members bad."

We all laughed: it was the old joke.

"So," Harlem said, eyeing me in the mirror. "Whatchou doin down here, Billy? Not here studyin, are you?"

"Nah," I said. "We're on spring break. I came down with a bunch of guys from school. Beer on the beach. Girls in motels. We figured we'd get lucky."

"An'?" asked Paul. "How you doing?" They were all listening.

"Come on," I said. "How're we going to get lucky? We got two rooms for seven of us, we got two-three guys in each bed. What are we going to do, get some girl in there, tell her to pay no attention to the guys in the next bed? Tell her not to notice the guy lying right behind her? Tell the other guys to hide under the spread and be real, real quiet?"

They were all laughing now.

"Real, real quiet," said Paul. "Yeah."

"Tell that girl to look the other way," said Fred, chortling. "Look away, look away."

"She don't care, someone else in bed," said Cash Money. "Why she care?"

Harlem looked at me in the mirror, grinning. "You ain't find nobody like that, Billy?" he asked.

"Not yet," I said, grinning back.

Harlem shook his head. "Surprised at you."

"Yeah, well, sorry to let you down," I said. "All we found so far are some great hangovers."

They laughed some more at that. Everybody liked the story, the idea of persuading a girl to ignore the two other men in the same bed with her. They all offered variations on this, and possibilities. We all laughed at them, and it lasted us a good long while.

We were on the coast highway, headed back to West Palm Beach. The Roadmaster tooled along, not so fast but very powerful and smooth. Jimmy Smith was on the radio, playing a Hammond B3, the great blues organ. It all felt perfect to me, as though, with all of us in it, in that big solid car, we could go right through anything. Nothing could stop us. Beyond the highway, to the east, the ocean flashed in and out of view. There were palm trees, suddenly against the night sky, ragged and wild, and then a string of neon lights, bars, motels, lit-up places with lights in tropical colors; then the palm trees would hit the sky again, black and uneven. Cash Money got out some weed and passed it around and we put it to our mouths. I hadn't had any since the summer, with Harlem. We took that heavy magical air into our lungs and right up into our brains, and things got funnier and funnier.

Right then, driving along, surrounded by my friends, I felt as though I were flying, as though I were rising up into the air, right up into that spangled sky. I felt so lucky, as though, miraculously, I'd managed to do things right. I had moved here, into this world, effortlessly. Somehow, I'd managed to get myself into this beautiful, invincible car, and we were rolling along past the dancing palm trees that heaved mysteriously against the heavens. Harlem had let me into his secret nighttime world again. I was here, I had climbed the stairs, said the password, and been admitted once more to this dark and radiant place.

When we reached the outskirts of West Palm Beach we turned off the highway and onto a broad avenue of large buildings. The car slowed down. The weed had quieted us, though it had made everything around us seem very funny. We weren't talking much, but we laughed easily, in low, gurgling chuckles. I was sitting in the corner, leaning against the window and feeling happy.

The avenue was lined with great palm trees, in solemn, symmetrical rows. Crossing the avenue in orderly succession were tidy side streets. It all seemed very grand, an ideal of order, and I felt my mood began to shift. I felt myself turn sober and responsible: this place spoke to me in a new way. I was an adult, I was a part of the world. I now felt just as pleased to be here, on this wide avenue, as I had been to be tooling along the honky-tonk highway.

We turned slowly off onto a smaller street. There were shops, and people walking easily down the sidewalks, shiny cars parked along the curb. It looked prosperous and calm, and in the warm evening, in my beatific state, it looked perfect to me, just as it should be: these small neat white stucco buildings, the clean streets, and high above it all the stately silhouettes of the palm trees.

We passed a movie theater, with stage lights glowing around the marquee. A Doris Day–Rock Hudson movie was playing. A couple was just going inside: they were both tanned and blond, and they wore matching madras shirts. For a moment they walked along the sidewalk in step, their tanned bare legs moving in unison. They noticed it just as I did, and they started to laugh. They broke stride, and their legs windmilled in slow motion. I had seen them laugh and change their steps; I had known what they were thinking, and why. I felt myself smiling with them. It seemed incontrovertible proof, right then, that the whole world was happy.

Our car seemed to be going slower and slower as we moved down these streets. At one of the stoplights I saw Harlem cock his head and look at me in the mirror. I grinned easily at him, my eyelids heavy, my head loose from the weed. I crooked my finger at him, but he didn't smile. There was purpose in his eye. I sat up a little straighter.

"What's up," I said.

"Billy, round here we going past some folks won't be happy to see you back there," he said. "Wonder if you could scootch down some."

"Sure," I said. I didn't know what he was talking about. It seemed like a joke, and I folded my arms on my chest and slid down a bit on the seat. The car didn't move. Harlem held my eye.

"Need a bit more, Billy," Harlem said. "Scootch down a bit more."

"Okay," I said. I sat up straight and then doubled over, crossing my arms and setting them on my knees, putting my head down on my folded arms. It seemed strange, what Harlem was saying, more than I could fathom. Who would be unhappy to see us here? To see me here? That tanned couple going into the movie? It made no sense. But I did as I was told and stayed still, my heavy head on my forearms.

Still the car didn't move.

"Billy," said Harlem. "Way it is, we going to have a little trouble, anybody sees you in the car with us. Going to have to ask you to get right the way down."

I sat up then, and stared at Harlem in the mirror. No one spoke. Beside me Nighttime Paul looked straight ahead, his face blank, his flat profile stone-still. Cash Money and Fred were silent.

"All the way down?" I said, not moving, baffled. "On the floor?"

Harlem said nothing, watching me.

I got right down then, climbing down into the well of the Buick, first kneeling on the old clean musty carpeting, then lowering myself farther and stretching out full length, flat on the floor of the car. Nighttime Paul and Fred moved their shoes as best they could, turning them sideways, away from my body.

When I had stretched out, as low as I could get, Harlem said, "Got your head down?"

My head was not down. I had set my face on my palms, bracing my weight on my elbows, as though I were lying on a bed and talking with friends. Now Harlem wanted me to give up my last vestige of uprightness, to put my head down flat. It seemed a significant change. All this no longer seemed funny; it seemed disturbing. It was humiliating.

I dropped my head all the way down. My elbows were tucked tightly against my ribs, and my cheek was set on my fingertips, which were right on the tops of Fred's shoes. The shoes were black wingtips. They were dry and dusty, with deep cracks in them. I could feel the leather, smooth and fine: they were expensive.

"Got to get you right down," Harlem said. There was no emotion in his voice. "You down now?"

"Yeah," I said.

I was down. I was entirely down. My nose was nearly flat on Fred's shoes. I could smell the leather, acrid and sandy. I could smell Fred himself, the innocent sweaty smell of his dark skin. He wore no socks. I thought of Harlem's clean, carefully chosen socks. I thought of Harlem's shoes, buffed and polished. I thought it was strange for Fred to have bought such expensive shoes and then let them turn dry and cracked, to wear such expensive shoes without socks.

Then for some reason I remembered saying good-bye to Harlem at the end of the summer. I remembered complaining to him about having to go off to college. I remembered teasing Harlem about his coming down here, to the sun, escaping winter. Now this no longer seemed funny. Now the memory made me uncomfortable, though nothing had changed.

The car had begun to move now, but very slowly, almost gingerly. No one was talking, and the chortling laughter had stopped. The four men were quiet, and we were driving as carefully through that clean, peaceful neighborhood as if it were a combat zone, full of mines and snipers.

Then, in the silence, as though this thought had been rising slowly through my consciousness, as though it had been months working its patient way upward toward this moment, those same months when I had been rising toward my sense of freedom, I understood about the shoes.

Fred hadn't bought this pair of expensive black leather wingtips. They were second-hand, they had been given to him. They had belonged first to someone else: a rich white golfer. Fred couldn't afford those shoes; he couldn't even afford socks.

Around me, the men were sitting in complete silence. No one moved, and I could feel from their rigid legs, their silence, their seriousness, that there was fear in the car.

I closed my eyes and lay still with the men. I was hardly breathing, and my nose was set against Fred's dry, cracked shoes. I lay without seeing, barely drawing in breath, as though this might keep me from something terrible, from finding out something I didn't want to know. But it was too late: I had already begun learning their shadowy secret. I was already moving into a part of Harlem's nighttime world where I had never been. It was a part I had never known about, a place I could not bear to think about, could not bear to see.

King
of the
Sky

I stood, that day, before the deep closet in the front hall, taking off my coat. The small domestic view gave me modest satisfaction: an orderly row of neat shoulders, our various selves. There was Gilbert's sleek and dressy herring-bone tweed, his grimy tan trenchcoat, my velvet-collared Chesterfield. No bright colors, nothing exciting, but everything was well made, clean, looked-after. Among the others I hung my everyday self, the dull green loden coat that I wear all winter—to the supermarket, to the small local museum where I volunteer three days a week, and on the twice-daily trips I make from Gramercy Park, where we live, to Jock's school, four blocks south.

"Come on, Jocko, take off your things," I said, turning back to the hall.

Jock, who is nine, didn't answer. He was in the middle of something private. His red boots still on, his jacket flung open down the front, he was kneeling next to a needlepoint-covered chair and aiming his gun-shaped hand at something in the distance. His eyes were focused, not on our meekly flowered wallpaper, but on a muddy battleground somewhere. He was talking urgently under his breath, and between the bursts of hissed and whispered words were periodic explosion noises.

In third grade, boys' fantasies are almost entirely violent. Mayhem and death lie at their cores, and all require the powerful and satisfying sound of an explosion. This noise is something all boys—and few girls—can do properly. It begins at the moment of detonation: the cheeks balloon slightly, and a deep gargle at the back of the throat produces a muted rumble. The lips part slightly to allow the sound loose into the world, and the vibrating root of the tongue and the arched roof of the palate produce a series of slow reverberations. The echoes continue deep in the throat, distant and sinister. Their majestic pace, their diminishing volume, their final lapsing into an elegiac silence, all suggest the end of everything. Nine-year-old boys need to suggest—particularly to their mothers—their dangerous capacity to end everything.

I knelt on the rug next to Jock's small, supple body. Ignoring me, he leaned on the chair seat and sighted along his extended finger, one eye closed for accuracy. I faced the pale clear skin of his cheek, the faint purple delta of veins at his temple, the fragile translucent whorl of his ear. Jock has Gilbert's high forehead and pointed chin, and his own silky gold-brown hair, which lies flat and fine against his skull.

I began easing his boots off. Jock allowed this, stretching out each leg in turn for me to grasp, but he continued to ignore me and what I was doing. It is as though the least hint of connection or cooperation with this large domestic female would destroy the secret, other, *real* life that Jock has so carefully created. I don't insist on recognition. I don't care. As long as Jock allows our worlds to function peaceably side by side, and occasionally to interlock, I don't complain. I have other parts to my life besides the part that contains him—why shouldn't Jock? And for him, it is a desperate matter, his independence.

When our things were off we got back on the elevator. We were going to the ninth floor, to visit Willie, who is one of Jock's best friends, and Willie's mother, Margaret, who is one of mine. We all live in an old building on the north side of Gramercy Park. It's a quiet neighborhood; the avenue stops there, and there's not much traffic. The park itself is small and elegant, and merely the sight of it—always a pastoral surprise among all that urban geometry—seems to slow the tempo. It's a peaceful, old-fashioned place, and our building is peaceful and old-fashioned as well. Our doormen are hushed and attentive, the lobby and halls are clean and well-ordered. It's safe, and we don't lock in the daytime. On nine I pushed open our friends' heavy front door and called out hello.

"Come in," Margaret called back. "We're in the kitchen."

Jock set off at a run. Margaret's apartment is bigger than ours, a duplex, with a terrace over the park outside the living room. Margaret has a great eye and has wonderful things; I ambled slowly down the long, book-lined hall, through the big square dining room with its modern mahogany table. I was admiring, as I always do, her style: the enigmatic nineteenth-century paintings, the complicated Oriental patterns underfoot. Margaret thinks of things that would never occur to me: she'd found a sculptor who worked in iron and commissioned him to make wonderful ornamental bars for the windows. The new ones were just being installed, and I could see fanciful baroque designs across every view.

In the big white kitchen Margaret was sitting on the tiled floor with Willie, wrestling with one of his boots. Margaret is tallish, long-boned, long-waisted, precise in her movements. Her hair is glossy blond and perfectly straight. She wears it blunt-cut, just below her jawline, and parted exactly in the middle. A small tortoise-shell barrette on either side holds it neatly in place. Margaret works nearly full-time as a lobbyist for an environmental group, and she was still dressed for the office. She was in a dark green long-sleeved buttoned-up blouse and black pants: very elegant. Margaret always looks elegant, in a quiet way. It's all in the details: black suede shoes, a high silk collar, a dull gold chain. Margaret likes details, and she's good at them. I'm told she's brilliant at work; lobbying means taking charge, planning strategy, changing people's minds. She's assertive and effective: I admire her for that; they're things I'm not.

Willie is Margaret's only child; she always said she couldn't manage with any more. He looks just like her, with the same pale skin, the narrow, brilliant blue eyes, and the sleek cap of blond hair. Temperamentally, however, they are fiercely opposed: Margaret demands order, Willie chaos.

Willie was lying on his side, propped up on one elbow. He was using his hand as a fighter plane and making jet-engine noises. Jock ran over to him with a nine-year-old's eccentric gait, haphazard and lurching. As he reached Willie, Jock knelt and skidded to a stop on his knees, his hands on his thighs. Willie gave him a sidelong glance and went on with the air war. Neither spoke.

"Hi, Margaret," I said. "Hi, Willie."

Willie ignored me, his puffed-out cheeks full of sound.

I would have ignored his ignoring, but at once Margaret said, "Willie, say hello to Mrs. Jamieson."

Willie did not look at her. He made more powerful jet-engine noises and set his plane on a dangerous course past his shoulder.

"Willie," Margaret said again. Willie ignored her. His eyes were fixed on his hand: this was aerodynamically flattened, and his fingers were split into wings. His engines revved, reaching a higher and higher whine.

"Willie," Margaret said ominously.

"Don't worry about it," I said, wishing I hadn't said hello to Willie in the first place. But now Margaret ignored me.

"*Willie!*" Margaret said again, her voice peremptory. Willie heard in it the end of the negotiating period. He looked up at me for a split second.

"Hi," he said, not quite insolent, his eyes flicking off my face at once. His voice returned to combustion engines.

"Hello, *Mrs. Jamieson,*" Margaret said.

"Mrs. Jamieson," Willie added airily to his flying hand.

Margaret shook her head, her lips tight. She looked at me grimly. "We've been having a wonderful time today. We're in such a good mood," she said.

Margaret's views about boys are different from mine. Willie's resistance drives her crazy. Of course, Willie's resistance might drive me crazy, too. There's something manic about Willie, something locked and frantic and driven. He lunges toward crazy, and then so does Margaret. They goad each other on. The more one insists, the more resistant the other turns, and though their goals are different, their methods are the same. They seem sometimes like two halves of the same fierce and indomitable personality, trapped in the same skin, battling for control.

I always thought it was just a phase. I think people are better parents at some ages than at others. I'm probably at my best right now, with a nine-year-old. Though I adore him, though I know he adores me, with Jock I can sleepwalk through my days, each of us in our own world. When Jock is a teenager, and I have to pay attention and get into the real issues, I'll probably be terrible. But I always thought that when Willie became an adolescent, Margaret would come into her own. Once she was freer to work, once she could return to her own world, she'd encourage Willie to inhabit his. She'd admire his independence, she'd support his originality. She'd pull back and he'd relax. That's what I thought. All this conflict seemed temporary; they would just have to live through it.

Now Margaret yanked at Willie's second boot. Willie, loose-limbed, uninvolved, came along with his foot, and was pulled smoothly toward her on his back. Strands of his sleek pale hair lifted magically from his head, as though he were freefalling through space. Jock had joined him on the floor, and at Willie's involuntary slither they both began to laugh, the low irresistible belly laugh of the supine. It made me laugh too, that loose, jellyish gurgle, but Margaret didn't even smile. She ignored them, sliding her hand inside the boot and finally worming out the foot. Her face was dark and her mouth set, as though the resistance of the boot, the tactile cling between rubber and leather, was Willie's fault, part of his stubbornness.

She pulled the boot off at last and shook her head. "God!" she said, and put the boots side by side next to the wall. She stood up, wiped her hands on her black pants, and smiled at me. "Okay," she said briskly, and moved over to the big gas range.

"It's all airplanes here this week, we're all pilots. Willie's King of the Sky," Margaret said, turning on the flame beneath the kettle. "I don't know why. Before that we had police shootouts and drug runners, but suddenly it's all airplanes. Do you have airplanes, or is it only us?"

"We're a mix," I said. "We have some comic book heroes, airplanes, and a lot of space ships."

"I'm glad we're not Exterminators anymore, anyway," said Margaret.

"*Terminator,*" Willie said loudly, from flat on his back, still not looking at her. "Terminator."

"Terminator," said Margaret. She looked at me and quoted wryly from an imaginary report. "Mrs. Welch can't seem to keep track of her son's interests. She belittles him by forgetting the names of his favorite toys."

"What a name, anyway, Terminator." I said. "Why don't they just come right out and name them Death, or Hatred?"

"The kids would love it," said Margaret. "They'd all want one."

She fixed tea for us, and soup and crackers for the boys, and we all sat at the butcher-block table. The boys were on stools across from each other. They were involved in something, staring intently and mirthfully into each other's eyes as they ate. Pasita, Margaret's Colombian housekeeper, was doing the laundry. We could hear the steady lunging drone of the washing machine, and the faster, ringing sound of the drier. Pasita sat behind us at the ironing board, her arm moving smoothly back and forth over the clean cotton. Next to her was a pile of ironed clothes, white and crisp. Outside it was cold and windy, and the bare-limbed park trees showed light dustings of snow, but in there the air was steamy and warm. It felt entirely safe.

I grew up in New York, on East Seventieth Street. When I was little, in the afternoons, it seemed that all of Park Avenue was full of children walking home from school. The girls walked with their mothers, their hair in messy braids, their socks drooping around their ankles. The little boys, noisy, daring, walked without parents, dressed in blue blazers, carrying knapsacks. The doormen kept a watchful eye on them. The doormen had authority and would call out sternly to a group of rowdy boys, "That's enough, now! Settle down," as they passed noisily by on the sidewalk. And the boys eyed the doormen and did not answer. They did, for the moment, settle down. They knew that they were part of a neighborhood, that their parents had friends in those buildings, that they were part of a watchful, strict, benevolent network that commanded and protected its children.

But things have changed, though doormen still call out to rowdy boys, on upper Park Avenue and here in Gramercy Park. The world outside that network is more threatening now, and our children are at risk in a way I was not.

When I was little, accidents were the gravest danger to children. There was, at that time, a tacit agreement among grownups that children were to be cherished. Strangers risked their lives to save other people's children, pulling them heroically from burning houses, out of rivers and wells. That has changed. Now a stranger approaching a child is an enemy; children are targets. Now there are grown-ups and teenagers who harm children, deliberately. That fact is always, always, at the back of my mind, of all parents' minds.

When Jock was five, he and I had a fight. He stood in the hall outside his room and yelled up at me, a small fiery figure in brown corduroy pants and a striped cotton jersey, his slipping-off socks dragging beyond his toes. He shouted that he hated me, and I shouted back that I didn't care: these were loud, angry, pulse-pounding moments. I was outraged that he should challenge me, and I towered angrily over him. Compared with him I was immense, giantesque. My huge hands on my wide and powerful hips mimicked and ridiculed his own, his small hands set bravely on his narrow hips.

"I don't care that you don't care," he finished shrilly, and whirled away from me. He stalked angrily into his room and slammed the door. He stamped his feet with each step, but in socks, on the carpet, his small feet made only faint thuds.

I went into the kitchen to calm down, and a few minutes later Jock appeared in the doorway. He was wearing shoes, and his yellow slicker. The peaked hood was pulled up over his head, casting a deep, glowing shadow over his face.

"I'm running away," he announced.

I was no longer angry; I was ready to make up. I looked at him, this small defiant golden figure, and I was struck by how powerless he was. Children have control over nothing in their lives; everything is determined by us, who claim to have their best interests at heart. But who's to say we do? We have our own best interests at heart, as always: self-esteem, authority, convenience. It seems so unfair to these tiny people, who stand up to us so bravely, who struggle so hard to be real, to make us know that they are real.

I said, "All right."

Jock stood still, uncertain.

"Forever," he warned.

He had thought I would argue. He watched me carefully, for a trick, for a second thought.

"If you want to run away, you can. I can't stop you," I said docilely. "But don't forget you aren't allowed to cross the street."

"I know that," he said crossly. He still watched me, and I smiled at him.

"I love you," I added, and at that he regained his dignity and turned proudly away. He walked to the hall door. I stood in the doorway and waved as he got into the elevator, his arms crossed on his chest, his elbows cradled in his palms, the peaked hood shading his small brave face.

What I should have done was follow him; I know that now. I should have gone down right after him in the next elevator. I should have shadowed him around the block, stepping quickly into doorways like Sherlock Holmes when Jock turned around. But I had some notion of playing fair, and I thought I should not invade his adventure.

Instead, I went to the front window and leaned recklessly out, the sidewalk below drawing me dizzyingly toward it. It was early spring, and the trees in the park were just beginning to unfold the fresh green of their leaves. There weren't many people on the block. No one else was in a slicker: it wasn't raining. I could easily see the small yellow figure, the pointed hood—which he had always refused to wear before—addressed upward, to me. He was walking slowly, for someone with such a fierce purpose, and I wondered if the world now seemed larger, noisier, more arbitrary, than he had remembered it upstairs in our kitchen. I watched him until he reached the corner, and I saw him turn dutifully down the next side of the block. Then I waited, watching the clock, leaning out the window over and over, until finally I saw him again, coming from the other direction. He was at the far end of our block, making his steady way up the sidewalk toward the canopy over our door.

I was standing outside it when the elevator door opened to reveal him. His face, in the golden shadow, was meditative and pleased.

"I'm back," he announced.

He was back, unharmed, and proud. That was what I had intended. But at what risk! I still wake up in the night with the nightmare vision of someone stepping toward him on the sidewalk, taking Jock's trusting hand and leading him away. A stranger taking possession of this child who occupies my heart. Oh, God, I think at two o'clock in the morning, my limbs locked with tension and fear, how could I have let him go?

It is a puzzle to me, this memory, a riddle about freedom and safety, independence and responsibility. I don't know the answer to it. When I zipped up Jock's pale yellow slicker and sent him into the world, I meant him to know he could turn from me, that he was free. But I shouldn't have done it, I shouldn't have taken that terrible risk. When I think of it now, it seems as though his survival was a miracle, an extraordinary and undeserved piece of luck. It seems dangerous, that luck, something I may have to pay for later.

Now Margaret asked, "Are you going to the parents' meeting on Tuesday?"

"I think so," I said. "But we have tickets for the opera that night. So if we go to the parents' meeting, Gilbert will have to give the tickets to his secretary."

"Who likes Wagner, I'm sure. So, what will you do?"

"Negotiate," I said.

"Who will win?" asked Margaret.

"It depends," I said. "I always say we should go to those meetings, but I don't even know how important they are. You know you should go, but why? At the last parents' meeting we listened to Tommy Grimshaw's mother tell us how sorry she felt for herself, and how difficult her ex-husband is."

Margaret smiled. "I know what you mean," she said. "But I think you do it for solidarity. We're all in this together. Anyway, I go because I want to know everything the teachers know. I want to know everything they think about my kid. I want to know what their theories are and what they suggest. I may not do what they suggest, but I want to know what it is."

Actually, Margaret did need to know what the teachers thought about Willie: he was a discipline problem, and in constant trouble at school. But she was right, too, about solidarity: that's what mothers owe each other—support, complicity, humor. I felt ashamed that I was willing to offer so little, that I was so lazy and insular. I was chastened by Margaret's response, the fact that she was determined to do things properly, to take part, to be involved.

"You're much more responsible than I am," I said. "I still have the feeling that kids grow themselves up, that it just happens."

"But you're probably right," said Margaret cheerfully. "They probably do. I'm wildly overresponsible. What can I say?"

"What does Frank think?"

"Who knows what Frank thinks? I'm so crazed about taking charge of everything that he backs off. Who knows what he'd be like as a single parent?"

"Wouldn't it be awful if our husbands brought up our children?" And we laughed at the thought, full of shared horror.

"Nan Wallace was on a flight home from the Caribbean last winter. It was just after she and Steve had gotten married, and her kids were with their father. The plane started bumping, which Nan hates. It got worse and worse and finally Nan grabbed the stewardess and said, 'Could you please tell the pilot to quiet this plane down? If it crashes, there are two wonderful children in New York who will have to grow up with their father.' "

We both laughed again, and I said, "It's a chilling thought, isn't it? But why? It's not that the fathers don't love them."

"Oh, no. Of course they love them. It's just that they don't know anything. They don't know *anything*," said Margaret firmly. "They have no clue. They'd get everything wrong."

"But wouldn't they learn?" I pictured Gilbert widowed, bravely quelling his grief, earnestly attending school meetings, soberly walking Jock to school.

"Please," said Margaret. "Frank knows every corporate law precedent going back to 1900, but he can barely remember what Willie's name is. The two of them living alone together would be a disaster."

Willie and Jock were in the middle of some sort of contest. Their heads were lowered over their bowls, and they were staring intently at each other, slurping from their soup spoons, and laughing raucously. Still staring fixedly at Jock, Willie said, "Daddy knows my name."

Margaret looked at him, irritated. "Of course Daddy knows your name. That was a figure of speech."

"Daddy knows my name," Willie repeated, "and I *want* to live with him. I'd *like* to live alone with Daddy." He put a huge spoonful of soup in his mouth. At once he lapsed into a high cackle. The soup, deliberately or accidentally, it was hard to tell, came spraying out in a wild fan, all over the table and over Jock. This was a declaration of mutiny, and Jock, of course, began laughing as well, rocking dangerously on his high stool and kicking his feet.

"Oh, *Willie!*" said Margaret. "*Look* what you've done." She was really cross. She stalked to the sink and got the sponge. "Get down off your stool," she snapped, "Willie, get *down*. Now."

Willie still did not look at her. He got down off the stool and then put his hands on the table. He began little springing jumps, kicking himself off against the floor, as though he were going to heave himself up and sit in the middle of the soup-sprayed surface. He was flopping his head from side to side and laughing wildly. Jock was doing the same: hysteria had set in, the last refuge of the child-about-to-be-punished.

"Willie, *look at me,*" Margaret said, kneeling in front of him, the sponge in her hand, trying to mop the soup off his shirt. But Willie would not look at her. He kept flopping his head from side to side, and laughing.

"Jock," I said, "stop laughing and come over here." Jock shook his own head wildly, closing his eyes. "Jock," I repeated, and without looking at me, still with his eyes shut, he slid off his stool. He began making his way over to me, holding out his hands like a blind man. He wobbled and staggered, deliberately missing my stool, while Willie screamed with laughter.

I grabbed Jock by the arm and pulled him over next to me. "Jock, stop," I said sternly, but I wasn't really cross.

Willie was still flopping his head back and forth, and he had closed his eyes too. Like Jock, he feigned blindness, groping with his hands in front of him. He touched Margaret's face, roughly bumping her nose, and he screamed joyfully.

"Eeeyeww! What is it?" He went into high-pitched giggles. "What weird, squishy thing is this?" He bumped Margaret's face again, rudely.

"*Willie,*" Margaret said, angrily. She grabbed him by the shirt and shook him. "Stop it. I mean it."

Willie's hand strayed away from her face, but he did not open his eyes, and he did not stop his laughter, shrill and false.

Margaret now took hold of his shoulders, and her voice rose. "Willie, stop it. Stop it right now."

Willie's eyes were still pinched shut. He shrugged his shoulders violently, away from his mother's hands, and began jumping wildly up and down, his voice in a high whine. "Eeeyew," he said, over and over, "eeeyeww, what is it? Is it human?"

By now Willie and Margaret were deep inside the thicket that they had created and shared: thorny, isolate, barbaric. Within it, each of them struggled fiercely to destroy the authority, the reality, of the other.

Margaret grabbed Willie's shoulders again and shook him, hard. He went limp, wobbling bonelessly. I felt sorry for both of them, both so angry, now so committed to their struggle. But Willie was being so awful, so wild, so arrogant, so contemptuous, that part of me felt just like Margaret. There was a part of me that felt mean, tyrannical, swollen. Part of me wanted that child subdued, wanted him shaken until his teeth chattered, until his will was broken and he stopped his derisive whine. I knew the feeling, all parents do, of the rage that threatens sanity. I knew why there was child abuse. We've all come close.

"Willie, listen to me," Margaret said, talking through her teeth. "*Listen to me.* If you don't stop this, right now, this minute, you are spending the rest of the afternoon in your room. Alone. Jock will have to go home. Now *stop it!*"

There it was, the big threat. I try not to use it, because Jock always rises to the challenge. And following through on it is always inconvenient. Now we all waited, suspensefully: everyone's afternoon hung in the balance, Jock's and mine and Margaret's, to say nothing of Willie's. But Willie never hesitated.

He yanked himself away from Margaret again and began springing up and down into the air, crouching, and then shooting up into the air. His eyes were still screwed shut, and over and over he made violent explosion noises. He was a rocket, a cannonball, a space ship, a bullet, anything but a submissive child.

"All right," said Margaret, furious, "all right. Is this what you want?" But she didn't move. "Is this what you're trying to do? Stop it, Willie, I mean it," she said.

He bounced up, landed, crouched, and launched himself again, unimpeded.

Margaret stood up now and shook her head. It was as though nothing had happened, no wildness, no threat, no feeble retreat. She cleaned the soup off the table and sat down again at the table, ignoring the boys.

"Honestly," she said to me, "it's like having lunch in the lion house."

Jock watched, interested: this is not what would have happened at our house. And I watched, unhappy: Margaret's strategy baffles me. It seems that if you don't follow through, there's no point in making threats at all. It seems to me you're just teaching a child that there's no risk to rebelling. But I said nothing to Margaret. No matter what she says about all of us being in this together, I know that you never tell another mother what to do. And besides, how do I know I'm right? Why is my instinct better than hers? What about letting Jock go off on his own, at five years old, in New York City? What kind of sage and responsible act was that? No, we all make our own mistakes; we all act crazily, indefensibly. We are saved by time passing and by miracles, not by the interference of our friends.

But Willie was not to be denied a climax. Behind Margaret, in a dazzling throwaway gesture, he upset his bowl, sending heavy split pea soup in a great floating wave onto Margaret's back, soaking her elegant silk blouse.

"All right!" she shouted. "All right, Willie! That is enough! You come here with me." This time she took Willie's arm and yanked him along behind her, out of the kitchen. Again, Willie relaxed all his limbs and let himself be dragged, limp, letting gravity declare his reluctance.

When they were gone, Jock and I looked solemnly at each other.

"Poor Willie," I said. "He doesn't seem very happy."

Jock shook his head, but he would not speak to me, he would not take my side against his friend. He sat silent and mournful, taking small spoonfuls of his soup, his head down. I drank my tea. When Margaret came back, she was brisk and glowing, her cheeks pink with fury. She had changed her shirt and put on a thin cashmere sweater. I wondered if you could ever get split pea soup out of silk.

"Sorry," she said, sitting down again. "I'm sorry, Jock, but Willie forgot his manners and he forgot the rules. He's going to stay by himself for a while and think about them."

"When can Willie come out?" Jock asked. He seemed very small and quiet. It was now hard to imagine him laughing raucously, kicking his legs under the table.

"Willie has to stay in his room until his father comes home," Margaret said brutally. She picked up her mug of tea in both hands and brought it to her mouth. It concealed her face except for her eyes, which were blazing. She looked wild, distraught, and I thought she was close to tears.

Jock's face fell. His afternoon was emptied of color, and he played dejectedly with the cracker on his plate. He crumbled it messily, rubbing at its soft pale crispness until it collapsed in bits. I wanted to comfort both of them, but I could think of nothing to say to Margaret.

Finally I said, "Well, Jocko, you and I will go to the park, if you like, or we can go home and I'll play a game with you. Whatever game you like." He glanced up at me, weighing this offer soberly, though we both knew it didn't make up for his afternoon with Willie.

I waited before I moved, but Margaret didn't look at me, or answer, so I thought she was letting me know that she didn't want to talk about whatever she was feeling.

"I think we'll get going," I said to her. "Sorry this happened, but don't worry about it. I'm sure we played a part in it; it wasn't all Willie." I wanted to make her feel less isolated, less frantic, but she shook her head.

"Oh, don't *you* worry about it," she said, walking us to the front door. "It wasn't Jock's fault. Willie has to learn what the rules are, that's all." Her face was stiff now, her head was up, and she had her hands deep in the pockets of her trim black pants. She looked very cool, very much in charge.

"Well, don't let it get you down. God knows, it happens all the time," I said, shaking my head slightly, as though Jock spent all his daytime hours shut in his room. But Margaret looked politely uncomprehending, as though she didn't know exactly what I was talking about. I couldn't think of any other way to reach her, and it seemed clear that she didn't want to be reached. So we left her alone, in her apartment, with Willie on the other side of a grimly closed door.

I should have stayed with her, I see that now. She had said, We're all in this together. What support was I giving her by leaving her alone, by letting her pretend that everything was all right?

What happened was that Willie decided to escape. The new window bars were being installed that week, and in Willie's room the old ones had been taken out and the new ones set in place. They were only set there, they hadn't yet been bolted into the window frames, but only the sculptor knew this. The bars looked solid, but as it turned out, a bold nine-year-old could dislodge them.

Willie opened his window wide. It was cold outside—it was December—and when he opened the window he must have paused at the damp winter wind that swept into his room. Like Jock, he bundled up dutifully before he set out, as his mother would have asked. He got a sweater from his bureau and put it on by himself, backwards, the label under his chin. His room overlooked the terrace, and when he climbed out onto his windowsill, the terrace must have looked inviting. It was diagonally beneath him, not directly below, but on the way there were window sills, ledges, cornices, safe things to grip. The climb would have looked dangerous but feasible to Willie, and it was both. There were places he could cling and balance as he clambered down and sideways through the singing air, the wind holding him against the building, until he had sidled far enough over to drop the last few feet onto the terrace.

This is the part that is hard to think about. The French doors to the living room were locked. Willie stayed on the terrace, maybe shivering, maybe hoping and not hoping to see his mother. She passed the living room several times that afternoon, but she heard nothing, she saw nothing. She tries to remember, now, if she might have heard something. If he had called, if he had knocked, would she have heard? But she heard nothing. Perhaps, when she passed, he was there. Perhaps when he saw her he hid, sobered by his climb, fearful at last of her rage. Perhaps he had been sobered by what he had done: going out into the real world, he had felt himself flattened against the cold brick side of the building, he had felt the terrible singing call of the drop, the rush of the sidewalk, nine stories down. Perhaps, after this, he had lost his nerve; perhaps the thought of facing her rage as well was too much for him. But he was there on the terrace for a while. He left a plastic superhero there, balanced on the sill outside the French door, waiting for it to open. He didn't knock on the door, he didn't shout out loudly for his mother to let him in. He made no demands. For some period of time he stayed alone out there, in the wind, his sweater on backwards. Maybe he played for a while with the superhero, under the lowering December sky. But it's hard to imagine him playing, it's hard to imagine him, by then, as anything but subdued.

At some point Willie decided to climb back up. He was trying to undo his mistake, to be good. He was trying to put himself back where Margaret wanted to find him; he had thought better of his escape. When Margaret finally knocked at his door, calm, her heart no longer closed against him, her rage no longer in charge, Willie wanted to be sitting in his room, the window shut, the sweater off.

He clambered first up onto the broad parapet. There he stood, his sneakered feet tiptoed and teetering as he stretched for the first window ledge. But climbing up is very different from climbing down, and this time the ledge was slightly too high, slightly too far, for his grip to hold his weight.

We are not in this together. The things that separate us are terrible and irreversible. What lies now between me and Margaret will lie there forever, a chasm nine stories deep.

These things should not happen. With luck, any luck at all, things would have gone differently. Margaret would have seen him, the terrace doors would have been unlocked, the window ledge would have been closer. And neither Margaret nor Willie ever wanted to be in that thicket of hostility. They love each other, mothers, children, no matter what they say, what they do. That should count. And repentance is meant to save.

Most often there are miracles; most children are saved. When a miracle doesn't happen, when you hear that a child is lost, the terrible sound of it echoes within your mind, a series of slow reverberations. They continue, deep inside you, distant and sinister. You feel terror, the vertiginous pull downward, the drop that you escaped for no reason. And you hold your own child close to you, close, no matter how he struggles.

About the Author

ROXANA ROBINSON is the author of the novel *Summer Light*, the biography *Georgia O'Keeffe: A Life*, and the short story collection *A Glimpse of Scarlet*. Her fiction has appeared in *The Atlantic*, *Harper's*, and *The New Yorker*, as well as in *Best American Short Stories*. She is the recipient of a Creative Writing Fellowship from the National Endowment for the Arts.

She lives with her husband in New York.

About the Type

This book was set in Bembo, a typeface based on an old-style Roman face that was used for Cardinal Bembo's tract *De Aetna* in 1495. Bembo was cut by Francisco Griffo in the early sixteenth century. The Lanston Monotype Machine Company of Philadelphia brought the well-proportioned letter forms of Bembo to the United States in the 1930s.